I0694266

KAMP KROMWELL

A Novel

A.J. GREA

Published/Created: Knoxville, TN: Oakberry & Inkwell, 2025.

Edited by R.M. Collins

Front and back cover design by A.J. Grea

Library of Congress Cataloging-in-Publication Data

Grea, A.J.

Kamp Kromwell: A Novel by A.J. Grea – 1st ed.

p. cm.

Summary: A teenage boy must escape the vengeful entity unleashed upon his summer camp while accepting his sexuality and the horrific memories of the deviant who tried to silence him.

ISBN-13: 978-1-968152-14-7

2   3   4   5   6   7   8   9

[1. Horror — Fiction. 2. Demons — Fiction   3. Monsters — Fiction
4. Summer Camp — Fiction]

OAKBERRY & INKWELL

DEDICATION

This one's for me...

ALSO FROM A.J. GREA

THE FORGOTTEN FEDERATION

"Within the superhero genre, so often dominated by darkly serious tales, *THE FORGOTTEN FEDERATION* is a breath of fresh air." – *Indie Reader*

"Exuberant and entertaining…" – *Kirkus Reviews*

Haunting Thelma Thimblewhistle
The Chronicles of Dead Anna

"A detailed gothic world beyond the realm of mortals." – *Kirkus Reviews*

"The pages come to life…like a Harry Potter book especially for girls, a must read, but maybe not alone at night, unless you are really brave like Thelma." - *GoodReads*

VICKIE VAN HELSING

"Vickie is smart and tenacious…" – Publishers Weekly

"…this NOT a shiny shimmery vampire novel. Oh no. The vampires are REAL SCARY vampires." – *Amazon*

"This is not a sweet sparkly romantic vampire…it's the old school Drac from back in the day, and he hasn't aged well!" - *GoodReads*

1

THE CROOKED TREE

July 1994

If you were to ask the townsfolk of Jasper Mill about the stretch of land known as the Robinson Farm—*and you wouldn't*—they'd say, "Nothing grows in that dirt but pain and regret." Ghosts in the foundation. Demons in the mud. Older folks who lived during the alleged incidents on the Tennessee property claim the soil is cursed, infested by death and disease.

Younger ones will tell you that's bullshit.

But they stay away from it, all the same.

The Robinson clan and their kin have owned those lonely acres for over a hundred years, decades that have managed to amass a great deal of legend. Since 1910, when old Jedd Robinson flew into a rage and murdered his entire family with a sawed-off shotgun, there has been one tall tale after another.

Lester Wilkens thought all that was all crazy talk. Every bit of it. Dirt was dirt. That was that. Dirt couldn't be evil, corrupt, or possessed. And with each black-soiled acre priced at just $21.00 total monthly rental, he didn't give two shits what manner of devil crawled around in it. Especially seeing the local monthly farmland rate was anywhere from \$55 to \$60. For a measly \$21, he felt he'd make *something* grow in that dirt, something he could sell at a pretty profit. That's how he felt in early March. He felt differently now.

Lester hiked his leg over one of the red leather-covered stools inside Jasper Market and felt himself sink into the thin cushion. He glanced up at the dusty menu behind the counter and perused the selections, even though he knew he would order what he always ordered.

"Jody," he called out. "I think I want to try something different today."

Jody Jenkins, who had worked at the market nearly all her life, rounded the corner and plucked the Bic ballpoint pen behind her ear. "Oh, this I gotta hear."

Lester hesitated and said, "How about a Tuna Melt with slaw?"

Jody's eyebrow bowed. "You know you don't want no Tuna Melt."

"I like tuna," Lester pressed.

"You'll just throw it away, Lester," sighed Jody. "Just like my Country Fried Steak last week. You want a cheeseburger, plain, cheese only, with fries. No salt." She began to scribble on her order pad. "Damn shame. Somebody else would have appreciated that steak."

"The tuna seems—"

Jody spun toward the kitchen window and said, "Cheeseburger, plain, cheese only. Hold the salt on the fries."

"Wait!" said Lester. Jody glanced over her shoulder. "I'll take *Swiss* on it."

She shook her head. "You *daredevil*, you." She went to the kitchen window and shoved the order ticket on an empty spike. "Make it *yodel*, Charlie."

"Swiss cheese. You got it," called a voice from beyond the window. The cook's furry hand reached through the window and snatched the ticket. "How ya' want it?"

"Medium-well," replied Lester and Jody in unison.

Jody placed a tall glass of Coca-Cola in front of Lester. She plucked a broom from the adjacent wall and pretended to sweep, even though it would have taken a snow blower to clean that floor. Lester sank a straw into the cool, bubbling glass and took a sip. Then he turned and gazed through the window into those distant open fields. Those barren hills looked much like the spreading scalp of a balding man.

He was sitting in that spot staring through that exact window when he thought of renting a couple of acres of Robinson land to grow tobacco. One acre of tobacco would bring in over \$900, and he could have used the money.

That's for sure. Minus the land rental fee and seed, that was to be a net-profit of $1650. Enough to buy that Ford pick-up truck from Dan Green, who had taken excellent care of it. It seemed like a win-win situation. But nothing grew on Robinson's land. Nothing but patches of crab grass. Weeds. Poison ivy. Nothing.

Well, there was *one* thing.

The old, crooked oak tree had been planted in 1878, one of the only things ever growing on the Robinson farm. Once a modest sapling, the decades had forced the tree upward and outward, sprouting branches strong enough to support Jedd Robinson's two-hundred-and-ten-pound frame when he hanged himself from it in the Fall of 1910, just moments after slaughtering members of his own family. These days, the trunk was nearly six feet wide. It stood an ominous forty-three feet high, with long winding branches that reached toward the ground like withered fingers clawing at the earth. No one could ever explain how such a big tree had grown under such adversity, but it had. It sure had.

It didn't start with the Robinsons, you know. Some two decades before Jedd Robinson purchased those twenty-one acres for $83.00 in 1887, the land had seen one of the most baffling incidents of the Civil War. The week before Major General Nathan Bedford Forrest would lead his Confederate soldiers into Johnsonville, Tennessee, as part of his twenty-three-day raid on Yankee supply bases, he sent fifty-two of his troops with orders to form a blockade along the perimeter of a small logging town seven miles outside of the Johnsonville border called Jasper Mill. Forrest received word the troops had made it without incident, but when he arrived with the rest of the soldiers three days later, no one was on that stretch of land. The only thing that alluded to the fact that his soldiers had been there at all was the empty tents scattered around the fields. Personal belongings, clothes, medical kits, and weapons were left behind. It was as if the soldiers set up camp and walked away into nothingness.

Some claimed they were deserters, cowards who had taken the opportunity to flee the fight. The general wasn't convinced. He knew those soldiers, like Clint Bishop, who would have given his arm for the cause. Soldiers like Duke Jones, who had led his division to victory in Georgia. Those two would have remained even if fifty cowards decided to throw down their arms and join the Yankees. Dead or alive, they would have been there.

Decades later, long after life had moved on from the tragedies of war, Jedd Robinson, then a handsome twenty-four years old, plowed and sowed some seven acres of that land with tobacco and corn, the very ground where those empty tents had once drifted in the wind. By late March of 1887, with the crops planted, Jedd and his two eldest sons began work on what would become their new home. By August 10, they finished the three-room hall and parlor log structure covered by weatherboarding. But still, nothing had grown. Not one sprout.

For six months, Jedd tried to grow all sorts of things on that land, everything from green beans to tomatoes, but nothing took root, nothing but a wayward acorn his four-year-old daughter, Ruth, planted some fifteen hundred feet from the family house. The tale was that Jedd was surprised to see the sapling springing from the dirt in that field, so much so that he built a small fence around it to keep it from harm's way.

Over the next few years, the Robinsons met with one tragedy after another. Just over a year after making a home on the land, little Ruth was stung to death by a swarm of wasps nesting in the same ground where she had planted her acorn. Two years later, in 1890, their eldest son shot himself in the barn. In the fall of 1894, their second daughter died in the family parlor during childbirth. In 1898, their grandson fell to his death from the rooftop of the family house. The winter of 1905 saw the passing of their second son, who froze to death after mysteriously wandering into the fields in the middle of the winter night. Still, nothing had prepared Jasper Mill for what would follow during the holiday season of 1910.

Everyone tells the tale differently, of course. There are alternate times and various motives. But facts are facts, and the facts are more horrible than anything you could concoct.

On Christmas Eve, at approximately five forty-five that evening, Jedd Robinson finished his dinner and excused himself from the table. He returned to the family dining room seven minutes later armed with a shotgun and shot every remaining family member, including his wife, his two surviving children and their spouses, and even his six grandchildren. With the deed done, he carried the bodies into the parlor, doused them in kerosene, and set them ablaze before making his way to the crooked oak tree, where he hanged himself just before Christmas dawned.

Folks will tell you they know why.

They don't.

No one does.

Two weeks after the murders, the remaining Robinson clan had the remains of the house demolished and placed the land for sale, but there wasn't a single soul willing to take that gamble. If a potential buyer came along who wasn't aware of the land's sordid history, they were told tales soon enough, long before any ink had the opportunity to dry on a contract.

Legend and folklore continued to spread about the Robinson land like winding vines, each thorn darker than its predecessor. By the 1930s, the crooked oak became a place you dared others to venture, a test of bravery for the young and foolish. And the stories kept coming, adding to the legend.

1931—the teenage boy who dared to climb to the highest part of the tree was attacked by crows and fell to his death.

1940—the hanging of George Jackson, who strung himself from the very branch Jedd Robinson had used.

1952—the ritualistic murder of the girl by two of her friends.

But these tales paled in comparison to John Tate.

In February of 1966, Tate, a lifelong resident of Jasper Mill, was accused of killing and dismembering more than thirty women. The exact number may never be known. The authorities found the bodies of four of those victims in Tate's barn, which ironically stood less than three miles away from the crooked oak. He was arrested and tried but was released on one of those "technicalities" we hear about now and again. The people of Jasper Mill were outraged. Even though Tate would be retried, folks were taking no chances.

Less than a week after his release, town members kidnapped Tate in the darkness of night and took him to the deserted acres of Robinson Farm. They tortured the man for hours, strapping him to a car bumper and dragging him for miles through the gravel, branding his body with hot irons, and finally castrating him. They sewed his mouth shut with gunny thread, nailed him to the crooked oak, and covered his head with a burlap sack.

It took two days for the man to bleed to death. Over forty-eight hours of hanging there, suspended on that oak in the blistering summer sun. After Tate's corpse was laid to rest, the townsfolk took his burlap mask and nailed it to the trunk of the crooked oak, a reminder of the horrors that follow us like shadows. And there it has hung ever since.

After that, the crooked oak never again managed a single green leaf. Not one. The only thing that held onto those bare, withered branches were hordes of black crows that somehow found a home in the tree's shadow. The scavengers were kept company by swarms of bald-faced hornets who dwelled in the deep, winding hollows of the trunk. From a distance, those slick, black feathers gave the illusion of shadowy leaves that stared at you and knew what you were thinking. And the angry buzz of those wasps sounded like a rumble. A deep, menacing growl warned onlookers to beware.

By the early seventies, Wilbur Robinson, Jedd's brother who inherited the dirt, began renting out some of the outlying acreage for piece farming. Sometimes, the farther away from the crooked oak you sowed your crop, the better your chances were for yield. That left a mere seven acres of the land that stood any chance of turning a suitable harvest, but even reasonable crops were thin. Corn was weak, fragile, and infested with worms. Tobacco would only grow waist-high, no matter how many times it was topped. That was if it grew at all. But those low rental prices kept fools coming, all the same—fools just like Lester Wilkens.

"Here you go, honey," said Jody as she slid the steaming plate before Lester.

"Looks good," he said with a smile. It was then he noticed that the burger had American cheese on it. "I asked for Swiss," he said with confusion.

Jody snatched her broom. "And you'd have took two bites before leaving it to rot. Now, eat your burger and hush up."

Lester smiled because she was right. He was a creature of bland habit. He was particular about many things, and his food topped the list. Some folks had adventurous palates. Lester's palate was content to sit on the couch and watch episodes of Andy Griffith for the rest of its life. He sank his teeth into the fresh burger and appreciated its commonality. He was glad it was American cheese. As he plucked a steaming fry from the plate and moved it toward his mouth, something from beyond the market window drew his eye.

A dark figure wandered down the road, making its way toward the gravel lot of the store. At first, Lester thought it was a dog, some shaggy canine roaming the plains. As it grew closer, however, it appeared to be something else, something almost human. He couldn't be entirely sure, but the thing seemed to be about four feet in height and shaped like a person—a child, to be exact. It meandered in the summer heat, stumbling about like a drunkard, swatting aimlessly at the strange cloak covering its body, which moved and pulsated with a life of its own.

"Well, what in all hell ya' suppose that thing is?" muttered Lester.

Jody, who had managed to hear the query, paused. She glanced at Lester and then through the storefront window. "I have . . . no earthly idea," she replied, slipping the broom handle against the counter.

The red-and-black figure entered the lot and fell to its knees. They caught a glimpse of swollen, red flesh underneath the churning shroud. Jody walked to the front doors and stepped onto the walkway, with Lester close behind. Without the foggy glass hindering their view, they saw insects whirring around a body. Wasps, angry, buzzing like the engine of a 747 jet.

"*Heeelp meee,*" mumbled a young, weak voice burdened with agony.

"Dear God," said Lester. "That's a kid! A goddamned kid!"

Snatching an apron from the coat rack inside the doorway, Lester bolted toward the boy lying across the gravel. He swung the apron at the wasps, whirling it about as if he were putting out a fire. The fat, buzzing wasps began to disperse into a thick cloud of yellow and black, rising into the air in a churning mass. The swarm floated toward the sky and scattered, with a few angry troops remaining behind. Some soldiers charged Lester and stung him about his hands and neck, but his adrenaline raged too wildly for him to feel it. As Lester bent toward the child, he heard gravel crunching behind him.

"Jesus Christ!" murmured Charlie, gaping at the sight. "Call the ambulance, Jody!"

Lester had no idea who the boy was, but the child's once bright yellow shirt was now stained with dirt and jagged trails of dried blood. Plastered on the shirt's front in large wood-like lettering were the words KAMP KROMWELL 1994. A few of the bees crawled wearily within the boy's mussed hair, digging to find their way free, spent from an assault that left the boy gasping for air. His body had begun to swell so intensely that the flesh of his ankles puffed around the cuffs of his socks. The digital watch around his left wrist looked like it was about to snap. There wasn't a square centimeter of the child's body that wasn't claimed by oozing, inflamed welts. His eyes were swollen shut, barely allowing his long eyelashes to sprout through. A white, foamy drool trickled from either side of the boy's mouth. His breathing sounded like the blade of a saw chewing through wet wood. Lester stared at the poor soul, wanting to reach out, touch him, and comfort the boy somehow but fearing any caress would only cause more agony.

A single crow landed on the pavement about six feet from where Lester sat, holding the child's hand. The massive bird looked at him with those black, knowing eyes, aware, as if it knew precisely what tragedy had befallen the boy. It squawked with a loud bark, causing Lester's insides to shudder. It hopped forward and attempted to peck at something clenched in the child's hand. Lester swung the apron into the air.

"Get outta here, ya piece a'!" he boomed.

The crow hopped backward, fluttered its thick wings, and cried at

Lester in reply. Lester glanced down at the boy's shivering hand. Woven in the child's fingers were coarse strands of fabric, a thick cloth, like burlap from a death hood made of an old potato sack. Lester looked to the distant oak that held the mask of John Tate.

And the tree looked back.

2

9:07 A.M.

My story begins with a troubled man named Samuel Barnes. You've not heard of him, but he's there, all right, filed away with all the other shameful events of Knoxville, Tennessee. If it hadn't been for the ordeal with Sam, I don't think I would have ended up at Kamp Kromwell in the first place.

Sam was the uncle of my childhood friend Jeremy Tidwell. Jeremy and I discovered each other early in life. We met at the onset of third grade when his parents moved to the city from Plunket County, a little rural town about an hour outside of Knoxville. Before that time, my only friend in the whole world was Leslie Cooper, who lived just behind me. I could tell Leslie most anything. *Most* anything. But I had shameful secrets that I felt no one could know.

Just like Jeremy.

Upon sight, Jeremy and I knew there was something different about each other, something that set us apart from other boys at school. It drew us to one another, this gravitational pull of scandalous commonality. We were too young to know precisely what being homosexual entailed, but I had enough older brothers to know that being "queer" was allegedly harmful. Armed with this knowledge, I learned to keep my true self hidden in the shadows, shrouded under the guise of someone else—someone who liked baseball, big boobs, and Matchbox cars.

On the other hand, Jeremy was an only child with an overzealous mother who convinced herself that her son's affinity for twirling batons, pompoms, and Barbie dolls were traits of childhood innocence he would eventually outgrow. It certainly didn't mean her only son was *home-o-sexual*, God forbid. And no one could tell her different. But I had news for her—Jeremy was as queer as a *football bat*. And so was I.

Though Jeremy and I were the only two gay people we knew at the time, we didn't necessarily share a romantic bond with one another. Contrary to popular belief, just because you lock two gay guys in a room doesn't mean they'll jump each other's bones. For all intents and purposes, Jeremy was just a "girlfriend," someone with whom I could speak freely about my crushes on the baseball players at school, my never-ending fascination with male underwear ads in the Sears catalog, and my burning desire for Chris O'Donnell.

I taught Jeremy to dull his vivid personality to navigate the rednecks, and he taught me how to be comfortable in my own flesh. We complemented each other. We kept the other from feeling so different, alone. As we got older, we started to confide more deeply in each other and exchange our maturing views on ourselves and the world in which we existed, like two stoned hippies sitting around a smoldering bong, pondering perceptions of life. During one of these existential conversations, he told me about Uncle Sam.

When I first heard the tale of Uncle Sam—this suspiciously single thirty-five-year-old man serving as Plunket County's only mortician—I was just over fourteen years old. According to Jeremy, the two of us had something in common with old Sam, something that piqued my curiosity. Apparently, Sam also liked members of the same sex. I questioned how Jeremy had learned such a thing, and he said Sam had told him. He swore that nothing physical had occurred between him and his uncle. But after pressing the subject, I learned there had been displays, various acts of "show-and-tell," and confidential phone conversations while Jeremy's parents were away.

To anyone with common sense, these flags would have burned red and deterred further exploration into a grown man who not only dealt with dead bodies but enjoyed having dirty talk with his young, effeminate nephew. But fourteen-year-olds don't have common sense. I found myself obsessed with Uncle Sam for many obscure reasons. Most importantly, he was the only other homosexual I knew existed.

I had learned of an animal in Vietnam, a rare breed of mammal discovered in 1992 called the *Saola*, a small antelope-like thing with two long, parallel horns. Some call it the "Asian unicorn." Later in life, I'd learn Knoxville housed a technicolor funscape of gay folk, but in those days, it felt like Jeremy and I were the only ones in the world. Two rare, neglected unicorns, all alone with our magic.

Shortly after I learned of Sam, summer arrived with a glorious splendor, and with it came the liberated sense of adventure felt only by the young and stupid. One late June afternoon, while Jeremy's mother and stepfather were exploring yard sales, Jeremy called me to come and keep him company at his house, which sat just four houses down from my own. As the two of us sat there eating sandwiches, the subject of Uncle Sam floated to the surface of conversation. I can't quite remember how or why he came up, but I learned that Jeremy had told his uncle about me, and Sam wanted to meet me over the phone. I want to say that I was warily curious, reluctant to participate in such an inappropriate thing. And I think there was a small part of me that *did* know better. But at that age, the voice of reason was soft and weak, often drowned out by the booming commands of the adolescent id.

I don't recall much of that initial conversation with Sam. Just his voice. This deep southern drawl rambled through rasping breaths as if the man held the phone receiver directly under flaring nostrils. He asked my age, what I looked like, and I asked the same of him. Before the conversation sank further into depravity, Jeremy snatched the receiver from my ear, bid Sam a quick farewell, and hung up the phone before his mother entered the house with an armload of gaudy secondhand clutter.

Over the following days, the notion of Sam gnawed at me. I felt I had to speak to him again and needed to do so without Jeremy present; I just wasn't sure why or how. I didn't know what I wanted to say, really. I felt I just had to talk with the man again, to hear the voice of the only other unicorn. Finally, as my mother napped one summer morning, an idea crept into my mind. In the privacy of our den, I picked up the phone, dialed Directory Assistance, and obtained the phone number for Odell's Funeral Home in Plunket, Tennessee: Sam's workplace. As I scribbled down the number on the back of the thick phone book, my hand trembled so much I could barely read what I had written. And . . . then I sat there. I sat there for what felt like hours staring at that phone number, wondering what to do, what to say. Losing my nerve, I returned the phone book to the stand and ventured to other distractions. Three days passed before I found the courage to take the next step.

A woman answered the phone, and I politely asked to speak to Sam Barnes. After placing me on a brief hold, I heard his voice enter the line. He was somewhat surprised to hear from me, but he seemed delighted. He told me he was just about to take a lunch break and asked if I would call him at home. I agreed. I jotted his home number just underneath the number of the funeral home. Then, as he requested, I gave him ten minutes to reach his apartment just down the road from the mortuary. With a nervous lump in my throat, I called his apartment. He picked up the phone after the first ring.

The conversation was innocent enough. I learned Sam had a dog named Roger and a parakeet named Lucy. He lived by himself in a one-bedroom apartment in Plunket, and he liked comedy movies. Sam said he wasn't "out," which meant no one knew he was a unicorn. I told him I wasn't "out" either. His favorite food was anything spicy, his favorite candy was Hershey's chocolate bars, and his favorite color was yellow. All these things seemed harmless to me, normal even. We ended the call with the understanding that I would not tell Jeremy that the two of us had spoken, and I never said a word.

Sam arranged for me to call him at his apartment on Tuesdays and Thursdays between noon and one in the afternoon. For the next three weeks, I did so like clockwork. With each discussion, the subject matter became more personal and intimate. It happened so gradually that I barely noticed at all. In some ways, it was as if I was talking with another teenage boy who also liked guys. I was too young and enthralled by my new friend to comprehend the sickness of it all.

After receiving a rather hefty phone bill, my mother severed my connection with Sam. Since I was a child, and children can be *stoo-ped* (with two "o's"), I hadn't pondered the consequences of making long-distance calls twice each week, some of which lasted nearly an hour. I also hadn't prepared for my mother's sudden interrogation, but I managed to avoid awkwardness by claiming I had been calling Jeremy while he was visiting his family in Plunket.

I wouldn't reencounter Sam until mid-July.

On Saturday, July 16, 1993, I rushed to Jeremy's house bright and early at eight a.m. to join him and his parents at Landers Water Park, an aquatic paradise just forty-five minutes outside Knoxville. Within minutes, we piled inside the rattling station wagon, stuffed to the brim with inflated floats and salty snack foods, heading to what we called "the mountains" of Pigeon Forge,

Tennessee. As we made our way, Jeremy's mother, Gina, claimed she had a "surprise" for us when we arrived. Neither Jeremy nor I could imagine what it could be, but we anxiously waited.

By ten that morning, we pulled into the vast lot of Landers and found a parking space among the sea of automobiles. As the four of us trudged toward the ticket booth, Jeremy's father began to wave as if he saw someone he recognized. That's when I saw a short, plump, balding man wearing neon-green swim trunks and a yellow tank top waving back at him. His smile shone through his short beard. He wiggled his round sausage fingers enthusiastically as we neared him.

"Surprise!" the strange man sang.

When I heard that voice, a voice on which I had focused so intently for weeks, I realized two things: first, this person had to be Uncle Sam, and second, Uncle Sam *was a damn liar.* This creepy fellow was all but a vague impression of the person he had painted himself to be. From our previous conversations, I had understood Sam to be of medium height, "stocky," with a beard, who had been told he "reminds people" of Bruce Willis (the *Die Hard* Bruce, not the *Death Becomes Her* Bruce). This dude was *not* Bruce Willis. This was Bruce Vilanch! My jaw hung ajar, and I turned to Jeremy, who seemed just as stunned by Sam's presence as I was.

"Uncle Sam," chuckled Jeremy. "You're coming, too?"

"Yep," he said as he joined us. Jeremy rose, and the two of them loosely embraced. "I was talking to your mom the other night, and she said you were going to Landers, and, well, I just couldn't pass that up since it's so close to me." Then, Sam turned to me with a smile. "And who's this fine young man?"

Jeremy glanced at me. "Joey Carpenter. My friend I've told you about."

Sam held out his hand to me, and I instinctively hesitated. At last, I forced my hand forward, and he took it into his. "Well, nice to meet you, Joe!" Sam said enthusiastically. His eyes locked onto mine. He smiled. There was something about that smile, something bizarre. I imagined if lions could smile before they devoured a wounded gazelle, it would look just like Sam's smile.

The five of us got tickets and entered the water park. For the first couple of hours, things were rather ordinary. We played in the wave pool, slipped down several long, winding water slides, and even took a moment for lunch. The first time Sam hovered close to me was as we waited in line for the Water Whipper, a long winding slide with several tunnels. Sam lingered behind me, edging closer and closer to where I stood. I would nudge my feet forward each time he did to maintain my distance. This game continued until I nearly found myself nestled deep in the ass crack of the round lady before me. After I stepped on the heel of her turquoise flip-flop, the woman turned and gave me a disapproving scowl, forcing me to take a step backward. With nowhere left for me to turn, Sam pressed himself against me. He reached forward and wrapped his hands around my arms to hold me in place. And there was that breathing again, that loud, rattling nostril breathing that ruffled the hair on the crown of my head.

At this moment, I realized what was happening between Sam and me. It had never been a casual, friendly conversation. Not for him. It had been grooming, a period of discovery and planning. He had intended to find a way to get near me all along, this portly, hairy, bald man who tinkered with dead bodies.

Suddenly, I was unable to remain in place. I wriggled myself free of Sam's grasp and ducked out of the line. He called me as I scurried away, though I couldn't quite hear what he said. From the corner of my eye, I saw Sam leave the line to follow me. That's when I ducked into a crowded restroom. I slipped to the last stall, closed the door, and locked the latch. Then, I took a seat on the toilet lid and waited.

As the minutes passed, the bustle of conversation grew softer and softer, eventually slipping into disconcerting silence broken only by the light *plink-plink* of a dripping faucet resonating off the cinderblock walls. I didn't move. I intended to remain in that stall until the end of time if I had to—anything to steer clear of old Uncle Sam.

I don't know how much time had passed before I finally emerged, but the sunlight was no longer shining through the open doorway of the restroom, and my swim trunks were bone dry. I decided to feign a stomachache and sit with Gina for the rest of the time there. Then I would never allow myself to be in the presence of Uncle Sam ever again.

Stepping to the sink, I had just plunged my hands into the stream of water when I heard a voice.

"Well, there you are!" Sam said as he slipped through the doorway. "We were all wondering what had happened to you."

"I think my stomach is upset," I said without looking in his direction.

"Oh, well, that's not good. Bet it was the wave pool." Sam stepped deeper into the bathroom, allowing the door to swing closed behind him. He joined me at the sink next to mine. After some silence, he said, "I didn't know you were such a cutie." He let out a nauseating snicker. I didn't reply. "I'd like to be your friend, Joey. If you'll let me."

"I think I've got enough friends, thanks," I said.

Sam glanced at the doorway of the vacant restroom, and then he slid his hand into his swim trunks. He exposed himself to me and nervously cooed, "Are you sure? I can be an *awfully* good friend."

I can't tell you the precise moment when raging anger ruptured through my fear, but I seem to recall it was about *one-point-two seconds* after that shit. I glanced down at Sam's crotch and then looked him straight in the eyes. "Okay. But I wonder if Gina would be okay with us being friends? Maybe I should go ask her." Immediately, Sam slipped himself back into his trunks, and his eyes gaped with fear. Feeling ripe with power, I added, "Something tells me Jeremy's parents wouldn't like—"

Sam lunged at me so suddenly that I didn't have time to think, let alone react. His hands snapped around my throat, and he dragged me backward as I fought, choking and flailing against his grip. I felt the blood pool in my skull. My head began to pound so hard I thought it would rupture.

"*Why, you little fucker! You little fucker!*" he hissed at me repeatedly. "*You little fucker!*" Veins bulged around his temples. His once pale complexion burned fiery red. He maneuvered me around the urinals and hauled me behind the lines of lockers at the rear of a rest area. A green hue began to fill my vision. I realized I was about to lose consciousness. I quit fighting. At first, I wasn't sure why. I had strength left. I think I began to feel I deserved what was happening to me. I was a unicorn, after all. Less than. Unworthy. Even God had turned his back on me. Why else would this be taking place? So, I let go. As Sam fought my swim trunks down around my knees, I held my breath, allowing the darkness to take me and spare me the details.

God, I know you don't care for people like me and that answering my prayer is the last thing on your mind. But please . . . please give me just one last thing: let me die quick.

I awoke to the blare of sirens as the ambulance rushed toward Saint John's Hospital in Pigeon Forge. I began to wane in and out of consciousness, my eyes creaking open like rusty hinges. I heard a voice call, "I have a heartbeat!" And then, the darkness swept over me again.

Two days later, I woke up with my mother beside my hospital bed. My father circled angrily around the room, buzzing like a wet hornet. Officers occasionally slipped into the room with sympathetic expressions and asked me questions, queries I couldn't answer. They would shy away from my eyes, which had somehow transformed from bright, blue irises into deep, blackish-red orbs of nothingness. I couldn't remember the ordeal. I couldn't think about it. All I could think of was God. Somehow, he/she/they had found it best to allow me to live, to come through it. I wasn't sure why, but I was convinced there had to be some reason God spared me. Could it have been that God loved unicorns, too? It was too soon to say for sure.

Over the remainder of that summer, I would learn several things about the attack, pieces I would hear my mother whisper about late at night while talking to my aunt, things my parents would say when they believed I was asleep, things that fortunately didn't sit in clear view of my memory. As Sam assaulted me, two boys slipped into the restroom to smoke and heard the commotion. They immediately alerted their father, a lovely man who later introduced himself to me as Steve Maples. Mr. Maples found Sam, tore him away from me, and pummeled Sam until he lay unconscious on the sticky concrete floor. I suffered two broken ribs and a dislocated shoulder. I couldn't swallow for several days. The EMTs declared me dead for nearly thirty seconds en route to the hospital.

The state charged Samuel Barnes with attempted second-degree murder, open and gross conduct involving an underage person, and statutory rape of a minor. Further investigation of his apartment in Plunket County uncovered disturbing images involving lewd pictures of young boys in various stages of undress and numerous Polaroid photos he had taken of nude deceased bodies at Odell's during his tenure. With that revelation, the state added the charges of possession of child pornography and lewd and lascivious behavior involving a deceased person.

The prosecutor, Laura Finch, urged my parents to allow me to testify about the attack in open court, but I refused. The whole truth would surface in a courtroom; a reality I wasn't prepared for anyone to know. Also, I felt the more distance I could put between myself and good old Uncle Sam, the better off I would be.

The assault and resulting charges turned into a scandal that clouded the skies of Knoxville and the surrounding counties. Landers Water Park closed after the media's crucifixion. My mother and father immediately shifted the blame to Jeremy's parents, which led Jeremy and his family to move from Knoxville a little over a month after the incident. I never laid lay eyes on Jeremy again.

Things changed for me after my encounter with Samuel Barnes. I became dull, listless, and faded. I regressed into myself, turning inward. I only found comfort at home in the solace of my room, away from my friend, Leslie, who couldn't help but bring up the attack. I could hardly blame her. Everyone wanted to know more, more details, more gore. The truth was I didn't remember the particulars, and that suited me just fine. I very well couldn't let others know the truth—that I was, in fact, this rare unicorn, much unlike the other mules around me, a one-of-a-kind creature who had sought out my attacker.

My father transformed the incident with Sam into a reason for my "differences," a motive for me being unlike my brothers. It certainly wasn't because I had been a unicorn all along. Sam had hunted me, taken me from the herd, and drilled that winding horn directly into my forehead. I wasn't different because I was *born* different; I was different because Sam had turned me into something else, something hideous, something shameful.

But I had always been a unicorn.

Sam just stole my magic.

3
FLOPPY MOSSY

"She is like a cat in the dark. And then she is the darkness."
— *Rhiannon*: Fleetwood Mac—

January 1995

Earl Drummond sat at his desk staring at the thick pile of counselor applications as if gazing into some dismal abyss, a blackhole of infinite despair. Finding one suitable counselor was challenging enough. Five seemed impossible. Did any of these little asshats take a moment to read what they had written? Hell, no. That'd be too easy.

One girl had said she was "edger" to be part of the "Cochran" family. Drummond didn't know who the hell the *Cochrans* were but could only assume the girl was *eager* to be part of their brood. Another applicant claimed she had "a lot of beauty tips" she could share with "less fortunate girls who ain't naturally hot." *That's all we need*, thought Drummond. One young fellow, who happened to be the son of a city councilman from Stone Creek County, claimed he had done "a dime" for dealing drugs, and he could share this experience with other kids to keep them "on the straight and narrow." In this case, the *dime* meant the kid had suffered ten grueling days in a juvenile detention facility in Oak Ridge for selling Tylenol PM capsules disguised as quaaludes. The buses would chauffeur in enough trouble that summer. Drummond didn't need to add any to the payroll. How had it come to this?

Drummond had once been the vice principal of a posh private school on the upper west side of Atlanta, Georgia. The job, which Drummond held for nearly five years, had been so tranquil that he sometimes felt he took advantage of the high-dollar salary. Things went south in November of 1985. Persil Academy made national news when Judith Havers, the "happily married" middle-aged principal, allegedly had affairs with not one but *three* of the academy's teenaged students. It damned Persil Academy. Just ten months after the guilty verdict hit the papers, the school locked its doors forever, and Drummond, then thirty-eight, found himself without a job.

For thirteen months, he bounced from job to job, searching for something suitable, somewhere he could lie low, do the job, and coast into retirement. He tried the public school system, but the salaries were far too thin, less than half of what he had been making at Persil. He even attempted retail management, but the bustle and aggravation of the first holiday season sucked the wind out of those frail sails.

Since the two had married, Lucy, Drummond's wife of thirty years, had worked at National Trust and Savings. She had started as a teller and had worked her way up to senior director of her division. So, with Lucy's experience leading the way, Drummond decided to try his hand at the banking institution. While this paid better than public education or retail, the severe stress and excessive work hours often outweighed the compensation.

In September of 1987, Lucy announced that National Trust had offered her the role of senior vice president of operations in their call center in Knoxville, Tennessee, some four hours away from where they currently lived. It seemed silly not to take the gamble. For the first time in a while, Drummond caught the scent of promise hovering in the cold winter air of the Tennessee valley, and it smelled sweet.

With its distinct balance of rural and city life, Knoxville seemed like the perfect place to begin anew, and it was. Just four months after their arrival, Drummond stumbled upon an opportunity with a place called Kromwell Industries, a company that specialized in property management. Kromwell was in desperate need of leadership for their camping and recreation facilities, which included camping sites in Pigeon Forge, Gatlinburg, and an enormous summer camp in the heart of a tiny town called Jasper Mill, which sat just an hour or so outside of Knoxville. With Drummond's significant experience with youth, the company was quick to offer him the position.

In the fall and winter, Drummond would manage the RV and cabin sites in Gatlinburg when skiing at Ober Gatlinburg was at its peak. In spring, his attention would turn to Pigeon Forge, where the warm weather always led to a boom of tourists eager to rush to the *home-spun fun* of Dollywood. It would be the summers that would nearly drive Drummond to drink. He'd spend several weeks deep in Mother Nature's cleavage as director of operations at Kamp Kromwell, a practical paradise of natural wonders. Really, the damn place was more trouble than it was worth, a public relations nightmare.

During his first year in the 1988 summer season, it was difficult for camp counselors to keep their clothes on. It was worse than Woodstock. Drummond had much creative explaining to do when several children, some between the ages of ten and twelve, witnessed a group of counselors partaking in a vodka-fueled skinny-dipping orgy in the middle of the night.

Yes, Bobby, that's called a va-gi-na.

Three teenage campers smoked a joint the following year and accidentally set fire to Cabin Seven, which nearly burned to the ground. Two parents threatened legal action during the 1990 season when their precious daughter broke both ankles after falling from the unstable rope bridges lining the north end of the campground, even though the counselors had expressly said the bridges were off-limits that year. And in 1991, Drummond narrowly averted what could have been a crisis of biblical proportions when a delayed background check revealed one of the new cooks, who had been on site for three weeks, was hiding a rape conviction in his boxer shorts. However, nothing would compare to the tragedy that befell Kamp Kromwell during the summer of 1994.

During his time in Jasper Mill, Drummond had heard nearly every bit of the folklore creeping through the town. In the first summer alone, campfire tales had told him everything there was to know about the madman named Tate, who had haunted Jasper Mill when he was alive in the '60s. The rumors, while different in plot and pacing, all boiled down to one story and one story only. Tate had been a homicidal fiend who had butchered countless women, some native to the area, others unfortunate enough to get his attention while passing through. A mistrial led the townsfolk to take matters into their own hands. They turned Tate into a tormented scarecrow, sewing his mouth shut, nailing the maniac to a tree, and wrapping his face in a burlap sack, a sack that remained fixed to the same tree on which they crucified him.

And yadda-dadda-bullshit.

A group of overzealous counselors decided making a game out of those legends would be fun. The "scary scavenger" hunt included locating twisted items like dead animals, rubbings from gravestones of Jasper Mill Cemetery, and keepsakes taken from the land of the town's self-proclaimed wicked witch, an infamous old bat known to all as *Miss Floppy Mossy*. But the most valuable item in the hunt, the most treasured token, was the death mask John Tate wore, dangling on the trunk of a winding oak about two miles from the campground.

No one dared go near the old tree that seemed to have a life of its own except George Peterson and Davey Abrams. The boys decided they would snatch that rotting old burlap hood nailed to the broad trunk of the massive oak tree, win the scavenger hunt hands down, and relieve themselves of camp chores for the remainder of the season. While attention was focused elsewhere during the hunt, the two boys slipped into the dusky afternoon to claim their prize.

As George and Davey approached the dark, twisted tree, they discovered they weren't quite as brave as they had thought. George would later claim that the oak seemed to know they were there. And it knew they were up to no good. George pleaded with Davey to abandon the quest, but Davey was a determined little shit. He scaled those twisting branches to where the burlap hood hung, gazing down to the ground below with that one dark, empty eye. Watching them. Waiting. Knowing. Neither of the boys realized that the tree was not only infamous for being the final resting place of John Tate, but it was also known to house massive nests of angry, bald-faced hornets. The only reason the town hadn't chopped the tree down years ago was that it was older than Jasper Mill itself. Many folks considered it to be a landmark of sorts. But everyone knew to keep their distance.

The wasps took less than five minutes to cover Davey Abrams's small body like a venomous wetsuit. George took off like a shot when the wasps emerged and still suffered over twenty stings along his arms and legs. The counselors had just begun searching for the missing boys when they happened upon a stunned and shivering George Peterson, huddled behind the campus auditorium, pale and in shock at what he had witnessed.

"The tree," muttered George in dazed bewilderment. "The tree got him."

Minutes later, Sheriff Fred Dunham called the campground to announce that the body of Davey Abrams had been recovered. Somehow, while covered in hornets from head to foot, the boy had found the strength to wander to the Jasper Market parking lot. Lester Wilkens, who was having lunch at the market then, would later tell Drummond it was the most horrifying thing he had ever witnessed—and that was a lot coming from Lester.

It was the first recorded death at Kamp Kromwell since it opened its gates in 1967, and news spread through Jasper Mill like wildfire through wheat. All the counselors were dismissed immediately, apart from Beth Hawkins, who hadn't known of the hunt.

Miss Mossy, who had threatened some form of legal action or another on Kromwell Industries for decades, didn't hesitate to threaten suit after learning her land had been part of the sordid game. Although the woman couldn't name a single item stolen or prove anyone had trespassed on her property, it still didn't stop her from bitching. Little did.

Though everyone agreed it was a tragic misadventure, the camp closed for the last half of that season and refunded admission fees. After the boy's mother attempted a lawsuit, Drummond wondered if Kamp Kromwell would open for the new season. Still, those marketing campaign materials landed in his mailbox like clockwork. The year 1995 would focus on watersports at Lake Ellington, which lined the perimeter of the campground, where brand-new Yamaha Wave Blaster jet skis would be available for use. In addition, the company would be upgrading the maze of rope bridges to include various slides, including three new winding water slides that would empty into the lake.

Finally, the company would provide new equestrian stables in the southern half of the grounds that would hold ten riding horses managed by a woman named Susan Brooks, who had herself competed in the equestrian games in the 1984 Summer Olympics. *Great,* Drummond thought. *Now we get horseshit, too.*

Kromwell Industries was doing everything it could to put the tragedy of Davey Abrams to rest, but it did little to rest Drummond's mind. He had to fill five counselor positions for the season. There was always at least one open counselor position. Unlike Beth, who had worked at the camp since 1992, the younger people tended to come and go. She was hardworking, intelligent, and very good with the kids, especially the junior campers who tended to miss home upon arrival. If only he could find five Beths. With five Beths, he could . . .

"Earl?"

The voice startled Drummond, who sat focused on the applications scattered over his desk. He jerked and looked to see Beth peeking through the door at him.

"Damn," he muttered. "You about scared the hell outta me." A giggle dribbled from his lips.

Beth smiled. "Sorry. I didn't mean to."

"Come on in," he said with a wave. "How did the interview go? The one with *Teresa Ambercombie*, or—"

Beth giggled. "Tracey Abernathy." She rounded the desk and took a seat in front of him. "It was a bust. The girl is nuts. I told her that she didn't pass the background check, and she *literally* lost her mind. 'I gave you references. You were supposed to use those!' References I'm sure she paid for, no doubt. Said she didn't agree to a background check, but I told her that the application clearly stated one would be conducted."

Drummond shook his head. "She can't be more than eighteen. How much of a background could she have?"

"More than you'd think. Let's just say she's been in her fair share of 'facilities.' We don't need mentally unstable people running around a campsite filled with axes," Beth concluded.

Drummond scoffed. "Amen."

"Any luck on your end?"

He sighed. "Not much. I've found a couple who might work."

"Who?"

He slipped his fingers around two applications resting on the plastic mail shelves in the corner of his desk. "Um . . . a Rosetta Samuel from Memphis and a Daniel Thorogood from Maryville."

"You know Jack keeps talking about that nephew of his who wants to come," Beth offered. "It'd be free labor."

Drummond rolled his eyes. "I love Jack. God knows I do. But we don't normally offer counselor jobs as Community Service. Dewayne was here in 1989 when he was a kid, and he was a shit." Drummond snatched a stick of gum from his desk and folded it into his mouth. "Foul-mouth little hoodlum with a stutter. If I do decide to let him come, he can stay in the kitchen, where his uncle can be responsible for him. A kid only has to tell me to *st-st-stick it up m-m-my as-as-ass* once."

Beth doubled over with laughter.

Jack Burns had managed the kitchen staff at Kromwell since 1981. He was one of the hardest-working men Drummond knew. But that nephew of his, Dewayne—that kid was hell on wheels. The boy couldn't string a single sentence together without cursing, and his speech impediment at the time made his profanity dangerously comical. Drummond was not a fan.

"What's this pile?" asked Beth.

"That's my '*Oh, God if I have to*' pile."

Beth turned through the pages. She paused at one. "This one doesn't look so bad. Bonnie . . . Evans?" Beth turned the page. "She's from Chattanooga. Twenty. Graduated from Notre Dame High School *with* honors. Says she teaches CPR. Works with the children's hospital. Going to the University of Tennessee in Chattanooga to be a social worker." Beth looked at Drummond. "What could possibly be wrong with her?"

"Read the letter," said Drummond.

"What letter?" Beth turned to the last page, a recommendation letter from the girl's mother. It was three typewritten, single-spaced pages describing in painstaking detail Bonnie's purity. The girl was a model citizen, a Christian who believed in God and abstinence. Bonnie could be a "good, Christian example" to "irresponsible girls who struggle with temptation." Beth's eyes moved to Drummond, who stared back at her with a raised eyebrow.

"See?" he said as if the letter told Beth everything she needed to know.

"What? I mean, it's . . . it's not *that* bad."

"Obviously, that girl has devout parents." He immediately threw up his hands. "Now, there is *nothing* at all wrong with loving the Lord. My wife and I go to church every chance we get. However, we'll have many folks on this campus who do anything but. You have to set all that aside at a commercial summer camp. Something tells me that girl, not to mention her mother, would be a liability, and Mr. Kromwell always says to—"

"Beware of liabilities," said Beth and Drummond in unison.

"Exactly," agreed Drummond. "Best case scenario: This Bonnie is a good girl who'll set a good example others may choose to follow. *Not-so-best* case, she spends her time wandering the campus, passing out God-fearin' flyers, and trying to convert us sinners. Worst case—Bonnie Evans is a pot-smoking party girl who listens to Dead Lepper, looking to escape her overbearing mother and raise a little hell. And when she gets caught—and she *will* get caught—she'll say the camp led her into temptation. Whole thing just gives me the shits."

Beth chuckled. "*Def Leppard*," she corrected.

"Who?"

"Def Leppard. That's the name of the band," Beth added.

"Whatever. Trash music."

Beth smiled. She reached down and plucked another application from the mix. After reading it over, she began to smile. "You could always bring the girl with all the beauty tips for us ugly folks."

Drummond snickered. "I don't think she could help this old mug."

The door popped open. Jack Burns slipped into the room with a disconcerting expression. "Earl?"

"Oh, God," was all Drummond could manage. "Don't give me bad news, Jack."

"Your girlfriend is—"

"See," said Drummond, raising a finger. "I said no bad news, man."

Jack sighed. "Miss Mossy. She's out in the lobby having herself a fit over those horses."

"Well, what the hell are the horses doing to her?" asked Drummond as he rose.

"She said the whole town smells like horseshit," Jack replied. Beth chuckled.

Drummond rounded his desk. "Well, the whole town smelled of horseshit long before the horses got here. What's her problem?"

Beth covered her mouth to hide her smirk.

Drummond and Beth followed Jack from the office into the dining concourse, where the woman everyone knew as Floppy Mossy paced back and forth like a sinner at a synagogue. She wore a threadbare wind coat with a tattered fur collar over her short, stout frame. A light brown dress with a faded floral pattern was under it, which, like Mossy, may have once been bright and vibrant. Thick, brown leggings peeked from underneath the dress's hem, which emptied into bulky black combat boots caked with dried mud. A dirty white gardening hat with a wispy peacock plume on the brim sat on her head. Tattered red hair peppered with streams of gray hung down the middle of her back. Traces of hay from her long day of winter yardwork hid in those luscious locks. The woman owned nary a brassiere, allowing her ample bosom to swing from her chest like two fleshy pendulums.

A massive old tom cat strolled around her feet, a ragged creature Mossy called *Rascal*, who accompanied her everywhere she went. Mossy noticed Drummond and waggled a finger in his direction.

"*Youuu sonuvabitch,*" Mossy hissed as she stomped forward in those boots, tossing dried mud along the floor. "Did you get approval for livestock on this land?"

Drummond sighed. "Everything is in order, Mossy. I can get the permits if you need them."

"I sure as hell *will* need them!" she shouted, hoisting her finger into the air. "I have my police report right here." She shoved her massive handbag into Drummond's arms. "Hold this." She dove into the bag, rifling through the contents. She removed various oddities, which included a curling iron, three Twix chocolate bars, a Phillips head screwdriver, shotgun shells, rubber bands, a feathered cat toy, an electric razor, and a copy of the TV Guide.

"Jesus, Mossy, what do you need all this for?" Beth posed.

"I got *everything* in this fucker, honey."

Drummond's brow furrowed. "Mossy, we've talked about that mouth. You can't use that language here. We'll have kids all over the place soon."

"Ain't no kids in here now, is they?" asked Mossy. She pointed to Beth. "That ain't no kid." She snatched her items from Beth's arms and stuffed them back in her bag.

"Well, it still isn't nice to hear!" said Drummond, this time with a bit of force, which seemed to pull the woman from the rafters.

"And what about all those damn rope bridges? All that beating and banging and what-not going on all hours of the night. I ain't too far away from this place, you know. I can hear every whack!"

"Oh, we'd move farther from you if we could," said Drummond, causing Jack to snicker.

Mossy squinted her eyes and strolled forward. She raised a brown, crooked fingernail to the tip of Drummond's nose. "Don't you get smart with me, Earl Drummond. Remember, I got me a pair of your personals. Snatched 'em right off the clothesline. I'll use my ways to render you useless to the missus."

"Your *ways*, huh?" smiled Drummond.

"You know I got 'em."

"You sure do," Drummond said with a shake.

Mossy snapped her fingers. "And *don't* you try and sweet talk me either. That ain't gonna work no more, Earl."

Drummond sighed and ran his hands over his face. "Look, Mossy. I can't do anything about the horses. I wish I could. I don't much care for the smell down that way, either. I'll tell the men to lay off the hammering when it gets dark. But that's all I got for you."

Mossy stared angrily at Drummond momentarily, and then her face softened. "Good." She bent forward and scooped Rascal into her arms. She squinted her eyes and leaned into Drummond. Finally, as with every encounter with Earl Drummond, she whispered, "Give me a little kiss."

Beth broke into silent giggles.

"How's about I owe you one?"

With a shrug, she turned on her heel.

"You don't know what you're missing, Earl. I'd blow your toes off!"

Mossy marched through the doors with that cat draped over her shoulder like a mangy mink stole.

4

10:15 A.M.

February 1995

The year following my ordeal with Sam Barnes was rife with trials and tribulations. It was as if my mind was lost in a constant storm, a subconscious hurricane that racked my thoughts with gale-force winds beyond my control. I spent my days feeling less than, undeserving of anything positive, worthy of only misfortune. That's not to say I rambled along, blaming my troubles on everyone except myself. On the contrary, I blamed *everything* on myself, including the events that landed me next to my mother in the office at Chamberland High School.

The two of us had an appointment with Principal Larry Harold about my recent absences from class. "Excessive absences that have warranted truancy." That's what Mr. Harold had called it. I had skipped *eleven* consecutive days of school, and they had been the most serene eleven days I had experienced in quite a while. There had been no bullies from whom to dodge, no threats to "hunt me down" in the hallways, and no sudden shrieks of *"faggot"* or *"queer"* in my direction. Mom, who had uncovered this covert vacation, had initially told the office I had been battling a case of strep, which, in turn, led them to request medical documentation we didn't have. So, the cat was out of the bag.

I had concocted every way possible to skip school, some quite ingenious. To this day, I can't tell you how much of my junior year I missed. I hadn't always hated school. Quite the opposite: I enjoyed the social aspect of the school environment throughout the seventh grade. Granted, I'll admit I wasn't a big fan of school at the onset of first grade, but within a few short weeks into the school year, it became an adventure for me, a place where I could meet other children, make friends, learn, read, and play. It wasn't until high school that I discovered how the hungry jowls of adolescence devoured childhood innocence, leaving only a confused and anxious teenage shell.

I see today's unicorns, and I can't help but notice the striking differences in our life experiences. The explosion of social media and advancements in digital communication have led to sharing events in the blink of an eye. In significant, essential ways, the world has grown more socially conscious. News of injustice that would typically take weeks to reach us—if at all—now blips onto our mobile devices mere seconds after it occurs, leading to widespread exposure and hastened action. I've watched today's teenagers come out to parents and others via text messages, emails, and PowerPoint presentations. Some have even scribbled, "Mom, Dad . . . I'm GAY!" in bright, rainbow-colored icing on chocolate cakes. With each example I've witnessed, the person or persons receiving this news have exploded with elation, like they've found winning lottery numbers hidden in the fabric of a Gay Pride flag. It clearly indicates that the world, at least as I knew it, has changed and *is* changing for the better.

That shit just wasn't *my* experience.

In my youth, I learned quickly that it was in your best interest to meticulously hide any "imperfection," any indication of originality or variation. Society largely viewed homosexuality as evil, an abomination, a scar on the face of humanity. Those who did speak of it only did so to mock its existence, like Christian, the "disco-dancing, Oscar Wilde-reading, Streisand ticket-holding friend of Dorothy" in *Clueless,* or the desperately and offensively flamboyant "Men on [Insert Subject Here]" of *In Living Color.* We were punchlines. Jokes. The world could no longer deny our existence, so they had to ridicule it.

We hid in the shadows, desperate to become, to belong. But unicorns can only hide so much. Those who attempted to transform themselves into straight people buried their true nature underneath layers of feigned masculinity/femininity only to wind up broken, scarred, drowning in a quicksand of identity crisis. We often drank ourselves into oblivion, abused drugs, or even used suicide to escape the pain. Those brave enough (or stupid enough, depending on how you look at it) to remain true to their inner selves became exposed, easy targets for the vile and vindictive who spied those winding horns hidden beneath our thin masks.

"Mrs. Carpenter," said a meek voice, shaking me from my thoughts. Mom and I turned to see Mrs. Moore, the school admin, standing at the counter. "Mr. Harold said he would be with you in just a moment. He's finishing up a phone call."

Mom didn't reply. I looked at her, unable to tell what was going through her mind. I imagined she was furious at me, and I could only ponder what hell awaited me within Mr. Harold's office. I turned my attention to the checkered floor beneath my feet, allowing my mind to wander along its patterned maze again, and I drifted.

Four months after Sam's arrest, Prosecutor Laura Finch and Detective David Simpson arranged to obtain my official statement, which they would submit as the state's evidence. Finch warned that, while credible, recorded testimony would lack the weight of live testimony that could be heard by the audience, felt by the jurors, and cross-examined by the defense. At the time, I didn't give two shits. I lacked the courage necessary for such feats of strength. A videotape was all they were getting. And even that was a chore.

I begged to give the account without family members present, but Finch said Tennessee State law required at least one parent or guardian to be in attendance. After some discussion, my mother agreed to allow my older sister, Anne, to attend the testimony in her place.

I was born two months after my mother's fortieth birthday, the youngest of six children. Anne, ten years my senior, was practically my full-time guardian. She was the only girl in our sea of boys, which, in a way, made her an honorary unicorn.

In February 1995, several months before *Tennessee vs. Samuel L. Barnes* was heard in court, my parents drove Annie and me to the downtown law office where Finch worked. Mom and Dad waited in the lobby while Finch, Annie, and I joined Detective Kelp in one of the meeting rooms hidden along the winding corridors of the building.

We entered a white room with no windows. There was a table with five chairs in the middle of the room. At the far end of the table stood a black video camera, which seemed to look at me with a stern frown as we entered. Prosecutor Finch held out a Bible and asked me to place my right hand upon it. "Do you solemnly swear that you will tell the truth, the whole truth, and nothing but the truth, so help you God?"

"I do," I said, suspecting God didn't listen to unicorns. I then gazed into the camera lens, watching its dark, glimmering eye focus on me. My mouth wouldn't open. I knew what to say but couldn't force the words to come out. It would be the first time I had spoken about the attack. I turned to Annie.

"Don't tell Momma."

Annie shook her head with a benevolent glimmer in her eyes and smiled. "I won't."

At last, I started to speak, and the shame and guilt rose to the surface. I told that camera every sordid detail—how I had come to know Sam, the phone conversations I had initiated, and the dazzling horn on my head that I had tried so hard to conceal. Though some details of the assault lay muddy in my mind, I relayed every element I could recall. Once I started, it was like a dam had broken, spilling out my secrets and flooding the room with my truths. Looking back on the incident with an adult mind, there were ways in which I could have navigated around my sexuality. It wasn't pertinent to the statement. But it felt wrong not to tell the truth, the whole truth, and nothing but the truth.

Finch seemed quite proud of what I had conveyed. Even Detective Kelp seemed pleased. We finalized the testimony, closed the recording, and Finch advised that the hearing would begin on October 17 of that year. Finch told me before we left that afternoon to call her if I changed my mind about testifying. That didn't matter at that moment. What did matter was that at last, someone—someone other than Jeremy Tidwell, someone other than Sam Barnes—*someone* in my family knew that I was a unicorn. Annie didn't seem to mind one bit. It brought that little hint of magic back into my life.

Unfortunately, the return to school severed that joy. At least once every two weeks, I found myself nursing a bloody nose or a busted lip, resulting from relentless bullying and my inability to shut the hell up. There were several occasions where I could have avoided an altercation if I could have just remained quiet and kept walking, but that, too, felt wrong. It felt wrong not to defend myself. To try. Even when I knew speaking up would result in a pulverized ass, my mouth was always ready to come to my defense, and it *always* came to my defense. No one else would defend me—not the adults, not Principal Harold. Certainly not Vice Principal Pikes, an allegedly devout "Christian," who seemed to have this innate loathing for me. I was convinced that if Pikes could get away with it, he would join the rednecks in their assault, burn me at the stake, and give me to his devils.

A sharp, musical titter jingled in the air, and I left my thoughts to see Mr. Pikes entering the office accompanied by another man I had never seen. The stranger wore a somber black suit and was quite tall and severe looking. He smiled a welcoming smile and nodded at my mother, who returned the gesture. Pikes's eyes met mine, and I noticed that shitty smirk he always had where I was concerned. I saw that Bible in his hands, the one he loved to carry around the hallways of Chamberland High School like some sword of morality. They disappeared into Mr. Harold's office, and my mother turned to Mrs. Moore.

"Mrs. Moore," said my mother. "We've been here for an hour and a half. The meeting was supposed to be at—"

Mrs. Moore raised her hand. "I apologize, Mrs. Carpenter. It's been a very—" The phone on Moore's desk twinkled, and she picked up the line. After a second of hushed conversation, she turned to us and said, "Mr. Harold will see you two now."

We rose and followed Mrs. Moore to the office. I saw Mr. Harold sitting at his desk with an uneasy face. In fact, he looked like he could vomit. Pikes stood propped against the windowsill, arms folded and that same smug smirk under his righteous nose. The man in black nodded to us as we walked inside and gave us another friendly smile. Mom reached out a hand to the man, who took it without question.

"Hey, Carl," she said to him.

"Hello there, Bobbie," he replied.

"How's Jessie?"

The man nodded. "Oh, she's Jessie."

Mom giggled as she took her seat.

"You two know each other?" asked Mr. Harold, who seemed as stunned by these pleasantries as I was.

Mom nodded. "Mr. Turnmire and I went to school together when I was Barbara Gleason."

I later learned Carl Turnmire, the Knox County school superintendent then, had been my mother's schoolmate from middle school through high school. Mr. Harold turned to Mr. Pikes, and the two exchanged hesitant glances.

"Um, Mrs. Carpenter . . . Joe," said Mr. Harold. I sat down in the chair next to my mother. She looked at her lap and took a deep breath. When she lifted her eyes, I noticed something brewing, an eclipse of the senses. Clouds had entered her eyes, gray clouds, angry, turbulent. She stared back at Mr. Harold with a determined glare. Taking note of this glower, Harold shifted nervously in his seat. "Now, Mrs. Carpenter, I think you know why we've called you in today."

"I've an idea, yes," Mom said.

Mr. Harold opened a manila folder on his desk, which sat pregnant with multicolored pages, forms, and documents of my indecencies. "Joe has . . . well, he's had some challenges lately, which have greatly affected his school studies. Most notably, his absences." Harold plucked a page from the folder and slipped his glasses over his eyes. "This year alone, Joe has been absent a total of . . . *fifteen* times, eleven of those that remain unexcused due to the recent truancy incident." Harold confidently removed his glasses and looked at my mother. "Do you have any explanation for that, Mrs. Carpenter?"

My mother's eyebrow arched with an elegant flair. "I do, in fact. So, the better question is why my son is so terrified to enter this school that he feels the need to hide from it."

Pikes, anxious to enter the conversation, rose to his feet. "Did you lie for your son and tell the school that he was out for eleven days because of strep throat, Mrs. Carpenter?"

Mom turned to Mr. Pikes. "Did you tell my son that maybe the bullies in school would leave him alone if he could find ways to be '*normal*,' Mr. Pikes?"

Pikes stepped forward. "No, I did not. I said that if he tried harder to fit in, the other children might be more accepting of him."

Mom smiled and slid back into her chair. "You realize that's the same thing, just with bullshit on it." The room remained silent. "Tell me, Mr. Pikes, do you find my son . . . unacceptable?"

"Sometimes, yes," said Pikes.

"Tom," warned Mr. Harold as he turned toward Mr. Pikes.

"And just what is it about my son that you find unacceptable, these things he could change to *fit in*, as you say?"

Pikes plucked a yellow pencil from the holder on Harold's desk and began to waggle it at my mother like a conductor's baton. "Well, he could be more of a *boy*, for one thing," spat Pikes before he could stop himself.

"Tom," said Mr. Harold once again.

"More of a *boy*, you say," my mother reiterated.

Pikes hesitated. "Well . . . meaning, maybe he could leave that Drama

Club and join a sport that would foster a team spirit. Healthy camaraderie. He could even come to my church, take part in some of the social groups there. A lot of the boys from Chamberland go there. It could be—"

Mr. Harold raised his hands. "I think what Mr. Pikes is trying to say is that we just want to find ways to get Joe to belong, is all, Mrs. Carpenter. That's all. Maybe if we could find ways for him to get along with the other boys, they wouldn't be so apt to tease him so much."

Again, my mother's eyebrow raised, and she leaned forward. "*Tease* him, you say." She chuckled. "So . . . so, when that Dickerson boy was kicking my son in the face a few weeks back while that fat one, that—"

"Goober," I whispered.

"*Goober* boy was sitting on his back," Mom continued. "That was just teasing, correct?"

"Mrs. Carpenter," Mr. Harold pleaded.

"And tell me, gentlemen, just what did you do to those boys after that light-hearted teasing?"

"They both got suspended," said Mr. Pikes proudly.

"In-school," I whispered. "Two days."

"*Two days in-school* suspension," Mom giggled. "Lord, help. How did they survive?" She turned to me. "And how many times had they *teased* you like that before, Joey?"

"I don't know," I shrugged. "Six or seven."

Mom again glared at Mr. Harold. "*Six* or *seven* times. And after six or seven times of 'teasing' my son with busted lips and bloody noses, you felt that a fitting punishment would be *two days* of in-school suspension?"

"Now, I'm sure there hadn't been that many altercations," began Mr. Pikes.

"Well, by God, let's just see," blurted Mom. "It's all right here, right? In your little folder?" She snatched the manila folder from the desk and began plucking out the bright pink pages, which indicated a rule infraction with physical engagement. "Let's see, four . . . five, six, seven . . . eight—"

"Mrs. Carpenter," Mr. Pikes attempted.

"Nine . . . ten."

"Mrs. Carpenter," Pike said again.

"Thirteen!" Mom declared at last. She slammed her hand down onto the desk with a jarring boom. "I'm sitting here with thirteen . . . whatever the hell you call them . . . *physical altercation* forms where my son is listed as the victim, and you gentlemen have the *unmitigated gall* to preach conformity to me? If Joey would learn to 'fit in' and be a 'boy,' this wouldn't happen? Well, that leaves me with questions, gentlemen. Lots and lots of questions. Namely, how my son, who spent the first eight years of his school career making the *damn honor roll*, is now so terrified to go to school that he hides in the woods to keep from walking through your doors? That! Now, *that* should be our agenda, gentlemen."

"No!" said Mr. Pikes abruptly, pointing the pencil at my mother. "Our agenda is that your son is truant, and, in case you didn't know, Mrs. Carpenter, that makes *you* liable. That's why we've asked Mr. Turnmire to join us today. You and your son are guilty of misdemeanor charges of educational neglect! And you're going to answer for that." He said this with such fervor and righteous abandon, I thought the clouds above would part and the divine resonance of trumpeted glory would blare through the room.

Without so much as a sigh or flinch of the eye, my mother reached forward and gently slipped that yellow number two pencil from Pikes's grip. She grasped it firmly in her fingers, stared into his eyes, and cracked it into two pieces with a sharp snap that caused my insides to recoil. There came that eyebrow again.

"*Like hell*," she hissed wickedly.

Pikes's face flushed red, and he pointed an accusing finger at my mother. "*Now, I've had just about enough—*"

"Quiet!" boomed Mr. Harold. "Enough, Tom. Enough. Stop it." Pikes fell silent and turned his stunned face toward Mr. Harold. "Tom, I think you should wait in your office for us."

Old Pikes couldn't believe his ears. This session had apparently been some holy crusade for him, a way to set some moral example using me as an unwitting model. He looked at my mother and then at me, and then he turned without another word and left the office, closing the door with a petulant slam.

Mr. Harold took a calming breath and turned to us. "Now, Mrs. Carpenter, to return to the subject at hand. You must admit, these absences are serious."

Mom began to gather her things. "What's *serious* to me, Mr. Harold, is that my son has endured just about all he can endure in these halls. It's obvious to me, and to everyone who knows the truth, this school has absolutely no plans whatsoever to protect Joe or take serious action against those who intend him harm. So, I'm left with two choices." She looked at Mr. Harold, and her expression softened. "Option number one would be to transfer him from

Chamberland and back into West Hills High School, which is where he *should have stayed* to begin with. We both know it. He spent the first six weeks of his freshman year there before all this zoning nonsense." She reached into her purse and handed a folded paper to Mr. Harold. "Just look at that. All A's with one B. If he could have just stayed there, he could have been with all his friends from our neighborhood, others he knows."

"Bullies are everywhere," added Mr. Harold.

Mom closed her eyes. "Yes, but he's *alone* here, Mr. Harold."

Mr. Harold pondered this and sighed. "Bobbie, you know that we can't do that. I really wish we could. But Joe is zoned for Chamberland by the county zoning laws. There's no way to change that."

Mom turned to Carl Turnmire. "Is that so?"

Turnmire took a deep breath, glanced at Mr. Harold, and turned to Mom. "Afraid so, Bobbie. Joe would have to prove he lived with another family member zoned for West Hills. There's no other way. The law is pretty clear on that."

"Fair enough," said Mom without missing a beat. "So, he's sixteen in two weeks. What do I need to sign just to pull him out of school altogether?"

Everyone paused, including me. Something had sucked the air from the room, the colossal vacuum of surprise. I was utterly stunned because, to be honest, I hadn't known leaving school was even an option. Mr. Harold and Mr. Turnmire exchanged worried glances.

"Bobbie, listen, are you sure you want—" began Mr. Turnmire.

Mom turned to him with a glimmer of tears in her eyes. "He's been through enough, Carl," she said quietly. "It's too much. It's just too much. You've heard enough today to know that he's got no chance here." She swallowed her emotion and snatched her purse from the chair. "Nope. No, best to let him find his own way."

"It'll ruin his future, Mrs. Carpenter," warned Mr. Harold. "College will be out of the question."

"Actually," countered Turnmire. "All accredited colleges will accept a general equivalency diploma, so long as the student has the proper SAT scores to back it up."

"And how much does it cost to take the GED?" Mom asked.

"Oh, 'bout fifty bucks, I think," said Mr. Turnmire.

"Done," said Mom as she snapped her purse closed. She rose and turned toward a very bewildered Mr. Harold, who seemed unaware of what had happened.

"Mrs. Carpenter, are you sure about this?" asked Mr. Harold.

Mom paused and looked at him. "I've learned we're not sure of anything in this life, Mr. Harold. But there's one thing I know for certain. The truth will stand while the world's on fire, and what you and Pikes have allowed those boys to do to my son after all he's endured is unforgivable." She pointed to his desk. "So, you keep that little file of yours handy, Larry. My attorney's going to want to see it. You can bet your sweet ass on that."

5
THE BURLAP FACE

"O', death . . . Won't you spare me over 'til another year?"
— *O' Death*: Ralph Stanley—

April 1995

A great horse will change your life; exceptional ones define it. Susan Brooks believed that statement with every fiber of her being. She had been around horses all her life, a relationship that began on a Montana ranch when she was four. There was a special bond Susan shared with horses. She wasn't sure how or why. It simply was. This bond allowed her to train even the most challenging animals, a talent that led her through competitive circuits toward the glow of the Olympic flame.

That's where it all went to hell.

It was still evident in her mind, though she had tried repeatedly to wash her brain of it. There she was, on that field with Blue, or *Blue Ribbon*, a liver chestnut Hanoverian gelding, a horse she had worked with for three years. There were one hundred and fifty-seven entries from thirty nations in attendance that year, all gathered at the Fairbanks Ranch Country Club in San Diego. Susan had noticed something strange about Blue that morning as she brushed him; something in his eyes, a tremor of tension. Her father said she was being silly. Nerves were getting the better of her. Still, there was a moment before the two of them took the field for dressage where it felt as if Blue was begging her not to lead him out. She should have listened.

Maybe it was the crowd. Perhaps it was all the cameras. The lights. The fervor of Olympic competition. Whatever the cause, Blue made one triumphant lap around the field, completing his jumps with ease. Then suddenly, he just stopped. Froze in place. He looked around at the eyes staring down at him and took a wary step backward. No matter what Susan did, Blue wouldn't move a muscle. To get him off the field, Susan and her father had to cover his eyes with her coat and lead him away. It was the single most embarrassing moment of Susan's life. It marked the end of her competitive career.

For the next few years, Susan found work here and there, caring for horses and stables across the country. The last place she had worked was a horse ranch in eastern Texas owned by Don Stevens, a rich, odious bigot sponsored by Satan. The grounds and stables of his farm were in disrepair, which confused Susan, considering the amount of money the man spent on women and whiskey. Time and again, she would ask Stevens for funds to tend to the animals, repair the stables, and groom the grounds, and each time she was denied.

The last straw came when Dodger, one of the six horses Stevens owned, developed a severe case of mud fever, which should have been expected given the humid, muddy conditions in which the animal lived. Susan was doing her best to clean the horses one day when she noticed the open wound on Dodger's rear leg. The animal started to vomit, indicating the infection had spread to the stomach. Without so much as a second thought, Stevens instructed Susan to have the animal put down and gave her money to make the arrangements. His lack of empathy didn't surprise her. What surprised her was that he didn't go down and shoot the horse himself. Rather than have Dodger murdered, Susan added her money to have a specialist treat the horse. Two weeks later, Dodger was given a clean bill of health. Susan quit the Stevens ranch three days later and returned to Lexington, Kentucky.

During the holidays of 1994, an acquaintance who worked for a company called Kromwell Industries in Tennessee told her about an opportunity to manage stables for a summer camp. It would be a year-round job, tending the horses on campus, providing riding lessons to campers, and managing the stables. She applied, and in January, she traveled to Jasper Mill, Tennessee, to speak with a man named Earl Drummond, who interviewed her for over an hour. Two weeks later, she was offered the job. The campus sat just a little over an hour from her home. The stables were sparkling new, and the eight horses were in pristine health. It seemed like a win-win opportunity.

Susan's favorite was an American Quarter Horse she had named Thelma. Thelma seemed to take to Susan from the start, following her around the fields and hovering near when she was at the stables. She allowed Susan to ride her without hesitation, especially if Susan had brought marshmallows with her, the big fluffy kind.

Spring was in full bloom. The air was crisp yet warm in the sunlight. Susan had awoken early, at ten past six, that morning, eager to get a start on the day. There were just a few more weeks before the first campers would bustle onto the site, ready for their turn at the horses. There was little time left for Susan to have them all to herself.

She stopped to get gas at the South Stop, a small gas station just outside the Tennessee state line. While in line, she spied a hefty bag of Jet-Puffed Jumbos on the shelf. She smiled and snatched a bag for Thelma.

She made it to the campus around nine fifteen. Leaving her car in the main lot, she boarded one of the open golf carts and headed west toward the stables. Her friend, Thelma, was grazing in the field just beyond the fence. The horse flicked its head excitedly and sprinted toward the stables to await Susan's arrival. As she rounded the corner, she spied Jack Burns, the campus's kitchen manager and groundskeeper, connecting water hoses near the stables.

"Good morning!" Susan called.

"Morning!" Jack replied. He gestured to the hoses. "I got you some new water hoses. Thought they'd be useful. Those old ones were starting to spring some leaks."

"I appreciate it," she replied as she parked the cart. She took her purse and her shopping bag from the passenger's seat. "I think I'll have to change out the trough today. That water is looking a bit stale."

"Yeah, you don't notice it as much in older, faded ones, but that shiny steel makes dirty water stand out." He followed Susan toward the stable doors, where Thelma stood in wait. "She's been waiting on you."

Susan smiled. "She's a sweetie." She approached Thelma, who tottered on her front legs with excitement. "Hey, you," whispered Susan. "I got you a present." She sat her bag on the bench by the door and opened the bag of marshmallows. She took three of them from the pack and held them out to the horse, who happily gobbled them up.

"Don't mean to be a party pooper, but are those good for horses?" asked Jack.

Susan nodded. "Oh, they're fine. They can have them in moderation.

You don't want them as a steady diet or anything."

"My grannie told me they were toxic to horses," he added.

"I think she was thinking of marshmallow plants," Susan clarified. "Those are, I think." She rubbed Thelma's head. "I thought about taking her out for a ride. Explore a bit."

Jack nodded. "Good to get some time in. Won't be long before this place will be overrun with crazy kids."

"What's it like?" asked Susan. "All the kids. I mean, I went to a summer camp, but I was, like, ten, so I don't remember much. You've been here a while, right?"

Jack smiled. "A while." He reached over and touched Thelma's nose. "It varies, I suppose. Some seasons are calm. Others, not so much. Just last year . . ." Then Jack trailed off as if he had thought better about his words.

"What?" asked Susan.

His face grew somber. "Kids can get into all sorts of things. Got to watch them. Especially those older ones. You'd think it'd be the little ones. Older ones, though—they're just curious enough to get into all kinds of trouble."

"I bet," agreed Susan.

"Overall, though, it's the usual things. They'll be some who don't like others, fights, disagreements. Someone always gets a scrape or a cut, and we have to take them over to Miss Conrad to patch. She'll get the duct tape out and fix them up." He noticed Susan's face and chuckled. "Joking."

Susan chuckled. "You sound like my dad. He thought he could fix the world with duct tape."

"Almost can," Jack nodded. He tipped his hat to her. "You have a good ride, now. Earl should be here around noon."

With that, Jack started on the path toward the campus square. Susan watched the man walk away, wondering about the things he had seen during his many years at the camp. She was also curious about what tragedy had happened the previous season and why Jack was reluctant to speak of it. Thelma nudged her arm, shaking her from her thoughts. She asked the horse if she wanted to go for a ride, and it seemed the animal was excited to explore beyond the confines of the grounds.

Once Thelma was saddled and ready, Susan led her to the main gate. Flipping the lock, she pulled the gate open and mounted the horse. With a gentle nudge to her sides, Thelma began to trot toward the main road leading away from campus. Susan headed east on the road and continued, passing a few houses scattered along the way.

About two miles down the road, Susan led Thelma to the left onto a narrow lane that stretched upward into the hills. Trees of various species lined either side of the path like soldiers standing guard over nature's domain. The day was warming as the sun ascended into the sky, so Susan tried to remain in the shade where possible. There didn't seem to be a single house or cottage in the distance. The vacant plain of untainted earth. At times, it felt as if she was riding into nowhere. She may have been. It wasn't as if she knew the area. What if she got lost? She couldn't leave Thelma in the heat without water. Just as a flutter of anxiety rose in her chest, she spied a small white house on the left surrounded by a rusty aluminum gate. She tugged on Thelma's reins to slow her pace.

The house's front yard was littered with various stone objects and small cement statues. Angels, frogs, and gnomes all faded and worn with time. A rocking chair on the front porch shuddered in the breeze. Suddenly, though she couldn't quite explain why, she got a bad feeling about whoever lived in that house. As her eyes continued to move around the property, she noticed someone gazing back at her through the broken blinds of the front door window.

"Tick-tick," clicked Susan without hesitation. She flicked Thelma's reins, causing the horse to trot forward.

She looked back only once, just in time to see the front door of the tiny house begin to open. A figure stepped onto the porch.

"Can I help you, missy?" called a gruff woman's voice. "You better get that stinky thing out of here."

Susan didn't reply. Instead, she led Thelma to take the first right off the narrow road, a dirt path that led into the trees. *God, don't let her follow me. Whoever she is.* She clicked her tongue again and urged the horse forward. Thelma increased her speed. Further and further down the path they went, winding up and down until Susan spied yet another structure in the distance to her left.

The house, if one could still call it that, lay in shambles. It seemed to have suffered a fire of some kind, though the years had added wear that no flames could match. It was old, ancient, from what Susan could tell. The roof was nearly gone. The back half of the home had caved into rot some years before. Still, through all the decay, she could see what had once been a sturdy, stable home. Someone had built that place by hand. Old craftsmanship.

Someone loved it.

The path took Susan and Thelma around the upper east hill and down to another road. On the edge of this road stood a tree with long, winding branches and black leaves, one of the largest trees she had ever seen. *What kind of tree has* black *leaves?* Curious, Susan pushed Thelma off the path. Slowly, the two of them headed toward the odd oak. Twice, Thelma neighed. And it wasn't the kind of sound that indicated contentment. It was a nervous sound, frightened, the same sound Blue had made so long ago on that field surrounded by eyes. Susan felt those eyes again, even though no one was nearby. Someone was watching her.

At last, Thelma paused some twenty feet away from the crooked oak. Then Susan realized that the tree wasn't draped in black leaves but covered in birds. Crows. They were all staring at her, motionless, silent. All sound seemed to drift from the earth, replaced by an eerie hum. The *wah-wah* drone of anxious anticipation.

Susan nudged Thelma forward, but just like Blue, the horse would not budge. She could feel Thelma's muscles shiver underneath the saddle's thick leather. She reached forward and stroked Thelma's mane.

"What's the matter, honey?"

The horse muttered a nervous neigh. *Don't make me go closer*, it said. *Let's leave. Let's leave this place.*

Unable to thwart her wonder, Susan threw her left leg over Thelma's back and hopped to the ground. She stood there, staring into those thick, black branches. Higher in the twisted branches hung a cloth of some kind, a sack nailed onto the tree trunk. She took three steps forward. Then she took four steps to the left. The farther left she moved, the more that sack took the guise of a human face, twisted and angry. It stared at her with one empty eye. And Susan realized it saw her. It watched her standing there. It was *aware* of her.

Something began to scurry from the gaping maw of the face, a pulsing, crawling liquid of yellow and black. The humming grew louder. Buzzing. It was wasps. Hundreds, thousands of thick hornets preparing to swarm her. Her trembling eyes turned to the crowd of crows staring down at her from the heavens.

They knew.

And they smiled.

Instantly, Susan spun on her heels and ran for Thelma, who began to step backward in fear. The buzzing grew louder. They were coming. She snatched the reins dangling around Thelma's snout, and she felt the horse pull her upward and onto the saddle as if it, too, knew they needed to escape the tree.

"Run, Thelma," whispered Susan.

Without further coaxing, Thelma broke into a full sprint, charging toward the vacant road. The buzzing grew so loud that Susan thought she would have to cover her ears. They were coming. They wanted her. She glanced back three times.

The first time, she saw the dark cloud of wasps churning against the blue sky above her, swirling like a venomous cloud. They reached the road, and Susan turned back once again. This time, the hornets seemed to take shape like a shadow, the figure of a man. A tall, hulking man with brawny arms and thick legs. But that couldn't be true. It couldn't be. She could hear Thelma's hooves pounding the pavement beneath them. She could feel the horse's chest expand and contract with breath. On the third glance, Susan thought the shadow reached for her, fingers outstretched, digits comprised of crawling masses of pulsing stingers.

Just ahead on the right, Susan spied the Jasper Mill Market, the store she passed each time she traveled to the camp. She knew they were close. The roaring hum of whatever pursued her began to fade away, retreating to the distance, returning to the tree. Returning home. She didn't know that. She *felt* it.

Susan didn't look back again.

6
11:05 A.M.

My mother was a curious soul. I wouldn't go so far as to say she was nosey, but she was most content when she was the one with the gossip. After giving my statement to Prosecutor Finch, for which only my sister was present, Mom acted as if she was not interested in the least as to what I had confessed. But I knew it gnawed at her. It was infrequent that Annie knew something Mom did not; she seemed to enjoy being the authority for once.

As the days stretched into weeks and the Magnolia tree in the front lawn began to bud into spring, my mother became less patient. She was starting to passive-aggressively interrogate Annie. To my knowledge, my sister never said a word.

"That's Joey's business, so you'll have to ask him," was all Annie would say.

That only further annoyed my mother. Not just because Annie wouldn't confess those secrets but because she was right.

About the middle of March, Mom's thin thread of patience finally snapped. The woman could not stand it one minute longer. Since leaving school that year, I worked part-time at Swan's Market, a small convenience store at the edge of our subdivision. Mrs. Swan didn't have much for me to do, of course, but it was at least some type of structure while I was adrift in a sea of possibilities.

I didn't have to be at the store until noon that day. I entered the kitchen, my mother's home base. No matter the day or time, Mom *always* sat at that kitchen table, one of those old fold-out contraptions bolted to the thick wood of the oak-paneled wall. The table and benches were white marble in black iron. On the bench next to her, stacked in two neat columns, stood a makeshift library of books of various genres. Mostly Harlequin Romance novels. I once asked her why romance novels?

"It's nice to read about *somebody* doing it," she said.

There was always a book in her hand. There was no limit to what she would read. I had seen her perusing everything from the Webster's Dictionary to the King James Bible. She was no stranger to the murder mystery. She had even read a dose of horror now and again.

I couldn't make out the title of what she was reading that day I entered the kitchen, but it was written by someone named Carole Mortimer. From the looks of the bare-chested man on the cover, it was yet another tale of "somebody doing it." Snatching the bread from the top of the refrigerator, I made a sandwich, grabbed a soda, and sat down at the table across from her. And for a while, the two of us said nothing. Mom sat there, reading glasses on the tip of her nose and that paperback woven into her fingers. At last, I saw the title: *Just One Night*.

Nearly ten minutes had passed before Mom broke the silence with, "Do you think you've *always* been gay?"

The bite of the sandwich temporarily lodged in my windpipe, and I coughed to maneuver it down my constricted throat. "Wh . . . what?" I asked in amazement.

"Do you think you've always been gay?" she repeated without looking away from her book. "I mean, *I* think so."

My first instinct was to deny any such rumor, and I opened my mouth to do just that. But for reasons I can't quite explain, what came out was, "Maybe."

Mom nodded, and again we entered silence, her reading and me picking over the tattered sandwich that was souring in my stomach.

"Yeah, I think so, too," she added.

"How would you know?" I asked.

She chuckled. "Oh, honey, mamas *always* know." She turned the page of her book. "You were always so sweet . . . sensitive. You couldn't bear the thought that you had hurt anyone's feelings, and your brothers couldn't have cared less." She paused and looked up. "You never liked to be dirty. You'd have taken ten showers a day if you could. You didn't like your toys to be dirty either."

"Momma, I—"

"Now, you never were one for Barbie dolls or anything, though you did love Wonder Woman. Lord, you were always out in the backyard, just spinning like you were about to take flight. You didn't necessarily play with girls' toys. But you had this unhealthy fascination with those half-naked He-Men dolls."

"*Action figures,*" I smiled.

"Well, whatever they were, they were muscle men wearing little fuzzy britches."

I looked at her, those glasses perched on her nose, and the minutes began to pass. Pushing her reading glasses along the bridge of her nose, she turned back to her book. Silence returned. That silence hovered in the kitchen, wanting us to say more. Finally, I forced the question through my dry lips. "Are you ashamed of me?"

She again lowered her book, plucked the glasses from her face, and slid them into the pages. Her eyebrow rose as it always did when someone said something she considered utterly asinine. "Are you a liar?"

"No," I replied with some confusion.

"You some alcoholic? A junkie?"

I chuckled at the thought. "No, I don't even—"

"Are you a thief?"

"No."

Her eyebrow lowered, and she leaned back. "Don't look like I'd have much to be ashamed of," she said as she lifted her book and turned the page.

I waited for the catalyst, that moment where the parent either explodes with anger or melts into a sobbing heap, blaming themselves for her child's attraction to the same sex, but it never arrived. Instead, Mom seemed content, pleased to finally know the truth, to know that now *she* knew something others did not. Most importantly, she wasn't at all ashamed. At least, she said she wasn't. I wouldn't go so far as to say the woman instantaneously transformed into a rainbow-flag-waving proud mother of a gay son before my very eyes, but she seemed to take the news rather well. Better than I had hoped.

We closed the conversation that afternoon with two express instructions. First, I was not to tell any of my brothers, especially Lee or Eddie, the church deacons, whose occasional association with righteousness and the Old Testament gospel would undoubtedly leave them with no recourse but to stone me to death. Secondly, and most importantly, my father was *never* to know for reasons all too obvious. My dad, with whom I had always maintained a rocky relationship, already looked at me differently. He had never proclaimed that I wasn't his ideal son, but he didn't have to. It had been evident early on that I did not fit into the mold he had fashioned for his other sons, boys of whom he was so proud. Strapping boys, football players, deacons, God-fearing men, and mules.

But I was unique.

I was a unicorn.

As the warmth of spring continued to seep into the air, my homosexuality became a fact shared only with my mother and sister. Nearly a month later, I confessed the secret to my friend, Leslie. Ironically enough, Leslie thought I was pulling some colossal prank. I don't know what she expected, really. Granted, I wasn't what I would call a "stereotypical" gay guy, but I certainly didn't convey the remarkable masculinity of the Marlboro man. Still, at least at first, Leslie found the revelation hard to believe.

Events would take an abrupt and unexpected turn a few weeks later. April 16, which so happened to be Easter Sunday. My family had always observed the Easter holiday, albeit sparingly. We would visit the family cemetery, carrying multi-colored arrangements of silk flowers to lay on the graves of those who had departed. Some too soon, others right on time. Then for the remainder of the afternoon, Mom would serve ham with various side dishes. My brothers brought nieces and nephews to collect Easter baskets and hunt for colorful eggs. And everyone wore their "Easter outfit," which included pressed clothing in the most troubling pastel shades. It was your typical mundane holiday. That year, however, the holiday would be different.

Two weeks before the day arrived, Mom reached nearly every family member we had to inform them that year we would *all* gather for a feast to celebrate the resurrection of our Lord. They seemed to believe Jesus himself would be appearing because nearly everyone was present and accounted for. We even had family who traveled some distance to join the festivities, even my then seventy-nine-year-old grandfather, my mother's father, who had himself once been a minister. The sun shone bright, the temperature was mild, and there was not a single cloud hovering in the pale blue sky. Still, a storm was brewing.

I sat at the round dining table in the living room with several of my nieces and nephews around my age. As usual, Annie was busy in the kitchen with Mom, finishing up the sides, which included corn on the cob, mashed potatoes, peas, and cornbread. Dad sat on his throne, a plump leather recliner he kept positioned directly in front of the television. My four brothers and their chatty wives were scattered around the remainder of the house, all engaged in various acts of self-praise and feigned adulation. My Aunt Carla sat in the kitchen with my mother, locked in conversation as family members fluttered around them. Conversations buzzed along the walls, the subjects overlapping and intertwining. At last, I heard a voice call from the kitchen to my right.

"Joey!" spat my Aunt Carla. "You're gay?"

My chest constricted, and my eyes popped open wide. The air around me dropped five degrees. I think I even stopped breathing for a moment.

"What?" I asked.

Condemnatory eyes turned in my direction, glaring at me, waiting for my response. My mother looked at me, content, at ease. She smiled and nodded. At last, I was able to will tongue into motion.

"Yeah?" I said in more of a question than a response.

Silence flooded the room so suddenly I thought I had gone deaf. Eddie's wife, Gertie, dropped her cupcake into her lap, and her mouth fell open with surprise. I felt a burning sensation explode in my chest and spread through my extremities, turning frigid as it crept over my flesh. My eyes widened, and I raised my head to see my sister Annie staring at the wall behind the stove like she was witnessing a traffic accident. Suddenly, she began to stir the mashed potatoes with such force I thought she'd take flight and zip out the window. Seconds seemed to span into minutes, minutes into hours, and hours into infinity as all eyes turned in my direction. I looked to Mom, who sat there quietly, ears to the ready, listening for any sound of objection.

But no one did.

No one made a sound.

My mother, who standing a plump four feet, nine inches reminded you of an angry Pekingese, rose from the kitchen table and sauntered into the living room, casting a wary glare at everyone in attendance. She stood there, hand on hip, watching, waiting, her eyebrow raised with anticipation.

"What?" muttered my grandfather, breaking the silence at last. "What's

Joey got?"

Cheryl, the nosey wife of my brother George, leaned over to him. "Joey's gay," she whispered as if I had three months to live.

His wrinkled face twisted with confusion. "Gay about what?"

"No, Pop-Pop, he likes *boys*," Cheryl continued.

My grandfather turned to me with a befuddled expression and said, "Well, hell, *I like boys*. What's everybody talkin' about?"

Annie suddenly dropped the spoon into the pot of simmering potatoes and slithered into the living room. Taking me by the arm, she led me through the sea of glowering eyes and into her room, where she shut and locked the door.

She turned, leaned against the wood, and gawked at me. "What . . . the *actual* hell," she muttered.

"Did she tell you she was going to do this?" I asked.

"God, no!" Annie whispered. "She didn't say shit!"

At that moment, a rumble rose from the floor beneath our feet. Upon hearing the news, I suspected that demons from Hell were clawing their way through the floorboards to collect my sinning soul.

Our nieces and nephews would later tell us that after Annie and I fled to her room, my father, who in direct contrast to my mother stood a hulking six feet, four inches, rose to his feet, walked downstairs to our den, and proceeded to toss every piece of furniture we owned while shouting obscenities at the top of his lungs. As he delivered what my mother would later call a "hissy fit," she waited patiently at the top of the staircase.

With his ravings echoing through the house, Mom smiled, holding her rolling pin tight. Everyone stared at her inanely while she engaged the room in polite conversation topics like the weather, upcoming local events, and recipes. After some time, Dad trudged up the stairs, panting and sweating like he had sprinted to Texas and back. Once he reached the landing, he looked down at my mother.

"Are you alright?" she softly asked him.

"Yeah," he huffed. "I'm alright."

"Okie dokie, then," she said, turning to the crowd as if nothing had happened. "Let's eat!"

Not a soul spoke about the magnificent horn on my head for the remainder of the day. Every time I would enter a room, a strange stillness would accompany me until someone would feel awkward enough to break the silence with inconsequential questions about work, what music I liked, or if I still planned to attend college. Or what the scholars call *bullshit*.

Later that evening, as the waters calmed, nieces and nephews secretly pulled me aside, each enthralled by the notion that I was gay. Yes, it was finally out; *I* was out. God knows I hadn't planned or even anticipated such a revelation, but I was utterly convinced that things had gone according to my mother's plan. In hindsight, it made perfect sense. She knew my sexuality wouldn't remain a secret forever. It couldn't. So, to her, it was best to rip the bandage off while she was in complete control of the situation. And control it, she did.

As the night closed and the family dispersed, I wasn't sure what would follow, but I had this naïve feeling that light lay at the end of the tunnel. Unfortunately, what did follow were weeks of passive-aggressive commentary, shameful gazes from my brothers, and brief, cold exchanges with my father. No one dared negatively mention my homosexuality lest they face our mother's wrath. But no one had to. They found a host of other creative ways to air their disapproval. In my fantasy world, I believed coming out would bring a great sense of liberation and happiness. While it had given me some sense of freedom, it had brought other unexpected forms of confinement.

Around this time, I heard of Camp—forgive me—*Kamp* Kromwell. My friend Leslie learned about the camp at school and afterward pleaded with her parents until they agreed to send her. Some two hours from Knoxville, the campsite was a "wonderscape" of nature spanning many acres, a literal nirvana for the outdoorsman. The place had a tennis court, sand volleyball, basketball, riflery, archery, and a mini golf range. Flanked by the "beautiful Lake Ellington," Kromwell also offered a host of water sports and swimming activities, including canoeing, rafting, and fishing. That year, the camp would be expanded to offer horseback riding in addition to jet skis. I knew all this not because I had studied the place but because Leslie talked about it ad nauseam.

The notion of attending a summer camp had never crossed my mind once in the sixteen years I had been alive. It wasn't that I didn't enjoy the outdoors. I did. In the summer months, I spent countless hours exploring the woods surrounding our neighborhood and inspecting the intriguing aquatic life dwelling in the creek beds. However, after each of these adventures, I had ample access to air conditioning, electronics, and showers. I could come home, eat what I wanted, scratch my ass without judgment, and lose myself in the trappings of a Super Nintendo. Summer camp could offer almost none of the amenities I had grown accustomed to. I suspected it would hold nothing until

Mom told me about a conversation between her and Danielle Cooper, Leslie's mother.

When my mother called me, I was just about to go and stock dairy products at Swan's Market. I entered the kitchen to find her seated at the table, reading glasses on her nose and a paperback in her fingers.

"Yeah?" I asked from the kitchen doorway.

"You'll never guess who I just spoke to," she said without looking away from her book.

"You're right," I said quickly. "I need to go. Mrs. Swan needs—"

"Danielle," she interrupted. "And do you know what she said to me?"

I sighed and rolled my eyes. "What did Danielle say?"

She looked at me over the brim of her glasses and slipped them from her ear. "She told me that Leslie is going to summer camp. How do you like that? I didn't know we even had a summer camp around here."

I could tell by her tone and inflection that she expected a response from me. I wasn't sure what I needed to say to escape the conversation.

"Yeah, Leslie has talked about it nonstop. Super-excited. Good for her." There was a pause, so I turned to leave.

"Wait a minute. Come here." When I heard that tone, I realized it didn't matter if I had to leave to get to a dialysis appointment; I needed to sit. I wandered into the kitchen and plopped down at the table. "What would you think about going to camp?" she added.

"Are you serious?" I snickered.

"Leslie's really excited about it."

"What would I do at a camp?" I asked.

Mom slid her glasses into her book and considered this. "Well, anything you wanted to. Danielle said it has everything. Swimming at this big lake, arts, crafts, campfires." Her eyes widened. "Stories . . . you love watching those ghost stories on the HBO."

"Tales from the Crypt," I corrected.

"They even have horse stables."

"What would I do with a horse, Momma?"

"Well, you'd learn to ride the thing. Don't be silly," she replied sharply.

"Just in case I need to make a quick getaway, and there's a horse nearby."

"Don't be a smartass."

I shook my head. "Momma, I'm sure a place like that costs out the wazoo, and Dad isn't going to pay for—"

"Don't you worry about your daddy," she interrupted. "I think it would do you good to get away from this place for a little while, be with some other kids outside, have fun."

My eyes moved toward the floor. "Away from the family, you mean."

Mom hesitated. "Don't you worry about *them*," she said softly. "I'll take care of them." She stared at me, waiting for a reply, but I wasn't sure what to say. "Well, never mind. It was silly," she relented. "I just thought you may like to go is all, but you don't have to." The guilt of one hundred Jewish mothers rang in her voice. She turned back to her book.

I decided to help her off that cross. I took a breath. "Well, when does it start?"

She smiled and reached for the yellow notepad by the phone. Straightening her glasses, she said, "Danielle said they have two sessions each year. Each is about four weeks or so. Leslie is going to the first session that starts on . . . June 9 and ends on July 7, and I knew you'd really like to go when she goes." She glanced at me, but I said nothing. "Of course, you could do the second session if you'd prefer. But I just thought you'd want to go when there'll be somewhere there you know." I still didn't reply. She regarded her notes. "Danielle said they have jet skis this year. I don't know if I'd want you to go on one of those. You could—"

"I'll tell you what," I interjected. "Let me think about it."

I had no intention of giving the notion further consideration.

My openness seemed to surprise her. "Really?"

"Sure," I said. "When do I need to make a decision?"

Mom looked at her notes. "Says . . . all applications must be postmarked by May 19, so you have a few days."

As I stocked the coolers at Swan's that afternoon, Kromwell seemed like an impossibility to me. I had my suspicions about the experience. I had seen the movie *Meatballs,* though I hardly thought that Bill Murray would be my counselor. There were pros and cons to the situation.

Pros:

- I would get to the camp, have a wonderful time, and maybe even make some friends.
- I would avoid the convictions of home life, which, after my revelation, had become unbearable at times.

Cons:

- I would hate it. I would *hate, hate, hate* it. And that would be too damn bad, because I'd be trapped in Kumbaya.
- It would be hot. *Scrotum-sweltering-hellacious* hot.
- It would be full of strangers I couldn't escape.
- I would be forced into social situations with said strangers—*mandated* interactions.

You know, I think I'll pass . . .

"Honey," said a soft voice, shaking me from my thoughts. I turned to see little Mrs. Swan standing at the store counter. She had the sweetest, most endearing smile. The kind of smile that made you believe she had never suffered an impure thought in her life. "Don't forget to put the newer milk cartons in the back now."

I glanced down to see that, in my hypnotic state, I had been stocking some of the new containers in the front. "Oh, sorry, Mrs. Swan. I'll fix it." I began pulling each half-gallon carton out and placing the newest cartons in the back.

"What's on your mind, sweetie?" she asked. "You've seemed about as distracted as a cat in a room full of field mice."

I sighed. "My mom asked me if I wanted to go to summer camp this year."

"Oh, my, that sounds fun," cooed Mrs. Swan.

"Yeah, I don't know if it's for me."

"Oh, I loved my time at camp," she added.

I turned toward her and saw her sweet face aglow with memories past. "You went to summer camp?" I asked with a smile.

"Oh, I sure did," she replied. "Well, not around here, though. We lived up in Indiana when I was your age, so I went to Camp Granada. Lovely place, just lovely. We did all kinds of things there. Biking, hiking, campfire stories, s'mores—oh, it was wonderful." Her smile turned into a playful smirk. She looked cautiously around the store, slipped from behind the counter, and joined me at the cooler. "That's where I met *Stanley*," she whispered.

"I thought Mr. Swan's name was Ernest?"

"No, no. *Stanley Rubenstein.* He was my first boyfriend. My—how do you say—*summer love*," she giggled. She clasped her hands together and stared into the heavens. "Oh, boy, was he something. Tall, tan, handsome. He was something to see out there on their field. Loved playing softball. Just to make me jealous, he would take off his shirt so the girls could ogle his chest. He was such a ham."

"And what happened to this Stanley guy?" I asked.

"Oh, you know. We lost touch and all. He was from New Jersey, so he went back home. We wrote for a while, but life went on, I suppose." Her smile faded for a second, but then she illuminated with happiness. "Oh, we were so bad, Joey. All of us girls used to sneak over and watch the boys. They act like only boys do that, but it's not so. Us girls are just as bad, maybe worse! Lord, those boys. All those boys. They would all wear those silky gym shorts, you know, and some of them wouldn't nary wear a pair of boxer shorts underneath. So, you'd just see all that down there just *a'swinging around!*"

I choked on the air I swallowed. "Mrs. . . . Mrs. Swan!"

This is one dirty old broad, I thought. *A dirty, dirty old lady disguised as some gentle Christian woman.*

She patted my back, took my shoulder, and giggled like a schoolgirl. "Don't you breathe a word of this to Ernest. But sometimes . . . honey, those shorts were so tight, you could *see* their religion. And some of those boys were *big* into religion, let me tell you."

I began to laugh. "You better stop. I'm going to choke to death!"

She didn't stop, though. She didn't stop for nearly forty-five minutes. My mind was filled with lurid visions of teenaged guys roped with muscle, all wearing silk running shorts cut to the thigh. In my mind's playground, they ran along a dirt field, dripping with sweat, tossing a volleyball, the sunlight glistening off their moist chests. Some were dark-skinned; some had nests of hair on their chests; some had pale skin littered with freckles. And you know what? A few of them had forgotten their underwear.

7

PLAYING NICE

"Exit light. Enter night. Take my hand; we're off to never-never land."
—*Enter Sandman*: Metallica—

May 1995

Dewayne Burns could play nice. Sure. It wasn't easy, but he could play nice. He sped along through the Podunk town of Jasper Mill at approximately sixty-five miles per hour on a road where the posted limit was forty-five. *Enter Sandman* by Metallica blared with ear-splitting vibrancy as he swung that rusty Camaro IROC Z-28 along the roadways, tossing plumes of gravel and dust in its wake.

Weekend Orientation, the old man had called it. *Whatever, man. What the fuck ever.* What type of orientation did Dewayne need to sweep the floors and sling hash to a bunch of dipshit kids? He could be doing so many other things at that moment—anything but driving through some hillbilly hollow for a weekend retreat. But it didn't matter.

Dewayne could play nice.

He had learned to play nice for his mother. He had learned to play nice for his teachers. He had also played nice for Judge Harrison. Yes, he had. It hadn't been Dewayne's fault. Things rarely were. You just didn't flirt with his girl. That would get you an ass-whooping.

Dewayne was paying for gas when some middle-aged codger wandered up to Samantha Tucker, who was now one of Dewayne's many ex-girlfriends. He loved her at the time. Maybe. Either way, Samantha had been his property then, so keep your hands off.

As Dewyane handed the clerk a twenty, he saw the drunkard pawing at Samantha, trying to get her to talk to him. Dewayne burst through the gas station door, one thing led to another, and the dude found himself on his ass.

Simple as that.

Judge Harrison knew the old man in question. Clive Dunn, who had a long history with the law. Dunn's record nearly burst at the seams with DUI and public intoxication offenses. That's not to assume that Dewayne's record was spotless. He was no stranger to the law, either. But at just eighteen, misdemeanors like petty vandalism and destruction of property hardly seemed to compare to Dunn, who, over time, had become a proficient vagrant.

The fight hadn't been necessary. It was just a bonus. Dewayne charged out of the gas station and yelled a few choice obscenities at Dunn, who immediately raised his hands in surrender. That was fine. It had been Dunn's addition of "fucking punk" that had pushed things into the red. Dewayne swore in a court of law that Clive Dunn had laid hands on him first, pushed him, threatened to—as Dewayne claimed—"whip his punk ass." It had happened so quickly that witnesses weren't sure who threw the first blow, and poor Dunn was too drunk to honestly know who had done what to whom.

Harrison sentenced Dunn to six months in jail, and Dewayne got sixty days of community service. Dewayne's Uncle Jack suggested he work with him in the summer camp kitchen to satisfy the request. So, now he would spend his summer slaving away in a sweltering, nasty-ass kitchen, serving a bunch of slop to kids. But it beat shoveling dead skunks off the road. He had Uncle Jack to thank for that.

Dewayne whipped into the gravel parking lot of Jasper Market, tossing shrapnel of limestone grime into the air. The head-banging hard rock anthem continued to roar as he checked his reflection in his rearview mirror. An elderly gentleman emerged from the market door with a brown paper bag of groceries in his arms. He looked at Dewayne disapprovingly, as most of the older generation did. Though Dewayne smirked in reply, the man's judgmental expression was enough for him to lower the volume. As a show of good faith, Dewayne raised an inconspicuous middle finger to the old man as he made his way to his station wagon. With a loathsome eye-roll, Dewayne killed the ignition and popped open his door, still humming along with the song ringing in his ears.

As he entered the storefront, Dewayne saw what he expected to see inside a little country market. It was the same shit store he had been to repeatedly, the same scene in all tightly knit communities across the South. There were lines of coolers along the walls stocked with sodas. The coolers in the very back contained various brands of beer. A deli counter stretched along the wall to the right, where Dewayne was sure you could pay to get food poisoning. Yes, the place was complete. Even some big redneck chick sat behind a counter surrounded by cigarettes, and that's precisely what he had come for.

The patrons inside delivered wary glances as Dewayne sauntered to the counter. He locked eyes with the plump clerk, a middle-aged lady who wore a blue blouse with white flowers. White roots littered her dry, overprocessed, black hair. A nametag that said "Jody" hung loosely off her right breast. Two thick paisley curls drawn in dark brown eyeliner sat where her natural eyebrows should have been. She looked at Dewayne, uninspired, just going to town on that Juicy Fruit gum in her gullet. He waited for her to acknowledge him and sing a cheery "Hello, may I help you?"

"What?" spat Jody at last.

Dewayne looked at her, taken aback by her abruptness, and said, "Uh, yeah. Do you have any Jolt colas?" Jody's listless eyes moved to the far wall to the glass doors of icebox shelves. He smirked. "Right. So, could you get me a pack of Marlboro Reds?" As Jody turned to the tobacco cases suspended on the wall behind her, the front doorbell jingled. Dewayne slipped to the icebox cases at the rear of the store and heard a fearsome sigh. Another customer had arrived.

The woman who had crept into the building stood just over five feet tall. Her ample hips rested upon a formidable pelvis. She had long, auburn-white hair piled into a loose bun. Hitched far above her plump waistline were blue-and-white striped pants with an elastic waistband, which she had nestled under her armpits like some nightmarish crop top onesie. A dingy white hat sat on her head, and a dusty feather hung from its brim. A dirty cat that looked as if it had just crawled out of the Micmac burial grounds paced to her right, and its hellish eyes were fixed upon Dewayne.

"Hey, Jody," sighed the woman.

"Hey, Mossy," Jody replied. "And how goes it?"

"Lord, help me; it still goes. I don't know how." As Dewayne stepped behind this Mossy character, she turned to her left and began to cough with a deep, mucous-ladened hack that sounded like his grandfather's old Buick starting up. Dewayne's face twisted in disgust, and he took a step backward.

"Reeooow," rattled the old cat to Dwayne.

Mossy wiped her mouth and turned back to Jody. "Gimme a pack of reds and a cuppa Skoal."

Jody slid the pack of Marlboro cigarettes on the counter to Mossy and snatched a tin of Skoal tobacco snuff from the container to her right. After punching various register buttons, she said, "Be $5.27."

Mossy handed Jody a ten-dollar bill, and Jody returned the change to her. The cat rattled again. "Oh, hush up, now," hissed Mossy. "We'll be home in a minute. You'll get your bologna." She picked up the cigarettes and the snuff and nodded to Jody. "You be good."

"Hell no."

The women chuckled at one another, and the Mossy lady wobbled out of the front door.

Dewayne cleared his throat as he stepped to the counter. He sat the plastic twenty-ounce Jolt cola bottle on the counter. He grinned. "She was pretty."

"Want her number?" said Jody, unmoved by his attempt at humor. She plucked the soda from the counter and punched it into the register.

"And that pack of Marlboro Reds."

"All out."

"What?" asked Dewayne in a panic. "I just saw you sell some to the *beauty queen*."

"Suppose she got the last one," said Jody. She turned to the nearly empty cigarette wall. "Got some Marlboro Lights."

"No," said Dewayne. "Got any Winstons?"

"Nope. You got Max 120s, Kools, Marlboro Lights, or Virginia Slim Light 120s. Other'n that, you're S-O-L."

"Fuck!" hissed Dwayne. "I ain't going all weekend without smokes."

Jody smiled. "You can try the Kenjo about thirty miles north. The Wally World is sure to have 'em, but you'll have to drive to Andersonville."

"Where the hell is Andersonville?"

Jody pointed behind her. " 'bout fifty miles that-a-way. Looks like you'll take what we got, or you could go ask the *beauty queen* if you can buy some off her." She giggled. "Bet she'd give you a fair price for 'em. May even trade 'em for a little kiss from a handsome fella like you."

Dewayne looked through the foggy window and saw the odd woman shove a wad of snuff into her jaw. She turned to make her way toward an old pickup truck in the gravel lot. He nodded to Jody, tossed two dollars in her face, and snatched the soda. He burst through the front door.

"Hey!" The woman didn't stop. "Hey, lady!"

Mossy paused and turned toward Dewayne. "What the hell do *you* want?"

Cigarettes, you fat bitch, he thought. But he forced a smile. He could play nice.

"Listen, uh, it seems that you got the last pack of Marlboro that this place had."

"Well," said Mossy as her eyebrow arched. "Ain't I lucky."

"Mmrrow," choked the cat.

Dewayne peeked at the cat and turned up his nose. "Pretty kitty." The cat began to rub its tattered fur around his bare ankles, causing him to squirm inside. But he could play nice. He turned back to the woman. "Well, the closest place I could get some is apparently Georgia. So, could you let me buy that pack off you?" She scrutinized him with a wary gaze. "I could give you five bucks."

Mossy hesitated. Then, she scratched her stubbly chin. "Don't know. I hear these is hard to come by."

"Seven," sighed Dewayne. He could feel his anger beginning to boil over. He hadn't had a cigarette in over an hour before entering this hellhole, and his patience was wearing as thin as rice paper. "Eight."

"Twenty bucks," Mossy posed.

"Twenty!" cried Dewayne. "Are you serious? I can get a fuckin' carton for twelve bucks!"

"Well, apparently, you ain't getting a carton here, sweetie," she said, nodding at the market.

"Ten," said Dewayne.

"Just 'cause you gotta filthy mouth, I say *twenty-five*."

That was it. Dewayne had the bullshit up to his eyeballs and wasn't wasting any more time on the woman.

"You know what?" he spat. "I *do* have a filthy mouth, you *fat bitch*. Take those smokes and shove them up your raggedy ass!" With that, he reared back and kicked the cat from around his ankles. The woman cried out. With her attention turned to the cat, Dewayne snatched the pack of Marlboro from her fingers and spun toward his car.

"Rascal!" yelled Mossy as she rushed toward the cat. "You little som'bitch! You kicked my cat!"

"Fuck you, lady!" shouted Dewayne as he jumped into his car. He fired up the engine, and Metallica blasted through the air. He threw the car into reverse, slammed his foot on the gas, and whipped the vehicle backward. He flipped the gearshift into drive and peeled forward, sending a shower of gravel in the old heifer's direction. Dewayne smiled with pleasure as he sped away, watching the woman wave her flabby arms.

Little did Dewayne realize that he had entered a new dimension, a hypothetical realm, a world of *ifs*. For instance, *if* his radio hadn't been so offensively loud, he would have realized the real cause of the woman's hysterics. *If* Dewayne had looked in his rearview mirror a split second earlier, he would have seen her lift the mangled body of her dead companion into her shivering arms. *If* he had ignored the woman, got into his car, and calmly left the market, he wouldn't have crushed the old cat under his rear tires.

If Dewayne Burns had played nice, he'd still be alive.

8
THE GATHERING

"Is there any just cause for feelin' like this? On the surface, I'm a name on a list. I try to be discreet but then blow it again."
—*(I Just) Died in Your Arms:* Cutting Crew—

On the surface, Bethany Leanne Hawkins seemed to have it all. Anyone looking at her would say so. And that's what mattered. But she knew better. Over time, that superficial appearance had become natural to portray. She had studied enough pop psychology in college to understand this stemmed from her own insecurities layered with needs for validation. But as Jackie always said: *Fuuuck them.*

Beth had *things.* Admirable qualities. What qualities, you ask? Well . . . brains, for one. And she intended to use them. Academically, school had come easy for her, unlike her older sister, Jackie, for whom studies were a mere notion. That's not to say that Beth didn't have to work for that honor roll. On the contrary, there were times when subjects were almost impossible. Like physics. She *hated* physics. How light and sound waves function, the principles of electricity and magnetism, the laws and applications of motion, forces, and gravity. *What. The. Hell.* Though she would never use those lessons in life, understanding them had given her brains, and she was thankful for that.

Also, Beth had looks. At least now. Her mother had once said Beth was a "late bloomer." Jackie hadn't bloomed late. Hell, no. Jackie was *born* in bloom. Boys fluttered toward Jackie like horny butterflies, so Jackie struggled to focus on anything that didn't involve a penis. That's not to say her older sister lacked intelligence. Jackie was smart. *Street* smart.

The boys overlooked Beth. Beth had been invisible to the male species, a cellophane figure through which affection and admiration quickly passed. It was a lonely existence, but it had served her well. When Beth turned sixteen, things changed almost overnight. She woke up one morning to find she had traded her acne for two perky C-cup boobies. *Who knew?* She hadn't necessarily been looking for boobies. She lifted her nightshirt one morning, and there they were. Boobies. *"Helllooo, gorgeous!"*

That May, her braces were removed.

Three days later, she met Jacob at Eastridge Mall.

Jacob was tall, thickly built, with short dark hair and chestnut eyes. He had a square jawline, the kind of jawline Beth had seen on the heroes of the comic books she loved to collect. She loved his laugh. He had the most fantastic laugh. Yet underneath his positive traits buzzed the nearly imperceivable vibration of obnoxiousness. She heard that vibration now and again when surrounded by his peers. It was how his tone would change when he spoke to her, the look he would give to other girls passing by, and the jokes he and his friends would make about others. Warnings. Red flags. Sometimes, Beth wondered if Jacob would have spoken to her if they had met before the boobs, those flat-chested days when her teeth looked like a rickety picket fence.

Jacob hadn't pressed Beth for sex, though he had spent much time pleading his case. There had been fondling, kisses, caresses in the back seat of his Toyota. During those intimacies, she had carefully assessed his—what did Jackie call it—oh, yes, his *rod*. It seemed to be an acceptable size. It wasn't as if she had much to compare it to.

She finally asked to see it one night, and he was happy to oblige. She stared at it, considering its length and girth, wondering what it may feel like if she allowed things to progress. Would it be painful? No, she didn't think it would be unbearable. It wasn't small. But it most certainly wasn't significant. At least by what she had seen in the magazines Jackie had shown her. It was . . . *nice*. Proportional. It didn't seem to bend in any freaky angles or anything. *It's a training penis*, she thought. *Yeah, like a training bra—just not as pretty.*

Two weeks later, she allowed things to move forward. There was a part of her that thought better of it, the part that knew Jacob was not the one, but her curiosity outweighed her judgment. And so, with Cutting Crew droning in the background, the two of them parked at the edge of New Gray Cemetery near the woods, and, as Jackie would say, they "did it." The song had just entered its second chorus when Beth felt Jacob tense and release.

Wait. Hold on. That was it? Really? That was sex?

She hadn't felt anything at all. Had anything even happened? With the deed done, he rolled away from her as if he had just scaled Mount Everest and asked her how she felt. She lied and told him she felt fine; it was great, he was great, the world was great, and she couldn't wait for them to do it again. But she felt lousy. She felt . . . wasted. At the time, she didn't believe she ever wanted to do that again with anyone, whatever it had been. The following day at school, she saw the consequences of her actions.

Jacob was distant, reserved, and cold. He looked at Beth like she had been a thing he had conquered, a punchline for his friends. She passed through the hallways feeling every set of eyes staring in her direction, judging her, knowing what she had done. And challenges arose. Beth began to retreat, withdraw.

That's when Jackie stepped in.

Her older sister was loose with her body *and* her opinions, attributes that Beth both loathed and envied. Jackie freely expressed herself in numerous ways and didn't give two shits what anyone else thought. And that wasn't just lip service; she *literally* didn't care.

"Oh, fuck them right in the ear," Jackie muttered around the cigarette dangling on her lip. She dug through her closet, looking for what to wear. "So what? You screwed a pencil-dick loser. So what? It's your body. You're a grown-ass woman."

"I shouldn't have done it," Beth said.

Jackie snorted. "From what you've said, you *didn't* do it, babydoll. I bet your honor is still intact." She turned to Beth. "I can check if you like?"

Beth chuckled and flushed red. "No, thank you. I'll pass."

"Look, if you want to try someone out, try them out. God knows guys do it to us enough. Better to know up front than waste time on somebody incompatible." She tossed a blouse to Beth. "Do whatever you damn well please, sister. But *own it*. Own it. Always own it. Own who you are, what you do, and the decisions you make. If you can learn to do that, no one can hurt you with your choices."

Jackie didn't know it, but those words would burn in Beth's mind.

They would give Beth Hawkins her most important characteristic—more important than brains and certainly more important than looks. Determination. Beth found the boiling heat of resolution in those words. *Own it*. And she decided to do just that. She would become free.

Maybe not as free as Jackie, but nobody needed to be that free.

Eight years later, strolling toward the sunlit parking area of Kamp Kromwell, Beth could still hear those words ringing in her ears. *Own it*. Beth had done just that. She regretted nothing and apologized sparingly. A blessing and a curse. Some considered her too rigid, firm, a bitch, even. It wasn't a perfect attitude, but it did offer protection. It had served her well at school, it had served her well in college, and it *definitely* served her well with the kids who attended Kamp Kromwell. This summer would be better. This summer would be the best.

Beth spied someone tall and thin sitting on the hood of a white sedan in the parking lot. The sunlight shone off the boy's red hair from that distance, looking like red flames glowing in the distance.

Dennis Fern, she thought. *That must be Dennis.*

Dennis Fern was one of the last applicants chosen for the season, and it wasn't without ample consideration. His application was less than stellar, and his phone interview was lackluster. But he had a saving grace. Dennis had worked with special needs children for three years.

"Dennis?" asked Beth.

Dennis held out his hand. "Beth?"

"I'm so glad to see you," she said. "Did you have any trouble getting here?"

He slipped a cigarette into his mouth and opened a silver Zippo lighter. "No, it's pretty straightforward, I think." He lit the cigarette and clenched it in his teeth. "So, this is the place."

Beth glanced at the rolling fields beyond them. "Yep, this is it."

A green sports car entered the lot before Beth and Dennis noticed it. As the vehicle stopped in a nearby parking space, Beth couldn't help but notice the guy in the driver's seat. With a bright smile, he stepped from the vehicle and walked to the trunk to gather his bags. The closer the guy came toward her, the more handsome he became. Standing well over six feet, he had sandy brown hair and thick legs.

"Are you Beth?" he asked in a husky Southern drawl.

"I am!" replied Beth enthusiastically. *I wonder what his penis looks like?*

He held out his hand. "Daniel Thorogood. You can call me Danny."

Daniel Thorogood had all the makings of a model counselor, at least on paper. A lifelong football player, he was apt at sports. He also held the assistant coach position in his local junior football league, so he was used to working with youngsters.

"Dennis," was all the introduction Dennis provided as he raised two fingers. Danny nodded in his direction and smiled.

Beth took his hand. "Hi, Danny. It's so nice to have you here. You're the football guy, right?"

"Yeah," Danny replied humbly. "I'll be playing for UTK come this fall."

Just then, another car came toward the lot. The red Nissan pulled next to Danny's car, and a young woman exited the vehicle. She had full cheeks, a lovely smile, and thin, neat braids lining her scalp. The girl also had the whitest teeth Beth had ever seen. She gathered her things and joined Beth, Dennis, and Danny.

"Rosetta?" asked Beth as the girl approached.

"Oh! Yes, that's me." Rosetta shook Beth's hand.

Rosetta Samuel also had a sports and recreation edge to her application. At one time, she had been a gymnast. Additionally, Rosetta taught sign language to deaf children, so she had all the experience one could desire.

Beth gestured toward the others. "Hi, Rosetta. This is Dennis and Danny."

"Hey there," said Rosetta. "Sorry I'm late. I had the worst time getting here. I was followed for a couple of miles by this idiot in a pick-up truck wearing a shirt that said CHUG NORRIS."

Beth sighed. "Gray truck?"

"Yeah," said Rosetta. "How did you know?"

"Has a bumper sticker that says SUCK GAS AND HAUL ASS?"

Rosetta burst into laughter. "Girl! I had to turn into this little market down the road. The woman running that place chased him off, though."

"Oh, yes. That's Jody. She could chase off a bobcat," Beth said. "And don't worry about that guy. Buster Harris. He's an idiot. He looks scary, but if you saw him out of that truck, you'd see he's just over five feet tall." Beth glanced at her clipboard. "Did I read in here that you're a gymnast?"

Rosetta placed her bags on the pavement. "*Was.* I don't really do that much these days. I had a little accident when I was fifteen." She raised the leg of her shorts. Rows of deep scars lined her leg.

"Wow," said Dennis. "Gruesome."

"Yeah, I was leaving the library in downtown Memphis when this guy dropped a cigarette into his crotch. And there you have it."

Beth gasped. "Oh, my God!"

Rosetta waved. "Oh, it's fine. I may not be able to do the uneven bars anymore, but I can walk, which the doctors swore would never happen again."

Another vehicle arrived, a new blue sedan with two people in the front seats. Beth could see the girl's excited smile from a hundred paces. Her carmate slid into her lap as she turned into a parking space. She shoved him forward, and Beth noticed it wasn't a person. It was a mannequin with a crooked brown wig on its head. Giggling with glee, the girl slipped out of the car and shut the door.

"Whew!" she said. "Hi, y'all. Sorry if I'm late." She tip-toed to where the three of them stood. "I'm Bonnie. Bonnie Evans. From Chattanooga."

Bonnie Evans had been another one of those lower on the list of potentials. Her mother certainly thought highly of her, which was evident in the lengthy letter included in Beth's submission. Ultimately, the camp needed one last female to watch over the girls' cabins. From the list packed with "harlots and junkies," as Drummond claimed, Bonnie seemed the least objectional choice. The main perk was that she was certified in CPR, so she could be helpful, if only in the worst cases.

Beth stretched out her hand. "Beth Hawkins."

Bonnie's eyes widened. "Oh, yeah! We talked the other week." She shook Beth's hand.

Beth nodded. "I'm so sorry about your friend." Beth noticed the confusion on Bonnie's face. "Tracey. Her application."

Bonnie managed to smile. "Oh! Oh, don't worry about that. Completely understood. Things work out the way they need to. Frankly, my mother was relieved she wasn't coming."

Beth turned toward the group. "Um . . . this is Danny, Rosetta, and Dennis."

"Who's your friend?" asked Dennis.

"My . . ." Bonnie seemed confused. "Oh! That's Axel. Like Axel Rose." Dennis was unamused. "I teach CPR at the Chattanooga Urgent Response Center. Mr. Drummond thought doing a couple of CPR classes this summer may be good." Bonnie turned toward her car. "Dennis, honey, would you care to help me get my bags out of the car? They're in the back seat."

Dennis paused. "Really?" Bonnie raised her brow as if she couldn't believe someone had denied her request.

"Oh," said Bonnie uncomfortably. "Okay. Danny?"

"Uh, yeah, sure," Danny said. Bonnie opened the passenger door, and Danny retrieved not one, not two, but three full-sized suitcases from the back seat. One of them popped open, spilling clothes and toiletries onto the ground. Beth rushed to help them.

"Um . . . I'm glad your mother let you come," said Beth as she helped gather Bonnie's loose items.

Bonnie paused and took Beth's hand. "And let me say I am *so sorry* about her. She's . . . well . . . *particular*."

In Beth's experience, "particular" meant anal-retentive, and Bonnie's mother seemed especially "particular" about her daughter. During Beth's phone interview with Bonnie, Mrs. Evans interrupted the call to address several topics, namely the "three Bs"—boys, beer, and bonfires. Beth did everything she could to assure the woman that the counselors would remain on their best behavior, but that did little to calm her.

"Oh, that's fine, Bonnie," lied Beth. *Because it most definitely was not fine.* "I completely understand." *And she most definitely did not understand.* "I've dealt with more than one concerned parent, and I tell them to rest assured the counseling staff at Kamp Kromwell is always thoroughly vetted."

The bluster of rock music and car engines spoiled the tranquil air. A dusty black Trans AM spun through the camp entrance and barreled up the road adjacent to the parking lot. It squealed to a halt approximately two hundred feet past the lot gate, reversed, and whipped into the area. Once parked, the music silenced, and the driver's door creaked open. Out stepped a young man wearing a black AC/DC tee shirt. A faded blue jean vest hung over his shoulders, and his long, windblown hair stood on end like a lion's mane. He fished a large duffel bag from the backseat, slammed the car door, and delivered a mischievous smirk to the young counselors.

"How the hell are ya?" called Dewayne Burns.

The new counselors slowly turned to Beth with stunned faces.

"Oh, he's not one of the counselors," clarified Beth. "Kitchen. He'll be working in the kitchen."

Dewayne meandered over to the group and dropped his bag onto the ground. "Dewayne," he proclaimed in more of an announcement than an introduction. "I'm here to do the dishes."

"You're Joe's nephew," Beth said.

"That's me." He fished the stolen pack of Marlboro from his pocket. Slipping one between his lips, he lit the end with a match. He blew a plume of smoke into the air. "I'm ready to be oriented."

A green shuttle came puttering down the roadway toward the parking lot. At the helm sat a broad, middle-aged man wearing an orange polo shirt. A wide smile appeared underneath his bushy mustache. He pulled to a halt beside Beth and leaned out the window.

"Good afternoon!" said the man as he killed the motor. "I'm Earl Drummond, director here at Kamp Kromwell. And I think . . ." His eyes scanned the young people. "Are we missing someone?"

"Um," Beth looked at her list. "Neil . . . Williams?"

"The fella I interviewed," Drummond said with a nod.

Neil Williams didn't have much experience with kids beyond the two of his own, but he was a carpenter, a skill that would be of good use at the camp. Drummond enjoyed the guy's playful attitude and kind demeanor. He suspected he would be a good fit with the children, if only teaching them how to make birdhouses.

A beat-up Volkswagen stumbled into the lot, backfiring as it entered the gate. The round car hobbled to a stop. A hefty guy with short brown hair and a neat beard slipped from the driver's seat. He snatched a bag from the car and jogged toward the group.

"Sorry!" Neil called. "Sorry."

"Neil?" asked Beth.

"I am so sorry," Neil said. "I had to stop and put water in that thing ten times. I never thought I'd get here. Please don't say I'm already fired, because I'll never make it home."

Drummond chuckled. "You're fine, son. You're right on time." A death rattle rumbled from the Volkswagen. It banged with a backfire reminiscent of an old man's fart. The last cry of a dying automobile. "Is that thing safe?"

"Oh, no, sir," confessed Neil. "Not at all, but it's paid for."

Drummond pointed at Rosetta. "You are Rosetta Samuel." Rosetta smiled and nodded. "You're Bonnie Evans."

"That's me," said Bonnie.

Drummond nodded. "Before I forget, your mother has called me . . . a *few* times. You need to call her when we get to the office." Bonnie blushed uncomfortably. Drummond turned to Danny. "This football player must be Dan Thorogood. The tall fella must be Dennis Fern." Drummond turned to

Dewayne and smiled. "And I never forget a face. Mister Burns! Good to have you back with us. Let's keep the profanity to a slow burn." Dewayne shifted. "Alright, everyone, pile your things in the back, and I'll carry you—"

Another vehicle came rolling into the lot. The dusty police cruiser coasted to where the group stood. Beth turned and looked at Drummond with surprise.

"Earl," said Beth warily.

"What is Fred doing?" asked Drummond.

Beth thought she spied a concerned look on Dewayne's face. Then again, she imagined that the sight of authorities always made someone like Dewayne nervous. His face lightened two shades, and he licked his dry lips. Those beady eyes of his darted back and forth as if he was getting ready to run. He moved to the side, slipping just behind Danny's broad frame.

The cruiser stopped next to Drummond, and Drummond leaned into the window. "Hey, Fred. What's going on?"

Sheriff Dunham sighed. "Earl, I hate to bother y'all. But is someone named Bonnie Evans in here with you?"

Staggered, everyone turned in Bonnie's direction.

"I'm Bonnie Evans," she meekly said.

"Little lady, the first second you get, would you mind calling your mother? She has called my station every thirty minutes for the past three hours hunting for you."

Drummond glanced at Bonnie with impatience and nodded to the sheriff. "Sorry about that, Fred. She's been calling here, too. You know how mothers can be sometimes."

A hiss of static rattled from inside the cruiser, and Dunham winced. He plucked the CB receiver from the holder and pressed the button. "Dunham," he barked.

"Fred," said a woman's voice. "You better get on back here. Mossy's in fits."

Dunham and Drummond looked at each other.

"Good Lord, what now?" asked Dunham.

"She saying there's been a murder."

Dunham's eyes widened. "A murder!?"

The CB crackled. "Oh, keep your drawers on. The victim's her cat."

"Son-of-a . . . shit!" Dunham muttered. "There goes my day." He pressed the button on the receiver. "Tell her I'm on my way and not to do anything crazy, please." He snapped the receiver onto the holder and turned to Drummond with a pained expression. "I'll give you a hundred dollars if you go deal with her. How much would it take?"

Drummond smiled. "I'm not sure you have that amount of money, my friend."

Dunham secured his seatbelt and placed the cruiser in reverse. "Oh!" he called out. "And speaking of Mossy, I hear she stopped by your stables this morning to complain to that new horse lady."

"Susan?" asked Drummond

"Did you not warn that lady about Mossy?"

Drummond sighed. "I hadn't gotten around to it, no."

"Well, you best make sure the woman didn't up and quit on you." He nodded to the group. "You all have a blessed day now. Say a little prayer for me." He pointed to Bonnie. "And call your mother."

9
1:03 P.M.

"We're spilling tea and dishing just desserts one may deserve."
—*Let's Have a Kiki*: Scissor Sisters—

June 1995

I stood alone with my suitcase in the Waverly Baptist Church parking lot at seven a.m. on Friday, June 9, waiting for my chariot to Kamp Kromwell to arrive. Everything had happened in the blink of an eye, leaving my mind feeling blunt and lethargic. As I swatted away the hungry morning mosquitos, I tried to arrange my thoughts into a timeline, a pathway to my current situation.

Just two days before Leslie Cooper would depart for Kromwell, her grandmother contacted the family with unexpected news. Leslie's maternal grandfather had passed in his sleep, and he had the nerve to do such a thing at his mistress's apartment in Atlanta. Needless to say, the revelation shook the very foundation of the Cooper family. Within hours, the family imploded with accusatory fervor. Apparently, a will existed that bequeathed significant assets to his twenty-seven-year-old lover. While the document's validity was most definitely in question, it made a bad situation much worse. Unfortunately for Leslie, Kamp Kromwell was out of the question.

To arrange Leslie's cancellation, her mother contacted the camp. She was referred to the corporate offices of Kromwell Industries, who advised with Leslie's registration well past the cancellation date, typically, a refund wasn't an option. Under the circumstances, however, the company "opened a case" that would be reviewed for either a partial or full refund *within thirty to ninety days*. Richard Cooper, Leslie's hot-headed father, flew into a ballistic tirade I could hear from my front porch. Richard Cooper didn't lose money. Especially that kind of money.

This is where I came in.

Leslie's father called us with an exciting proposal. During his fifth heated call to Kromwell Industries that day, the case worker advised that he was within his rights to sell the package to someone who could attend in his daughter's place. The scent of this potential bargain was like fresh blood to my shark of a father. The two men went back and forth for half an hour, negotiating and renegotiating. Finally, Richard Cooper agreed to sell Leslie's spot at Kromwell to us for *half* of the cost. A deal too good for my father to pass up. Frankly, I didn't care if Mr. Cooper had been *paying me* to go; the summer camp experience didn't entice me. Then my mother said something that caused me to think.

Mom stood at the stove, coating her meatloaf with a film of thick ketchup and tomato paste. Anne and I were busy at the kitchen sink, washing and drying dishes.

"Well, I think it may be good for you—for everybody, really," said my mother aloud to no one in particular. I looked at Anne. Mom slid the meatloaf into the oven. "It'd give you some time away . . . different environment." She began spooning blots of butter onto unbaked dinner rolls. Her eyes turned toward me. "And it'd give me some time to talk to your father . . . your brothers. Let them know how things will be from here on out." She slipped the spoon into the mashed potatoes steaming on the stove. "If they don't like it, me and Annie will just pack our things and meet you in the mountains."

I smiled and rolled my eyes at the ridiculous notion.

Anne shrugged. "It sounds like fun to me." Her eyes met mine. "If I were you, I'd be on that bus faster than you could blink."

Around eight thirty that evening, I fell onto my bed, watching the dying sunlight cast its orange glow across my ceiling, my brain heavy with thought. I lay there, pondering the implications and next steps. I started the day convinced there was no way in hell I'd spend weeks walking in the wilderness. But then came that quiet voice I've learned to trust implicitly in my later years. *Maybe you need to do this*, it said. I heard Anne's words again. *If I were you, I'd be on that bus faster than you could blink.*

I stepped into the kitchen, where, as usual, Mom sat reading. I plucked a cup from the cabinet, pulled open the freezer, and filled the cup with ice.

"I'll go," I said. She looked at me over the brim of her reading glasses. "I think I'll go." I noticed her surprised expression. I rounded the table and took a seat in front of her. "You're right," I said quietly. "I need to . . . be gone for a little while, I think. Let things process. If I don't like it, I'll just come home."

"Right," she agreed. "If you don't like it, we'll drive up there and get you." She slid her hand across the table and took ahold of mine. She squeezed it, and we smiled at each other.

"Okay!" I groaned. "Let me call Leslie."

The path was complete. Now I could clearly see how I had reached my destination.

The bus arrived, and I climbed aboard, feeling like I had just made the worst mistake of my life. Only one other soul was on the bus besides me, a kid with a goofy smile and big eyes. He nodded and smiled at me from the back of the bus as I slid into a vacant seat in the middle of the bus. As I heard his feet shuffling toward me, I felt this momentary surge of panic. *I could just jump off this thing and live in the woods for a few weeks. I could give up now, say hell no, let Dad lose the money. Who cares?*

But then I'd just be alone. Alone with my sanctimonious brothers while they attempted to exorcise me of the gay entity that had possessed me. Alone with my father's disapproving glares of shame he'd give before turning away, unable to bear my sight any longer. Alone, staring into an uncertain future that seemed to stretch into decades, all the way to the grave of an old, lonely gay dude nobody would remember.

It was *Schrödinger's Summer Camp.*

At that moment, camp was a wonderous adventure and a miserable experience. Only by remaining on the bus would I know which.

"Hey, man!" said the kid as he plopped down in the seat across from me.

"Hey," I replied. *Get up! Get up now before the doors close.* The doors to the bus rattled shut, and the driver shifted the bus into gear. *Oh, for shit's sake.*

"I'm Kenny Love." I turned to him, uncertain if I heard him correctly. "It's spelled l-o-u-v-e but pronounced 'love.'" This was the first of many fabrications Kenny would deliver. I'd later learn it was pronounced *low-vey.*

"Joe Carpenter," I replied.

For the two and a half hours it took us to reach Kromwell, Kenny took great pleasure in telling me about his life. And what a life it was. He and his two sisters, *Sweet* and *Good*, lived in Farragut with his parents, who were both neurosurgeons. He had a girlfriend named Victoria Valentino, who owned a red Lamborghini in which the two had "passionate sex." That was just his main girlfriend, mind you. He had several others. Kenny was undoubtedly a ladies' man, or at least he believed he was. I had doubts he could create relationships with anybody, let alone hot girls who liked to get it on in Lamborghinis.

The one true thing Kenny told me that morning was that he was terrified of insects. So, what better place for someone with entomophobia than a summer camp in the woods? I hoped Kenny wasn't going to make me regret my decision. That's not to say that I found him intolerable. Since I didn't take anything he said literally, he was somewhat entertaining. *Sort of.* When we neared the camp, I felt the *real* Kenny Louve was a lonely guy buried underneath several feet of bullshit.

Our bus hobbled into the parking area on the left and took its place among five other buses. Once parked, the driver advised us that it was safe to depart. I noticed seven individuals hovering around the parking lot's gate beyond the murky windows. They were all dressed in shorts with tee shirts emblazoned with the Kamp Kromwell logo. As the campers emerged, the older man among them began to wave for us. He called out, asking us to bring our belongings and assemble. Once everyone gathered, he wrung his hands together and smiled.

"Good morning," chimed the man. "My name is Earl Drummond, the director of Kamp Kromwell. And welcome to the best summer you're ever going to have!" He began to clap his hands, prompting everyone to join in the applause. "These are our counselors." He nodded to the girl in the end.

"Uh . . . hello, everyone. My name is Rosetta Samuel. I'm nineteen, and I'm from Memphis." Someone in the back cheered. "Thank you," she replied with a chuckle.

"What's something that most folks don't know about you, Rosetta?" asked Drummond.

She pondered. "Um . . . I used to compete in gymnastics."

"Have you ever been in the Olympics?" asked a girl from the crowd.

Rosetta smiled and shook her head. "Well, no, but one day maybe. So . . . anyway, I'll be looking after Cabins . . . One and Two?" she asked, glancing at Drummond, who nodded. "Yes, one and two, so I look forward to having fun with you." We applauded, and she motioned to the girl to her left.

"Hey, y'all," said the perky blonde as she raised her hand and wiggled her fingers. "My name is Bonnie Evans. I'm from Chattanooga, and I just turned twenty about two months ago. So, not legal just yet." I could feel the uncomfortable silence like a prickly sweater against my skin. Bonnie then smiled with a toothy grin. "Thank *yooou*," she added for some weird reason.

There was something oddly irritating about this Bonnie chick, though I couldn't place my finger on it. Something about her seemed rehearsed, overly energetic, as if her true self was anything but this bubbly, cartoonish specimen before us.

"And something no one knows about me . . . let's see. Well, I play the banjo for my church choir." Again, no one appeared roused. "Does anyone here play the banjo?"

Kenny immediately raised his hand.

Of course, you do, Kenny.

"I play electric guitar," he claimed.

And I'm sure that Eddie Van Halen taught you.

Bonnie smiled. "Well, that's *almost* like it. Anywhoo, I'll have Cabins Three and Four, and I look forward to getting to know y'all." We managed to clap as the guy next to her stepped forward.

"Hey, guys," he said in a deep, rusty voice. "My name is Danny Thorogood."

Now, that's a name.

Mr. Thorogood had my complete attention. He was tall, much taller than I was, and thickly built, a football player-type.

"I'm eighteen . . . from Maryville, and I just graduated two weeks ago *finally*." Several cheers sounded from the audience. "And something that people don't know about me is that I'm absolutely addicted to horror movies. Can't get enough of them."

"Ew!" declared Bonnie, throwing her hands into the air. "Not me. I don't do those."

"What's your favorite scary movie?" I blurted before I could help myself. I felt the flames of humiliation rush through my cheeks. I took a step back. *What the hell is wrong with you?* Two boys at the end of the group began to chuckle. One wore a dirty white tee shirt airbrushed with the words "Chester the Jester."

Danny's eyes met mine, and he smiled. And what a smile it was.

"Wow. Um, I don't know, man. That's a good question. I'd have to say . . . *The Wolfman*. The old one with Lon Chaney Jr." I beamed at his response and nodded, trying to quickly forget I had said anything at all. "What's yours?" he asked me.

I wasn't quite prepared for him to acknowledge me, let alone ask for my opinion. I suddenly found it impossible to open my mouth. I felt a gentle nudge against my back and turned to see a tanned fellow with curly hair smiling from behind me.

"Um, *Halloween*," I uttered at last.

Danny bowed and pointed at me. "Oh, yeah. *Awesome* movie, man. That's a good one. Anyway, I'll have Cabins Nine and Ten, so I look forward to rocking out this summer with you guys."

I turned back to the fellow who had nudged me. The faint traces of a juvenile five o'clock shadow were along his darkly tanned chin. To his left was a tall guy who towered above us. The tall one looked down at me and mouthed something like, "Don't pay attention to him." I stared at him, confused, until another voice directed my attention back to the front.

"Hello, all. I'm Beth Hawkins, and I've been a counselor here at Kromwell for several years now. Has anyone been to Kromwell before?" She pointed through the crowd. "I know at least two of you have: Lily and DJ." I saw a boy and girl wave at the counselor. "I'm going to be managing Cabins Five and Six. And we are going to have an awesome summer."

"Wait," said Rosetta. "What's something we don't know about you?"

"Oh!" said Beth. "Well, gosh, I don't know."

"You can cook a mean chili," said Drummond.

Beth chuckled. "Well, I can cook something *like* chili. I don't know if it's mean or not."

All eyes turned to the guy with red hair, who took an unsteady step forward. "Um, name is Dennis Fern. Eighteen. Originally from Indiana, but moved to Tennessee about five years ago. I'll have Cabins Eleven and Twelve." He began to step back but raised his hand. "Oh, and I play classical piano."

"Uh, what?" asked Beth, her eyes rolling in their sockets. Dennis looked at her and shrugged. "Like, really? You play piano?"

"Ever since I was five." Dennis offered a smile.

The bulky guy with a beard stepped forward and grinned. "Wow, Dennis. You're going to have to give me a lesson or two." The guy waved. "Hi, um, I'm Neil Williams. Cabins Seven and Eight. I'm the senior citizen of the group. I'll be twenty-two this year. I'm from Oak Ridge. I . . . do a lot with woodwork, but everyone . . . kinda . . . knows that. Oh!" He snapped his fingers. "I can speak Spanish and German."

"Ah!" sang Drummond, who then rattled off something that sounded German to Neil, though it could have been Klingon for all I knew. Neil laughed and replied in a manner just as incoherent.

Drummond chuckled and stepped forward. "I asked him how the weather was, and he said it was hotter than *Sahnemeerrettich*." No one knew what the hell that was. "Which is like a horseradish . . . cream . . . that's a bit . . . hot. Anyway! Let's go ahead and get everyone settled. Then, we'll meet at the dining hall for lunch. Each of you should have received a cabin assignment in your welcome letter."

Everyone began to rifle through their belongings to retrieve a letter I knew I did not possess. Various groups filed into assortments according to cabin assignments. Each counselor would manage two cabins—one for the teenagers or seniors and the other for the children, the juniors. I knelt and unzipped my bag, hoping that I would magically find something that resembled a welcome letter hiding amidst the socks and underwear and packs of Pop-Tarts my mother had sent with me. A piercing cry from my left caused me to jerk.

A hefty black bird sat on the fencepost beside me, a crow. But it didn't look like any crow I had ever seen. This thing was massive, dark—so dark it nearly shone blue. For a moment, I thought it was looking at me. After another moment, I was sure it was. It stared at me with remarkable curiosity, tilting its head left and right as if it were trying to determine what manner of creature I was.

"Son, everything okay?" Drummond called to me.

I rose to my feet and timidly stepped forward. "Um, sir, I don't have a letter."

He nodded to me. "Oh, let's see what we got. Name?"

"Joseph Carpenter."

"Joe," muttered Drummond as he flipped through his listing. "Joe, Joe, Joe . . . well, Joe, looks like I'm not seeing you on here."

Oh, my God, I thought. *Please don't say I have to get back on that rickety ass—*

"Wait! There you are. You took over for Miss Leslie Cooper. And you are in Cabin . . ."

And God, if you could please put me with Danny, I would greatly—

". . . Twelve with Dennis."

Shit balls!

I returned to gather my things with the crow's black gaze upon me, sensing the sticky sensation of its glare. Snatching my bag from the ground, I quickly joined the group surrounding Dennis, which included the boy with curly hair who had nudged me, his towering compadre, and, of course, my new best friend, Kenny Louve. The curly-haired guy peered at me with this sly, devious smirk as I walked toward them. Once all the campers were with their leaders, we began the long hike toward the center of camp.

Each counselor gave us details about the campground and surrounding area, but no one seemed to know more than Beth Hawkins. She regaled us with fanciful factoids, all the while being vehemently wooed by *Kenny Casanova*, who showered her with asinine compliments.

Constructed in 1966, Kamp Kromwell first opened its gates in 1967. At over three hundred acres, the camp boasted a tennis court, basketball court, golf range, archery range, riflery range, and even a horseback trail leading from newly constructed stables. Water sports and swimming activities would be held at the "beautiful Lake Ellington." Last but not least, the upper north side of the grounds contained the webbing of rope bridges, which weaved in and out of the vast forests surrounding bright green hills. I was relieved we wouldn't sleep in the trees and forage for food in the dirt.

As we reached the camp square, Danny, Neil, and Dennis led the boys west. There were six large cabins nestled under the canopy of trees. The counselors would bunk in the junior cabins, leaving the more capable teenagers alone. Dennis led us to Cabins Eleven and Twelve, belonging to the junior and senior boys under his assignment. We entered our bunk, chose our beds, and began to unpack as he led the younger children toward Cabin Eleven.

The interior was impressive, much larger than it appeared on the outside. It held ten single beds aligned in two rows of five. Four white fans suspended from the center of the ceiling turned at medium speed, circulating cool air blowing from a small air conditioner at the front of the room. Spacious windows lined every wall. They hung ajar, looking like gaping aluminum jaws, breathing in the purity of the outdoors. Without thought, I tossed my backpack and suitcase on the bed closest to the door.

"So, Beth," began Kenny. "I think she was digging the *Louve*."

I chuckled. "I'm sure she was, man." I placed my suitcase on the bed, but the curly-haired fellow appeared beside Kenny before I had even unzipped it.

"Hello," he said, hand outstretched. "I'm Asia Demarco." Kenny looked at me and offered his hand.

Your mom named you Asia?

"Um . . . hello. I'm Kenny Louve." Kenny was so stunned he pronounced his name correctly.

Asia shook Kenny's. "Kenny, I just wanted to tell you, you don't want that bed."

Kenny looked at the bed apprehensively. "Why not?"

"That's on the west side of the cabin."

"So?"

"So?" said Asia. "What about the bed bugs?"

"Beth said there weren't any bed bugs. I asked," Kenny confirmed.

And Kenny had asked. He had asked Beth about the size and species of every insect dwelling on the grounds.

Asia nodded. "But you heard what she said, right? She said there ain't no *east-side* bed bugs. She said nothing 'bout west-side."

I knew there were notable differences between the East Coast's theater and fashion cultures versus the West Coast's big-budget glitter. I was also aware of the hip-hop rivalry between East Coast and West Coast rap artists, such as The Notorious B.I.G. and Tupac Shakur, who would tragically pass in violent drive-by shootings. However, I never—not once in my life—heard of regional variations in bed bugs.

I raised a curious eyebrow and focused on my suitcase. As Asia prattled on, I thought I spied the glitter of a horn protruding from his forehead. Could it have been possible that I had stumbled upon another unicorn out here in the wilderness, lost in the forest, alone on the trails of Kamp Kromwell? I would later learn that this feeling was called "gaydar" and was a talent all homosexuals innately possessed. A biological *homo-beacon*, if you will.

"But then *you'd* have bed bugs," explained Kenny. "Aren't you worried about—"

Asia shook his head. "Ain't no bed bugs want any of this, friend. They don't do Mexican."

Apparently, west-side bed bugs were bigots.

"You're full of it," said Kenny, turning toward the open door. "Mister Dennis! Do we have west-side bed bugs?"

Asia took Kenny by the arms. "Look, look, look. Tell you what I'll do," he suggested. "Why don't you take my bed over there?" He pointed to the bed across the room directly underneath the air conditioner. "See, there is no way *any* bugs are getting around that bed. First, it's high off the floor. It's not under one of the windows. And see—it's right under the air conditioner, and you know how bugs hate that cold."

"I don't know."

Asia waved his hand and plucked Kenny's suitcase off the ground. "Oh, Keith, I'm just looking out for you."

"Ken—"

"Come on and let us get you settled in. My big ole brother gonna keep all those mean ole bugs away from you with his nasty feet. You're gonna thank me in the morning. You wait."

As the two of them made their way to the other side of the room, I thought I would miss Kenny, but not very much. I looked in my suitcase and spied a folded paper on my clothes. I opened it.

Call if you want to come home. It's all going to turn out. I love you! – Momma.

"Hello!" a voice sang. I jerked with a start and slipped the note into the suitcase pocket. Asia sat on the bed beside mine, legs crossed, foot bobbing. He held out his hand. "Asia Demarco."

I hesitated. "Joey Carpenter," I said, taking Asia's hand.

He pointed to his tall friend, who began to stroll toward us. "And this here is my brother, *Superhonkey*," added Asia.

I coughed uneasily. "Who?"

The tall boy rolled his eyes and reached forward. "I'm *Paul* Demarco. Asia's adopted brother. *He's* adopted. Not me. I always like to clarify we're not genetically linked."

"Your name is really Asia?" I asked with a smile.

He nodded. "My Christian name is Alberto Deleno Demarco, but my *chosen* name is Asia."

I shrugged. "Chosen by who?"

"By me, honey," Asia confirmed.

I nodded and returned to my unpacking. After a second or two of odd silence, Asia blurted, "So, where're you from?"

"Knoxville."

"Our cousin lives in Knoxville," said Paul.

"Where are you two from?" I asked them.

"Johnson City," said Asia. "Well, I was actually born in Columbia. I was imported to Johnson City when I was adopted. How old are you?"

"Sixteen," I replied. "You?"

"Old enough to—" began Asia.

"We're both seventeen, but he's two months older than me," said Paul.

Asia spun toward Paul and punched his arm. Paul's winced. "Boy! What did I say about aging me?" He turned back to me, and his brow raised with curiosity. "So . . . what's your *tea?*"

I chuckled. "My what?"

"Tea. What's your tea?" he repeated. "Everybody's got tea."

Paul rolled his eyes. "He's asking if you're gay. He asks everybody."

I felt a cold sweat wash over me like someone had poured a bucket of ice water over my head. "What? I mean, what would make you ask me that?"

"Well, you are, ain't you?" asked Asia. I didn't reply. He turned his attention to his shoes and began picking at the laces. "The way your mouth *fell down the stairs* when that handsome thing started talking about scary movies and shit, I just thought—"

Warm anger overcame my icy exterior. "I don't think that's any of your . . . How would you like it if . . .?" I fought to articulate a response. "Are *you* gay?" I asked with a shake of the head.

"Oh, sho' nuff," nodded Asia without hesitation.

"All day long," Paul agreed.

Asia's honesty stunned me. Not only was it his candor but also how this unicorn proudly showcased his horn without hesitancy. That didn't make my showing mine any easier. I wasn't sure why—it wasn't as if I knew either of these people. At that moment, I realized I could be anyone I wanted to be at Kamp Kromwell. Nevertheless, seeing Asia gawking at me with intrigue, I couldn't declare my truth. Not just yet.

Asia reached over and patted my leg. "You don't have to pour the tea right now, honey. You serve it when you're ready."

With that, Asia rose and began to unpack his things. I returned to my own suitcase. My mind wandered through possibilities and outcomes. It was true; I could be anyone I wanted to be at Kromwell. I didn't know any of these people and would likely never see them again. So why not be free? Free like Asia.

A stinging sensation drilled its way into the side of my temple. I turned to the far window. Just beyond the thin windowpane hovered the black eyes of the crow.

10

2:17 P.M.

"'cause sometimes, I said, sometimes I hear my voice. And it's been here silent all these years."
—Silent All These Years: Tori Amos—

Equivalent Energy. Positive manifestation. During her rebirth into the New Age, Anne stumbled upon a book called *Creative Visualization: Use the Power of Your Imagination to Create What You Want in Your Life* by Shakti Gawain. I can still see the cover of that paperback in my mind—a nomadic woman, staff in hand, eyes closed, lifting her head to the heavens. In it, Gawain detailed the ideology that we can manifest what we need in life by mentally conjuring these things into being or "visualizing" them.

Some believe our mental state draws analogous energy into our lives. Negative thinking brings undesirable consequences; positivity attracts success and well-being. While I'm not prescriptive about these principles, I am confident in one thing: people with like minds gravitate toward each other. I could see this reflected in the relationships between my intolerant father and his narrow-minded sons and the conservative partnership shared between Principal Harold and Vice Principal Pikes, and it was most certainly present in our small group of outcasts, the *Kromwell Krew*. Six quirky individuals who shared unconventional commonalities. "Freaks" who belonged nowhere else.

At the time, we were strangers to each other, but something higher than us, some energetic presence, was pulling us together.

The verbose Kenny Louve remained close to me, though I wasn't sure why. It wasn't like I had a lot to say to him. He had enough to say for the both of us. Things Kenny told me slipped into one ear and through the other, each of his tales a tad more implausible than the last. I was confused as to why someone would make up stories about nearly every aspect of their life. I thought that maybe Kenny was simply trying too hard to be liked. So, I tried to feign interest.

The Demarco brothers—Asia and Paul—orbited me like two curious moons, remaining distant but ever-present. Paul never offered much beyond a nod and a smile, but Asia always said hello, goodbye, or spat a cynical "Have fun, sister!" my way. I thought Asia was an obnoxious ass. Asia had spied the horn on my head, my shameful secret, and he now felt he had some right to patronize me. But my horn was *mine* to display, speak about, and declare. Not his.

The Foster twins, Lily and DJ, were the camp veterans. They, too, crossed my path occasionally, long enough for DJ to nod politely and Lily to roll her eyes and pull him in the opposite direction. Why? Did she feel they were better than I was? The two also needed to tell everyone they were not *identical* twins, which I thought was evident because they were brother and sister. But Lily especially was very passionate about the matter. She was the leader, and her brother the follower. I would often sit in the dining hall, observing them, watching her tell him what to eat, what not to eat, where they would be going, and what activities they would undertake for the day. DJ seemed perfectly happy to allow her that control over him, though I couldn't imagine why.

In contrast to our would-be club were two odious shits, Chester "the Jester" Henry and Lynn Reynolds, two mouth-breathing ignoramuses from some Podunk place called Rock City. At first, the two reserved their juvenile heckling for the Foster twins, though they eventually bestowed that gift on all of us. When Lily and DJ were nearby, the two would whisper to each other, peppering in the occasional passive-aggressive racial remark, then snicker like two booger-eating morons. Lily would tell one of the counselors, but Chester was always ready to explain. They hadn't meant it that way. They were just teasing. Lily had misunderstood. But it was not a misunderstanding. It was prejudice and microaggression intended to belittle and demean. Everyone knew Chester and Lynn were bad apples. It'd only be a matter of time before they were tossed from the barrel.

On the seventh day of camp, I awoke from dreams of Sam Barnes, lurid nightmares that would visit me now and again like an old friend. These visions came and went without rhyme or reason, and each time they appeared, I'd be transported back to Landers Water Park. I'd feel those sticky fingers pawing at me and that rancid breath on my neck. Fortunately, the campers were given a free afternoon to participate in special activities or freely explore the grounds. I chose the latter in hopes of being alone. I had no energy for imposed interaction. Solitude was what I needed—distance from others, certainly from Kenny.

While Kenny returned his tray to the bin after breakfast, I took the opportunity to slip through the kitchen without being seen. Making my way through the back door, I took a deep breath of fresh summer air and headed toward the lake with a book. I can't tell you what book it was. I didn't care. It was a prop to keep my hands busy and convey my preoccupation to onlookers. I had to somehow dig my thoughts out of the putrid soil of Sam Barnes. All I needed was the morning and a shovel.

I had just stepped onto the main pathway leading to the lake when I heard a voice that had become all too familiar.

"Joe! Hey, Joe!" called Kenny. "Wait!"

I paused and closed my eyes. *Oh, God, please go away.* "Hey, Kenny," I said with a sigh.

He trotted toward me with that goofy grin on his face. "Hey, where did you go? I came back to the table, and you were gone." He wagged a finger at me. "You were hiding."

"Not very well," I said, feigning humor. I turned and continued on my way.

"Where're you going?"

"Nowhere, really. I was just going to go sit and read for a while."

"Oh!" he said. "Okay. I thought we were going to the archery range. You said you'd teach me how to shoot."

We turned down the hill and walked toward the glistening water. "I don't know, Kenny. I'm not too good at it. Maybe you should find someone else to teach you."

He chuckled. "I'm sure you're better than me."

"How about later? Maybe I'll read for a while, and then we can get together after lunch and practice."

"You not feeling good?" he asked with concern.

"Yeah, headache." *A headache that* you're *giving me, by the way.*

"Ah, I gotcha," he said as if he understood.

He didn't.

Kenny hovered at my side like a fly buzzing around dog crap. Like clockwork, he began to rattle off one of his stories. Something about his dad having developed this magic cure for headaches or other foolishness. This inexplicable heat began rising in my face, the pressure of anger bubbling in the pit of my throat. Visions flooded my mind, images of me spinning on my heel and knocking Kenny flat on his ass. *Joe, you can't punch the guy for talking to you.* Maybe my patience with Kenny had run thin. Perhaps I was angry at Sam Barnes. Whatever the cause, I suddenly turned toward him.

"Listen," I said flatly. Kenny paused and gawked at me. "Dude, your dad doesn't work in medicine. Your mom did not dance on Broadway. Your parents aren't doctors. And you most *definitely* do not have a girlfriend named *Victoria Valentino. Nobody* has a girlfriend named Victoria Valentino. As a matter of fact, nobody has a name like Victoria Valentino unless they're a stripper." His eyes glistened with tears, but I couldn't make my mouth stop. "I don't know why you make this shit up, Kenny, but it's not normal. Do you even think about it, or can you just think of bullshit on the fly?"

"I'm not . . . I'm not lying," he struggled.

"Tell me *one thing* without the crap. Right now. Say one, single, solitary fact."

Kenny pondered this. His face flushed red. Then he said, "I thought you were my friend."

I winced.

I had asked, and he had delivered. Kenny Louve believed we were friends. And maybe, on some level, we were. But at that moment, I didn't need a friend. I needed silence. I needed solitude. Space.

I shrugged. "Maybe you need to find someone else to be your friend, Kenny."

Kenny stood there, staring at me with this blank, wounded gaze, unable to say a word. My anger was suddenly replaced by the sticky sensation of guilt. *What the hell is wrong with you, Joe?* Had I become so damaged that the only way I could be at peace was to make someone feel as bad as I did? Or, worse yet, had I finally become my father, allowing life's bitterness to sour my soul? I saw a tear roll down his plump cheek and wanted to stop it. Take it back. I had just broken a heart, which was pretty damn sad for someone with so many scars. Kenny raised his finger to my face and opened his mouth to speak.

Inane laughter echoed from the distant trees.

Someone yelled something I couldn't understand, but the phrase, "Screw you, Chester!" was clear.

Kenny and I looked at one another. He lowered his finger. "Um, was that DJ?"

"Beth!" called Lily. "Rosetta!"

Kenny and I turned on our heels and sprinted toward the trees ahead. We followed the commotion toward a clearing where we saw Chester Henry and Lynn Reynolds. The two held DJ captive, his back pressed against a tree. Lynn leaned behind the trunk, holding tight to DJ's wrists. There was old Chester, picking his fingernail with a rusty pocketknife that wouldn't slice butter with a hot blade.

"What do you think you're doing?" I asked.

"Bird watching," Chester replied.

Chester—King of Pricks. He had dark, greasy hair chopped into a mullet, which hung in thin wisps just past his ears. Faint traces of adolescent acne lay beneath the new stubble sprouting on his chin. While surprisingly straight, his teeth were severely stained by cigarettes and tobacco. Beyond the lousy hairdo and yellow teeth, he wasn't a bad-looking guy. All Chester needed was a flea dip, a haircut, and a pressure washer sprayed through his mouth, and he could have been okay, handsome even.

Lynn Reynolds, on the other hand, was a homely bastard. He was tall and lanky, and his face was covered in painful-looking acne. Like Chester, he had yellow teeth. Unlike Chester, Lynn's teeth were as crooked as a barrel of fishhooks. What made Lynn unattractive wasn't so much his appearance as his unhealthy adulation of Chester, which made him ugly and a little sad.

There was rustling in the trees. "Being a sack of shit!" Lily sat above our heads on what remained of an abandoned rope bridge. She clung tightly to the decayed rope, her feet dangling over the side.

Chester chuckled. "Either way, ain't none of y'all's business. So, why don't you two *girls* run along now?"

"Did you put her up there?" I asked Chester.

His brow furrowed. "Now, how would I do something like that? She got up there of her own free will."

"After he threw my journal up here," she called back. "Asshole!"

Kenny nodded toward the pocketknife in Chester's hand. "You're not supposed to have that. We weren't supposed to bring knives onto camp—"

"Oh, calm down, *porky*," Chester hissed. He held the old knife out for us to see. "I didn't bring it. Found it. Out by that tree."

"So, you thought you'd threaten people with it," I added.

Chester folded the knife and slipped it into his pocket. "No. I'm not threatening anyone with it." He turned to DJ. "Have I threatened you with it?" DJ didn't answer. Chester nudged him. "I ain't said I'd do anything to you with it, have I? Tell the truth."

"No," muttered DJ through gritted teeth.

And that was Chester's modus operandi. Indirect intimidation. I was sure he hadn't literally threatened DJ with the knife. That would have been too incriminating, like his little "jokes" about race and stereotypes. He didn't have to be direct. That would be too brave. All he had to do was talk smack while showing DJ the knife was in his possession. That was all the threat necessary. The calling card of the chickenshit.

"See?" said Chester.

"Let her down, Chester," I said, sounding intimidating.

He shrugged. "Hey, I'm not holding her prisoner. She ain't my *slave*." Lynn snickered like a moron. "She can get down anytime she feels like it. She's too scared to do it. We're just trying to get her over her fear."

Two figures emerged from the brush and stepped into the clearing. Asia and Paul strolled toward Kenny and me.

"Well, if it ain't Miss Thang," popped Chester, waving a limp wrist.

Asia rolled his eyes and turned to me. "We saw you two running up here and wondered what was up." He caught sight of Lily dangling in the branches above. His eyes moved to the tree where Lynn held DJ against the trunk. "Didn't know it was a party."

"Yeah," Chester replied. "And *fags* ain't invited."

"Then it ain't no party," replied Asia slyly.

I slipped my hands into my back pockets and stepped forward. "You know, looking at the odds, I wouldn't be running that mouth if I were you."

Chester sneered. "What odds?"

I bent forward and took a thick tree branch from the ground. "The way I see it, there's four against two, five against one after I split Lynn's head open with this tree branch."

"You got that right!" shouted DJ. Lynn gave his arms a sharp tug.

The seed of doubt shadowed Chester's grin. He slipped his hand into his pocket and whipped out his knife. "Oh, yeah?"

Asia's eyes widened, and he burst into riotous laughter. "And what the hell is that? That supposed to be a knife or something? You're not hurting anybody with that little thing." He gasped and raised his hand to his mouth. "I'm sorry. I bet you must hear that whenever you're with your *sister-cousin-girlfriend*."

"Kiss my ass, queer," barked Chester, but with a bit less of that ignorant enthusiasm.

I bounced the tree branch against my shoe, scowling at Chester, daring him to make his move. I wasn't quite sure how it would turn out. Could I crack him over the head with that branch before he could poke me with that rusty sticker? We'd see.

Asia and Paul armed themselves with wayward branches from the ground and held them like baseball bats.

Feeling particularly cocky, I pointed the branch at Chester. "Why don't you do yourselves a favor—let him go and walk away." I waited for Chester to say "or" like they do in all the movies, but he didn't. Still, I just had to add, "Or . . . the four of us can beat the shit out of you. Your choice."

Kenny rifled along the ground and armed himself with a branch as well. I couldn't help but notice that his stick was short and a bit too warped to be menacing. It looked more like a question mark than a tree branch, but he held it like a samurai sword.

There we stood, branches in our grip, looking like the starting line-up for the Cubs. Our eyes locked upon Chester and Lynn. There was a moment when I thought that Chester may call my bluff and launch the assault. My hands constricted around the tree branch in my grip, feeling its rough bark scratch beneath my fingers. In my mind's eye, I visualized it connecting with Chester's mouth, knocking his remaining teeth loose. *Envision what you want to see in the world.*

Ironically, Chester grinned. He closed the knife and returned it to his pocket. "Whatever, shitheads," he said. "You ain't worth my time. Can't take a fuckin' joke." He turned to Lynn, who dropped DJ's wrist. DJ stumbled forward. The two of them ambled past us, glaring at us. Chester paused at my side. "You'll get yours, queer," he added.

"If it's mine, I certainly hope so," I quipped.

Chester and Lynn disappeared through the brush.

Asia turned to me and swung the branch over his shoulder like a lumberjack with an axe. "And that's how you do *that*."

"Very good," called Lily from above us. "So, what's your grand plan for getting my ass out of these trees?"

"Well, girl, you look comfortable. You could just stay there," Asia called back. "We could come up a few times a day . . . throw you up some food and shit."

Lily nodded sarcastically. "Ha, ha, ha."

Without a word, Kenny dropped his branch and stepped forward. He had the analytical expression of a mathematician on his face as he approached a tall, winding tree near the bridge's center. His eyes moved to each branch, assessing their proximity to the tattered rope bridge. Placing his hands against the trunk, he lifted his right foot and pulled himself onto the tree.

"Wait! What are you doing?" I asked.

Kenny turned to me. "Going to get her."

Lily shook her head. "Get me? Why don't you get Rosetta or Beth instead? They'll know—"

"We'll get in trouble," Kenny said as he pulled himself upward. "Not supposed to be up here."

The higher Kenny climbed, the more anxious I became. "Kenny," I called at last. "I think Lily's right. We can go get one of the counselors. We won't get in trouble if we tell them what happened."

"Whew," muttered Asia. "Watch that boy go. Like a squirrel!"

Kenny didn't stop. He paused periodically, surveying the tree branches, deciding where to venture next. "My dad . . . used to be a Mounty . . . taught me to climb trees all the—"

"Aren't Mounties in Canada?" yelled Paul.

"Um, yeah," Kenny countered. "We . . . lived there . . . for a while."

Paul glanced at me. I rolled my eyes and sighed. When I turned back, Kenny was at eye level with Lily, who looked at the boy like he was a madman.

"I don't know what you're expecting *me* to—"

"Climb onto my back," said Kenny.

Lily's face twisted. "*What?* Boy, you done lost your entire mind—"

"Trust me," said Kenny. "I've climbed trees all my life. I've got you. Promise."

He spoke this with conviction, a tone that let me know it was true. Lily took a deep breath. She looked at Kenny, down at us, and then back at him. We watched in awe as Kenny took Lily by the arm and lifted her onto his stout back. Once she securely held him, he began his descent with the same calculated approach he had employed on his way up. Lily closed her eyes so tight I wondered if she'd ever be able to open them again. Every minute or so, I would hear Lily whisper, "Are we down yet?" Each time, Kenny confidently replied, "Almost."

As the pair neared the ground, I found myself overcome with this newfound feeling of respect for Kenny Louve. He was a bullshitter, no doubt, but he was a *brave* bullshitter. I glanced back at that mangled rope bridge—which had to have been nearly thirty feet from the ground—knowing I couldn't have forced myself to do something so courageous. With Kenny and Lily safe on the ground, we launched into applause.

"Whew!" said Asia. "Where'd you learn to climb like that?" Kenny smiled and opened his mouth to speak. Asia raised a hand outward. "Never mind . . . you can tell me later, friend."

DJ held out his hand, and Kenny took it. "That was awesome, man," DJ confessed.

Paul patted Kenny's back. "You're better than me. I'd have shit myself."

Lily nodded. "Not too bad, *Ken-nay Love*. Not bad at all." She stepped forward and gave him a hug.

Seeing adulation flow in Kenny's direction and his eager absorption of it pleased me. He needed it, especially after I had been such a dickwad to him.

The six of us emerged from the forest that afternoon, not realizing we had just been bound together, joined like links in a chain. Individually, no one on the campus cared about us. No one wanted us on their team. Alone, we were invisible, transparent. Together, however, we were bright—sometimes too bright. We didn't need to be on someone's team; we were our own. Together, we were the *Kromwell Krew*.

Lily had thought of the name. She asked Rosetta if we could get tee shirts with the logo, but Rosetta didn't suspect that would be possible. Therefore, DJ drew our moniker on the back of our Kamp Kromwell tee shirts in electrified letters that reminded me of an AC/DC album cover. I recall Drummond seeing the shirts and laughing to himself. He liked the name so much that he threatened to steal it.

Four days after our ordeal with Chester and Lynn, Kenny and I returned to our cabin after dinner. It was our first time alone since I had shown my ass. The two of us hiked along in the twilight, making small conversation that consisted of short sentences and forced snickers. I could sense that Kenny was still affected by what I had said.

"Kenny, man, listen," I began uncomfortably. "About what I said the other day. Um, I'm—"

"My dad's in jail," he said softly.

The weight of truth contained in those four words shook me.

"What?" I said, even though I had heard him clearly.

"Been there since I was two. My mom died of an overdose when I was four. My grandmother says that Dad used to beat on my mom and me." He stopped and knelt to a patch of wildflowers at his feet. "When I was little, I had issues with my teeth coming in, so I cried a lot. One day, Grannie said Dad started hitting me because I wouldn't stop crying. He kept hitting me until I stopped. So, they put him in jail. After that, Mom started drinking, got on drugs." He looked up at me. There wasn't a tear in his eye. His voice didn't waver. Emotionless. Factual. I could feel his truth bearing down upon me like an anvil. "I've lived with my grannie ever since." He plucked a flower from the ground and twisted the stem around his finger. "I'm not around people my age a whole lot. That's why she wanted me to send me to camp. My dad—he was supposed to get out this week, and Grannie thought it best I not be around."

"Have you not seen him?" I asked, not knowing what else to say.

Kenny shrugged. "He writes to me all the time, but I never read the letters." His eyes turned back to the flowers. "I keep them, though. Feels wrong to throw them out. That's not a story you want to tell over and over again when you meet people. So, yeah, I fudge a bit. I mean, I don't really like to. I'm not trying to hurt anybody. Just wish things could have been different. To me, they're just stories . . . *better* stories."

And I thought—*You know what, Mr. Love? That's just fine by me.*

11

SOMETHING WICKED IN THE WOODSHOP

"So many have paid to see what you think you're getting for free. The woman is wild, a she-cat tamed by the purr of a Jaguar."
—Maneater. Hall & Oates—

Exhausted, Beth dropped the last trash into the bin and dragged herself to the table where the others sat. She plopped herself onto the bench beside Rosetta. Her head rolled to the side with a sigh and rested upon Rosetta's shoulder. Week one was over. They had made it. Just six more to go. Rosetta reached up and patted Beth's cheek.

"Oh, come on, now," said Rosetta, taking a bite of her candy bar. "You can't be through already."

"It gets harder every year," Beth sighed.

"Girl, what are you going to do when you have kids of your own?" Rosetta added.

Beth rose and brushed her hair out of her eyes. "Well, I won't have *thirty* of them, that's for sure. I don't think I'm having kids. I don't think I have the willpower for it."

"You know, I'm not going to say I won't have kids, but I'm not running out to stock up or nothing," agreed Rosetta. "Now, I don't mind other people's kids. You can send them bitches home."

The group chuckled.

Danny took a sip of his soda and peered around the room. "Where's Bonnie and Dennis?"

Beth fell forward onto the table and laid her head in her arms. "I bribed her and Dennis to clean up the woodshop. It's a wreck after all the birdhouses. You'd think those kids built the Ark."

"What did you bribe them with?" asked Neil.

"My car," sighed Beth, prompting snickers from the group.

Rosetta glanced at Danny. "Do you want kids?"

"Two," Danny readily replied. "I've always liked that number. If I end up having more—eh, that's okay. If you have three, you might as well have a hundred," he added with a smile. "That's what my mom says. She had four of us. Two boys and two girls." He picked up his can of soda and took a drink.

Neil stretched. "She's not lying. People with one kid don't know what it's about."

"Oh yeah? And how many kids do you have?" posed Danny with a smirk.

"Right now, two."

Everyone paused with stunned silence and gawked at him.

Beth's head snapped upward. "Say what? You have *two* kids?"

"Twins," Neil chuckled. "They just turned two."

"You got to be shittin' me." Rosetta rubbed her hands over her face. "Two . . . the same age at the same time. Oh, I'd die. Just take me out and drown me in that lake, honey."

"How'd you get two kids, man?" Danny asked.

Rosetta scoffed. "If you don't know that by now, Dan, we got a problem."

"I married my high school sweetheart right out of school. A year later, there they were." Neil smiled. "I love it. I love being a dad."

"Oh, my God," muttered Danny. "I don't know what I'd do with two kids *right now*."

Rosetta raised her eyebrow. "Terrible twos. The whining. Like the kid in Cabin Eleven. What's his name . . . Craig?"

"*Greg Penborne!* Oh, Lord," said Beth with a nod. "Bless his heart. I thought he'd never get that piece of wood sanded today. Earl finally just took it from him and fixed it."

Danny pointed at Beth. "He's Dennis's. He said that kid is always whining about something. It's too hot outside. The lake is too cold. Today I think it was his bed or something."

Rosetta raised a finger. "Now, hold on a minute. Them beds are lumpy as hell."

"At least all of your campers are human," Beth said.

"Oh, yeah! Lindsey," Neil giggled. "The horse girl."

Rosetta laughed. "*Lindsey Rafferty*. God love her; does she gallop everywhere she goes?"

Beth's eyes rolled in Rosetta's direction. "Everywhere . . . all the time . . . galloping. Obsessed with the horse stables. I think Susan is going to take out a restraining order."

Drummond rounded the corner and poked his head into the hall. "Y'all making it?"

"Barely," Beth laughed.

Drummond scanned the dim dining hall. "Has Bonnie not got back yet?"

"Not yet," Danny replied.

Drummond's brow rose. "Could one of you go get her? I tried to call the woodshop, but no answer. Ringer must be off. Her *mother* is on the phone *again*."

Rosetta snapped her fingers. "My momma ain't called not one time since I've been here. Swear to God, y'all."

"Again?" Beth posed. "Has Bonnie not talked to her yet?"

Drummond rolled his eyes and shrugged. "Who knows?"

Beth sighed and dropped her arms to her sides. Rosetta nudged her.

"I'll go," Rosetta conceded. "You lie back down, precious."

"Bless you," said Beth as she lowered her head. "And when you get back, I'm going to call your momma and tell her what a terrible mother she is."

Rosetta laughed and squeezed Beth's shoulders. She threw her leg over the bench and jogged toward the kitchen. Jack Burns and his odd nephew, Dewayne, were busy stashing away the freshly cleaned pots from that evening's dinner. When Rosetta entered the kitchen, Dewayne turned to her with a frustrated gaze.

"Can I help you?" he pointedly asked her. Jack took him by the arm.

"Hey there," Jack interjected pleasantly. "Something up?"

"Nope, no, just passing through," Rosetta said. *Fucking asshat.*

She slipped around the kitchen island and through the back door. Her eyes caught movement overhead. Giant moths with dusty gray wings fluttered eagerly in the haze of the sixty-watt bulb. She peered out into the distance. The dark auditorium stood to her left. The nurse's cabin was to her immediate right. She noticed a shadow moving against the drawn curtains and recognized the generous shape of Nurse Conrad, who appeared to be filling a kettle with water. Or gin. Who's to say?

The woodshop stood some distance past Conrad's small cabin, buried in a thicket of short trees and bushes. Rosetta had forgotten just how far away it was. Walking would take forever. Granted, she could go back through the dining hall, grab the keys to the golf cart, then walk up and retrieve it from Cabin One, but that would take forever, too. Of course, she could run.

Maybe.

Running wasn't a guarantee, not after the accident.

It seemed unfair how details of tragedies remained clear to the mind while good moments tended to fade like old photos. Walking out the doors of Cossitt Library in downtown Memphis. Waiting at the crosswalk for the light to shine green. Taking that first step into the intersection. The second step. A third. On the fourth step, she felt whisked away, high into the air. Her eyes filled with bright light. The world around her spun on its axis. There was this wave of sharp, searing pain.

And then nothing.

Rosetta awoke some weeks later in Baptist Memorial Hospital with large sections of her body wrapped in plaster and suspended from wires. One day, she was a gymnast, an Olympic hopeful, and the next day, she felt as if she had aged decades in the future, doomed to spend the rest of her life in the withered body of an old woman.

Rosetta leaned to the right and left, stretching her hips. Then she took a deep breath and began jogging into the shadows. The sounds of nature churned around her. The humming of the crickets singing to the moon, the croaking of frogs calling to one another in the night, and the whirring of cicadas clinging to the trees. A dark symphony of solitude. With each footfall, she could feel her muscles tighten around the rods fused to her bones. But she was running. That's all that mattered.

The soft echoes around her were interrupted by a piercing scream that shook her insides. She spun to her right to see a huddle of black nestled in the tree branches above her. A mass of crows perched there, looking more like shadows than birds.

"Son-of-a!" she hissed. Her hand moved to her chest. "Y'all need to piss off." She said this in jest, but the creatures looked at her like they found little humor in her statement.

There was something about crows that both intrigued and repulsed her. It was their intellect and awareness. Especially these crows. These crows seemed different. She wasn't sure how, but they were different. It was as if they could see through her, into her, sensing her deepest secrets. Her mind recalled that final scene from the Hitchcock flick *The Birds*, a film she had watched when she was sixteen. A battered Rod Taylor leads the weary Tippi Hedren to the car. They drive away with thousands of birds watching them, waiting. But waiting for what? It was the same type of sensation Rosetta had now, looking into those black eyes.

With a deep breath, she shook away the notion and jogged onward. She forced her mind to focus on the following day. At breakfast, Drummond would revisit the season schedule, which included craft events, learning opportunities, and team-building sessions. There would also be traditional summer camp experiences, such as "Folklore Night" with campfire stories, "Field Day" competitions, and even the cliché talent show. With the rather interesting dynamic of kids in attendance, Rosetta suspected it would all be something to see.

Some stood out, like the clumsy little girl Missy Jelesky. After seven days, the child was already covered in enough Band-Aids to swaddle a mummy. One couldn't forget Beth's horse girl, Lindsey, who thought she was Mrs. Ed.

Not all the kids were quirky. Lily Foster. She was cool. Her brother was okay, too. Quiet. A bit reserved. Much unlike his sister. Rosetta liked Lily, mostly because Lily somehow reminded Rosetta of herself. *Because she can be a little smartass.* According to Beth, this year marked three consecutive years that Lily and her twin brother had attended Kromwell. Rosetta wondered how a kid wouldn't grow bored of the place after a while. She had been there a week and was already missing MADtv so bad it hurt.

Naturally, no group was complete without assholes, the bullies, those whose low self-esteem impelled them to pick at others. It hadn't taken Rosetta two seconds to peg Chester Henry and Lynn Reynolds. Chester, the leader, was trouble from the moment he stepped from the bus with that tacky airbrushed shirt that read "Chester the Jester." *Jester, my ass. More like Chester the Dipshit.* As the counselors introduced themselves on the first day, Rosetta had paid close attention to that Chester kid, who eyed the crowd, searching for the weak, the unique. Chester and Lynn would be trouble, but Rosetta was used to misfortune. She had fought scarier convicts than Chester or Lynn and was still around.

At last, she spied the woodshop ahead in the clearing. *Oh, thank God.* She stopped some twenty feet from the front deck of the building, placed her hands on her hips, and bent forward, drawing a deep breath in through her nose and exhaling out through her mouth. She rose.

"Hey! Bon—." Her voice trailed off, fading away as if someone had stolen her vocal cords.

Crows. Not just one or two, but dozens of crows. The mass of black covered the entire roof of the woodshop like tar. Her eyes moved to the dark windows of the building, and for a moment, she wondered if anyone was inside. Maybe Bonnie and Dennis had finished their cleaning and left already. She began to return to the dining hall, but something stopped her. It wasn't a noise or a sight but a *feeling.* Her eyes moved back to the woodshop. She stepped forward. Slowly and quietly, she ascended the four small steps to the deck. There was a faint glow of light seeping through the window on the left. She stepped to the glass and peered inside. The space was dark except for the washroom at the rear of the building. A light was on. Something was *moving* in there.

Rosetta approached the front door and took the handle. Locked. *Why is the door locked?* She instinctively raised her hand to knock but hesitated. She didn't know why. It was that feeling that whatever was transpiring within the walls wasn't supposed to happen.

She slipped from the deck and crept around the right side of the building. Those black eyes above followed her through the darkness, watching her movements. As she neared the washroom window, sounds caused her to duck underneath the windowpane. Sighs, breaths. She placed her fingers on the edge of the windowsill and pulled herself up. Her eyes widened.

Bonnie was bent over the washroom folding table, her breasts exposed, her Kamp Kromwell shirt up around her neck. Dennis was shirtless, his shorts around his ankles. His hand was covered in blood. For a moment, Rosetta thought Dennis had forced himself upon Bonnie, that violence had occurred. What other explanation could there be? Bonnie Evans was proper, chaste, and . . .

Bonnie took Dennis's hand and licked the blood from his fingers.

. . . a freak!

Bonnie Evans was a freak! Who was this bitch on the table? It certainly wasn't the bubbly blonde who had bounced to them in the Kromwell parking lot. Rosetta wanted to escape the scene but couldn't pry away her eyes.

Squawk!

The crow's sudden shriek caused Rosetta to shudder with a start. She saw Bonnie's head jerk upward from the table. Bonnie stared through the windowpane as if the bird had called out to her and told her an interloper bore witness to her despicable act.

Dammit!

Rosetta sank from the window, eyes wide, heart racing. Beads of sweat bled onto her forehead. She heard mumbled voices, then footsteps. She clung to the woodshop wall, her mind racing with options. The footsteps marched toward the back door. All Bonnie had to do was peer around the railing of the stoop and see Rosetta trembling in the shadows. She heard the door creak open and dove toward the adjacent trees.

Rosetta cowered there in the shadows, staying low to the ground. Bonnie stepped to the railing, and the moonlight illuminated her curious face. Her eyes scanned the night. Rosetta slid her palms over her mouth and calmed her breathing. Dennis appeared at Bonnie's side. Rosetta couldn't hear what the two of them were saying, but it was apparent the flames of their peculiar interlude had died. He took Bonnie by the arm, urging her to return inside, and she jerked away from him impatiently.

Squawk!

Rosetta shuddered. Her eyes rolled upward. One of the crows perched above her head, calling out, calling to Bonnie. *Here she is*, it said. *She's right here. Come. Get her!* Did it matter? What would Bonnie do if she caught Rosetta? Rosetta was no stranger to fighting, and she had undoubtedly fought more formidable opponents than this skinny bitch. Would Bonnie slap her? Would she attack her?

Kill her?

For reasons Rosetta couldn't quite explain, she felt frightened. *Why?* Maybe she felt this woman, this Bonnie—whoever she was—was capable of nearly anything.

At last, Bonnie followed Dennis back into the woodshop. Rosetta turned and rushed into the shadows, slipping through the brush and branches, running as fast as her legs would carry her. Faster and faster, she sprinted through the forest toward the distant glow at the rear of the dining hall. Her legs began to burn as her hand caught the storm door of the kitchen. Yanking it wide, she ducked into the kitchen, her chest heaving in and out, sweat dripping down her forehead.

"Hell," said Dewayne Burns as he stepped from the pantry. "What's after you? You see a bear or something?"

Jack stepped toward Rosetta and took her by the shoulder. "Are you all right?"

Rosetta's mind began to calculate a response. She couldn't confess what she had seen. Who would believe her? She didn't really believe it herself. Did Bonnie see her as she ran away? There was no way to know, but it was best to keep the secret to herself, at least for now.

"Running. I . . . just ran a bit too much. Got my leg aggravated." She smiled when Jack handed her a paper towel for her moist face. "Are they still in there doing as little as possible?" she added.

Jack managed a smile. "I think so. Been pretty quiet."

Rosetta walked toward the kitchen door, paused to collect herself, then stepped into the dining hall as casually as possible. "Well, I couldn't find her."

"Was she not in the woodshop with Dennis?" asked Beth.

"Not that I saw," Rosetta replied as she slipped beside Beth.

Drummond sighed. "Lord, what am I going to tell—"

At that moment, Bonnie and Dennis stepped into the foyer of the dining hall. Not a hair was out of place. No flushing of the skin. Her clothes were just as crisp as they had been earlier. In fact, Bonnie Evans looked so ordinary Rosetta wondered if she had seen the act.

"Okie dokie," Bonnie said with a cheerful smile. "Woodshop is all clean."

"Where were you two?" asked Beth. "We were looking for you."

"Damn," said Neil, pointing at Dennis's bandaged hand. "Dude, you all right?"

Dennis nodded. "Just cut myself on that saw up there. It's no biggie."

"Bonnie, your mother is on the phone *again*," Drummond said, his brow raised.

Bonnie hesitated.

For a fleeting moment, Rosetta thought she spied anxiety in Bonnie's eyes, though she wasn't sure if it was because she had been missed or that her overbearing mother was waiting for her on the phone.

Bonnie smiled. "Well, you must have just missed us."

As Bonnie followed Drummond toward the office, she shot Rosetta an icy glare.

12

3:00 P.M.

I've always enjoyed the art of storytelling. I inherited it from my mother. She could take any story and spin it into an epic odyssey. I loved how she never ceased to regale me with tales from her vast library. I especially enjoyed stories about the house on Rudolph Street, a boarding house owned by my great-grandmother long before I was brought into the world. My siblings claimed the three-story, twelve-room house was haunted, and my mother had plenty of stories to corroborate the claim. Spine-chilling stories. Stories you remembered.

My love for storytelling was why I was so excited about Folklore Night at Kromwell. It would be the traditional ghost story/campfire tale event, with roaring fires and gooey s'mores. And it was literally the one aspect of the camping experience I was looking forward to.

We divided into four groups that evening. The first group, overseen by Drummond and Bonnie, was for those fussy campers who'd remain indoors playing board games. Rosetta would spin family-friendly folklore for the second group of younger campers who didn't need to be exposed to grisly horror. Lastly, for the older campers who longed for the shadows, we could attend circles led by either Danny and Beth or Dennis and Neil.

I was front and center.

About eight-thirty that evening, Danny and Beth led us through the trees to a clearing at the lake's edge, where Mr. Burns had already started a bonfire. Boxes of chocolate bars, marshmallows, and graham crackers were distributed around the group. We all took seats on the surrounding logs, tree stumps, and folding chairs, eager for adventure. My mind was brimming with images of the Crypt Keeper rushing toward us, cackling in John Kassir's trademark screech.

I sat on the soft grass with my back against a log, with Asia and Paul flanking my sides. Lily sat on the ground to my left, with DJ behind her. Kenny, who was never far from me, sat to my right, positioned between Asia's knees. There were a few other familiar faces in our group. The horse girl, who had trotted all the way there from the lake, sat just across from me. The funny guy, David *Something-or-Other*, sat to our right.

Chester and Lynn lingered just behind David's shoulders. I remember Chester making eye contact with me. He grinned with his yellow teeth and gave me a cunning wink. I rolled my eyes and did my best to ignore him. *Dear God, man, buy a fucking toothbrush.*

This world should maintain a delicate balance of good and evil, light and dark, pricks and princes, but I can't help but feel that, as a society, we've suffered more than our fair share of assholes. And to me, Chester and Lynn were the epitome of assholes. They were the entire anus. The rectum itself. I don't believe a single soul on the Kromwell campus liked either of them. They didn't do much to win anyone over, that's for sure.

After the forest incident, no love was lost between Chester, Lynn, and the Kromwell Krew. Surprisingly enough, the two of them hadn't said much to any of us following our little altercation. There were the typical goofy glares and hushed comments when any of us was around, but nothing direct. It was uncharacteristic, especially for Chester, the type of idiot who couldn't leave well enough alone. While the Krew had taken his silence as a gift, I took it as a warning. It worried me. I was right to be concerned. Something was brewing that night, a story that would thrill everyone that Folklore Night, especially me.

Danny and Beth rounded the tree to applause as the fire roared before us. Danny, dressed in this flowing brown robe and hood, looked less like an old, wise storyteller and more like a lost Jedi from *Star Wars*. I appreciated his effort all the same.

"Greetings!" Danny dramatically announced. "Welcome to Folklore Night!"

Beth smiled and waved. "Everyone has stuff for s'mores, right?" Everyone nodded. "Good, good!" She and Danny sat on the short log before the fire. "Now, here is what we'll do. One of us will start off with a story. Then, afterward, we'll let one of you go. Then back to us, then you, and so on. Sound good?" She raised her finger. "Oh, and people, remember there's a fire here. Let's not get crazy and push someone. It could end badly. Okay?" She turned to Danny. "You want to go first?"

Danny pondered. "I think—"

"Tell us about John Tate," called a voice I didn't immediately recognize.

Beth's eyes widened with an unease she attempted to conceal. I wasn't sure why. Until that moment, I had never heard the name John Tate. Those unfamiliar with the area knew nothing about his legend and its darkness.

Danny shrugged. "John who?"

"Tate," sighed Beth. She waved her hands. "Come on, now. That's a little too much. I have one that's even better than—"

"Oh!" cried the horse chick. "Come on, please? I've been waiting all day for someone to tell us."

Asia took my arm and leaned toward me. "Who the hell is John Tate?"

I shrugged. "No idea."

Danny turned to Beth and smiled. "Okay, who is this John Tate? Somebody's going to have to tell me something."

Beth's eyes moved warily through the group. "Okay, look. If I tell you. *If.* Nobody better go telling on me to Mr. Drummond. If I get in trouble, *ev-er-y-bo-dy* in this group is going to be in trouble. Got it?" There was silence. "Everyone promise. Say, '*Beth*, we swear to God *that we won't say anything to Mr. Drummond.*'" Everyone joined in a humorous chorus of bumbling allegiance. "Scoot over."

Danny raised his brow. "Wow, okay. Let me give you some room, lady."

A deathly silence crawled over the ground. The fire even seemed to rise higher at the prospect of John Tate. A bone-chilling wind kissed the hot June air. I felt this unexpected catch of tension tickle my throat, though I couldn't have imagined why. Kenny scooted closer to me, sinking deeper into Asia's knees.

"All right. Has anyone *not* heard of John Tate?" asked Beth softly. No one spoke. "I'm not being dramatic. I'm seriously asking."

Asia raised his hand first. I followed. Soon, several others in the group held hands high. Last but not least, Danny grinned and raised his hand before Beth's face.

"Um, I haven't heard of him," mumbled Danny excitedly. "Ms. Maples, I've not heard of John Tate."

Beth grabbed his hand and laughed. "Okay, okay. I'll tell you." She cleared her throat. "I think some of us have heard a story about John Tate from someone through the years. I heard it from my father. In 1966, back when my dad was fresh out of college, he got an internship writing for the *Knoxville Journal*. After Tate was arrested, he came here to Jasper Mill to help cover the trial. It was the first and *the last* thing he ever wrote for the paper." She glanced at the firelight and peered into the flames. "Tate, when he did dwell among the living, did so about five miles from here on a little plot of land they called Harmond Hill. His was the only shack buried in the deep, dense forest. Dad said he was a tall man, big. He stood a fearsome six feet, seven inches in height, weighing three hundred and seventy pounds. Apparently, he was ugly as homemade sin, but his stature made him popular with the ladies of Jasper Mill."

"Must've had *big feet*," mumbled Asia. Giggles echoed around the fire.

"That could explain it," Beth said with a smile. "The town preferred that Tate stay on the hill, hidden in the depths of the dark trees, locked away like a shameful secret they wanted to avoid. But occasionally, he would wander into town searching for liquor and ladies. You could find the liquor. The empty bottles led to Tate's shack like a hobo's breadcrumb trail. The ladies: they were harder to locate."

I felt Kenny nudge closer to me.

"Dad said they found the first body in the early spring of 1966," Beth continued. "Some seventeen-year-old girl from Kentucky on her way to Nashville. The crew had just broken ground on Kamp Kromwell when—"

"Wait," said Kenny. "Like, *this* Kamp Kromwell? They found a body at this Kamp Kromwell?"

Beth nodded. Then she shrugged. "Well, more like *bodies*." Kenny turned to me with wide eyes. "This place was started by Conrad T. Kromwell, who bought this acreage of land from the township of Jasper Mill to bring mother nature to the masses. Once they started construction on the camp, people discovered what Tate had been up to in his spare time. As the crew continued to tear up the soil, bodies began to spring up like dandelions. Just two days after the crew found the first girl, the upper torso of another tumbled out of a wheelbarrow. After that, the detectives remained onsite. Over eight days, Dad said they found *nineteen bodies* and pieces of several others who authorities would never identify. Eyewitnesses identified Tate as the last person seen with at least nine of the victims found."

"That's not evidence," barked Chester, who I'm sure, in some way, identified with a homicidal maniac. "Just 'cause you see somebody with someone don't mean they killed them."

Beth shrugged. "Well, true. I think the evidence came when authorities arrived to question Tate. They found three more bodies in the barn on his property." She shook her head. "That barn. Dad said whatever was inside that old thing was too much for even the most seasoned detective. One officer told him it was a 'medieval torture chamber.' Rusty saws, broken hatchets, scarred leather bindings, and blood-soaked chains. But that wasn't the strangest thing the authorities discovered. The most bizarre thing—the thing that no one could explain—was Lois Greene."

"Who's Lois Greene?" Danny asked.

"She was the fourteen-year-old daughter of Elmer and Rose Greene," Beth replied. "Everyone in town knew her. She was Tate's biggest mistake. When a local girl disappeared, suspicions quickly turned to him. Lois had been walking home from the library when Tate jerked her into the cabin of his truck. But he kept her alive. For reasons no one could explain, Tate had allowed Lois to live. And not only had she survived, but Tate had apparently cared for her during the six months she remained there."

"Like Beauty and the Beast," said the horse chick in a wispy romantic manner. The girl beside her shivered in disgust.

"Really?" spat Lily. "Don't sound like no Disney movie to me."

"He must have loved her, though," continued Beth. "Dad said that each week, Tate brought Lois bundles of wildflowers to the attic where he held her. The room was filled with withered marigolds, daisies, and lilacs. The man cooked for her, washed her clothes, and gave her gifts taken from victims—bracelets, jewelry—stuff he thought she may enjoy. Some thought that John Tate loved the girl. Well, to the extent a thing such as Tate could feel love, I suppose. When authorities found Lois that night, Tate just fell to his knees and surrendered, like without her, there was no longer a reason to fight. An officer told Dad that as they led Lois past him, draped in a gray blanket, Tate held out his thick wrists and allowed the police to place not one but *three* sets of handcuffs around them. Tate waived his Miranda rights and readily admitted not only to Lois's kidnapping but each of the murders as well."

"What did your dad say the trial was like?" I asked.

"Dad said Tate just sat there. Quiet. The man never made a sound. He didn't even move. He just stared through the window at the willow tree on the court grounds. Every day, those officers would lead him into that courtroom, and he would take his seat just as politely as anything you ever did see. And he'd stare at the willow. The expression on his stone-cold face never changed at all. It was as if he was carved out of rock, sitting there like a statue, bound in chains, and dressed in this orange jumpsuit. Staring at that willow tree."

"So, how did he really die?" asked DJ. "Gas chamber? Electric chair?"

"He never went to jail," said Beth. Gasps hissed through the group. Beth nodded in confirmation. "Yep. Dad said the town expected an open-and-shut case, but some 'technicality' led the judge to claim a mistrial just halfway through testimony."

"Oh, my God!" exclaimed Danny, who was as enraptured with the stories as the rest of us. "You have to be kidding!"

Beth shook her head. "Dad said that even though Tate was declared mentally fit to stand trial, the defense claimed he couldn't *knowingly* waive his Miranda rights. That voided his confession, and for that reason, the judge said the case would have to be retried."

"Wow," muttered Paul.

"Well, the town went nuts," Beth said. "The prosecution demanded expedition, which wasn't going to happen. It would take months to arrange, and then everyone would have to relive it all again. Everyone was frightened that this man, this monster, would walk free after all he had done. But walk he would—at least for a little while."

"They let him go!?" exclaimed DJ. "No way!"

Beth shrugged. "The defense moved to have him conditionally released until the retrial, arguing that Tate's life was in danger in prison. Tate posted bail, and that was that."

"So, they shot him. Who shot him?" asked Kenny.

Bonnie squinted her eyes. "That's where things get a little ugly. Tate returned to that cabin on Harmond Hill, which had been all but demolished in protest after his arrest. The barn, though—that was in perfect order. No one dared go near that thing. No one saw Tate after that, and they didn't want to. In fact, some believed that he had fled from police and left town in the middle of the night, traveling somewhere new."

"They never found him," said a voice.

Beth looked back. "Oh, they found him, all right—just not alive. Dad said two teenage boys were returning home from baseball practice about a month after the trial ended. They decided to cut through Robinson Farm, which sits just over those hills. They saw this scarecrow nailed to the tree at the edge of Robinson's tobacco field. They approached the figure and poked at it with their bats."

"It was John Tate," muttered Kenny as he desperately clutched my arm. I pulled myself away from him and rolled my eyes. "It was him, wasn't it?"

"Tate was nailed to the tree and left there to die," Beth confirmed. "Dad said that every atrocity that one could do to a human had been done to that man, and I won't go into that."

"Oh, come on!" begged Chester. "That's like leaving the cheese off a cheeseburger!"

"Somebody wasn't happy that Tate was free," continued Beth. "Somebody took care of it themselves. After they tortured him, he hung in the summer sun for days. They made this hood out of a potato sack and covered his face. The tree he hung on seemed to die along with him. These days, the only things that go near that tree are the crows and bugs that call it home. That sack—Tate's mask—is still out there, nailed high to the tree trunk—a warning to stay away."

The group sat silently, our minds turning with horrific visions from Beth's story. What she hadn't said was even more unsettling—the things that remained secret. It wasn't until Chester stepped forward that I could pry my eyes away from the hypnotic whirl of the flames before me.

"Well, *I* have a story," smiled Chester. He slipped open a roll of newspaper and looked at me. "And it's a good one." He cleared his throat. "*Pedophile Arranged*," he announced, causing my stomach to lurch. "'Samuel L. Barnes of Plunket County, Tennessee, was arraigned today in the Knox County Supreme Court.'"

I felt my throat twist and believed I would vomit. I fought myself up from the grass and rushed toward him. Lynn snatched me by my shoulder. Chester held out his hand to keep me at bay and chuckled as he continued.

"'Barnes currently faces charges including lewd and lascivious behavior involving a deceased person, attempted second-degree murder, and statutory rape of a minor.'" He continued to read the article as I fought to free myself from Lynn. I could picture Chester announcing my name for the whole camp to hear. "Barnes was arrested in 1993 in connection with the rape and attempted murder of a minor at Landers Water Park. The boy was fourteen at the time of the assault. Barnes has been released on $750,000 bond, and his trial has been scheduled for September of this year." Chester folded the paper and tossed it into my face. "Thanks for getting the water park closed down, *queer*."

Lynn snickered and turned me loose. A frigid downpour of shame drenched me. At the time, I didn't realize the names of minors were omitted from publications. Maybe if I had maintained my composure, ridden it out, and appeared unaffected, I could have navigated around Chester's impromptu news report. But I had sprung to my feet so quickly that there was no way to avoid complicity now.

I spied Beth and Danny, who stared back at me with disbelief and pity, mouths ajar, eyes wide. Turning to the Krew, I noticed they, too, gaped at me, silent, unable to believe what they had just heard. Asia's mouth moved as if he wanted to say something, but nothing would leave his lips. Without a word, I disappeared into the trees.

13

SOMEONE'S IN THE KITCHEN

Dewalla Evans couldn't drive to save her soul from Satan, but you wouldn't tell her that. Carl, her husband, warned that if she had one more infraction, a fender-bender, so much as a speeding ticket, their insurance would cancel their policy immediately. Dee sped along I-75 like a maniac, not caring if Jesus himself flashed those blue lights behind her. She was getting to Camp . . . Camp *whatever it was* if it was the last thing she did. *You'll regret it if you do.* Her daughter's hateful words echoed in her ears. *She told me I'd regret it if I came. I'll show you who's going to regret it.* Why had Bonnie wanted to be at some silly summer camp, anyway?

Tracey Abernathy.

That's why.

At one time, Bonnie, Dewalla's oldest and only daughter, had been the model of Christian purity, a star upon the tree of Heaven. All through the child's life, she hadn't given Dewalla the slightest bit of worry. She never had to be concerned about what Bonnie was doing or who she was out doing it with. Her daughter was honest, a pillar of the Mount Zion Baptist Youth Group, and a beauty to behold. Sure, Bonnie wasn't the *brightest* star on

Heaven's tree, but the girl was undoubtedly book-smart . . . for the most part. Yes, she could be a little naïve, foolish, and maybe that was Dewalla's fault. Maybe Dewalla had spent so many years coddling Bonnie, making her believe she was better than those around her, that she didn't have to work quite as hard to get what she wanted.

But Bonnie had common sense.

For the most part.

Tracey changed all that.

We work the field of souls together, you and I . . . Some fields are blooming now, other fields are dry.

Wayne Watson, who had achieved a Contemporary Christian hit with his song *Field Of Souls*, was handsome, though Dewalla would never utter that to a living soul. Sometimes, Calvary 89.7 FM played music that she considered a bit too contemporary, but most often, they would play the classics, like The Kingsmen, Gold City, and the Gather Vocal Band. Some other music, like that of DC Talk or those long-haired hippies who called themselves Stryper, had no soul. Heartless. Borderline blasphemy.

Godless.

Godless, like Tracey Abernathy.

In Dee's opinion, Tracey Abernathy was a godless girl with loose lips and even looser morals. Dee begged Bonnie to attend college from home, only thirty minutes from the University of Tennessee Chattanooga campus. Still, Bonnie felt it best to take a more independent approach to college, learn to be alone. If Dewalla and Carl had been paying for this collegiate adventure, Dee would have said the dormitory was out of the question. Seeing that Bonnie had obtained a full scholarship and was over eighteen, there was little the woman could say on the matter, which really burned her ass.

Dewalla had only had to endure Tracey Abernathy's company once, when Bonnie had first moved into the dorm, and once was enough. The girl had tattoos and a shaved head, for the sake of Jesus! Well, she had *a* tattoo, but it was on her lower back, a *tramp stamp*, as Dee heard it called. Offensive symbols right on the girl's back, hovering just above those tacky, low-rise jeans. And, okay, her head wasn't necessarily *shaved*, just burred down around the sides and back. But Tracey had dyed it in various colors of the rainbow, and good Christian girls didn't go around looking like a technicolor Jezebel.

Dee hated the girl on sight, watching Tracey sit in that dorm room, legs apart, just like a *whore*. And Tracey knew Dee hated her. In fact, Dee would even go so far as to say Tracey enjoyed that she hated her. She believed it was why Tracey seemed determined to lead poor Bonnie down tragic paths.

Lead me not into temptation . . . I already know the road all too well . . . Lead me not into temptation . . . I can find it all by myself . . .

First came the absent Sundays. For most of the first semester, Bonnie was home every weekend. She would spend time with her family, just like Dee had raised her to do. They would attend church each Sunday morning, just like Dee had raised her to do. And they would conclude these weekend visits by attending Sunday evening services, just like Dee had raised her to do.

Suddenly, not long after Thanksgiving, Bonnie could no longer attend evening services before returning to campus. Said she didn't like driving that far in the dark or some other such excuse. By Christmas break, Bonnie wasn't staying for Sunday morning services either. Dewalla was lucky to see her daughter on weekends at the onset of the spring semester. Said she had to study, a test was coming—things like that. "You can study here," Dee would argue. But there was always some excuse. Always. She couldn't study because her brothers would annoy her, the lighting wasn't proper, or she needed access to materials available on campus. The list was endless. Excuses, excuses.

Dewalla merged from I-75 onto I-40 and continued onward. The putrid scent of a dead skunk crept through the air vents into the cabin, turning her stomach and reminding her of marijuana. Ah, yes, the *pot*. That's what really set the world on fire.

Just after New Year's Eve, Dee got a call from Dean Winskill at UT, who informed her that Bonnie—*her Bonnie*—had been "high on the pot" at some party where another girl was taken to the hospital with, get this, *alcohol poisoning*. Well, that was the first and last straw. Dewalla and Carl went ballistic. Dee demanded that Bonnie leave the dorm and come home. Bonnie outright refused. But that didn't stop Dee, who decided to reach out to Dean Winskill and demand Bonnie be transferred to a new roommate in a new dorm, one who would be less trouble and less of a negative influence on her little girl. Bonnie was infuriated about the relocation but agreed to it all the same. Little did Dewalla realize it would only reinforce Bonnie's dependency on Tracey. Bonnie didn't come home at all. Phone conversations, which Bonnie had promised would be at least once a day, now only happened two, maybe three times per week, and the time spent in those discussions was laughable.

A promise made that's a promise kept . . . There's a love so true . . . Just hold on; God is holding onto you . . .

It was Carl who had said Dee had made the mistake of trying to control

Bonnie, which immediately sent Dee over the edge. She didn't speak to her husband for two days, but she began to suspect he was right by the morning of the third day after she had time to think about what he had said. At least, partially right. Carl was never entirely right.

After soul searching and a glass or two of red wine, Dee called Bonnie and apologized for interfering with her relationship with Tracey (aka the Devil). It nearly killed her to do it, and she certainly didn't necessarily believe she was in the wrong, but it did seem to appease her daughter. Like Carl had said, if Dee wanted to have a relationship with Bonnie, she'd have to learn to loosen the reins. And she would. For a little while.

After the apology, Dewalla's relationship with her daughter slowly changed. Bonnie returned home on the weekends. Well, some weekends. There were even some visits to the church on Sunday mornings. During one of these Sundays, her daughter broached the idea of summer camp. Dee, who had been looking forward to the upcoming summer and having her daughter home, was not excited about Bonnie spending most of the season away at some godforsaken wilderness retreat in some little hole-in-the-wall county in northern Tennessee. Bonnie claimed that being a counselor would look good on her college transcript, especially her degree in social work. And for a while, that seemed like a sound reason. So sound, in fact, Dewalla had written a letter of recommendation for her daughter so that the camp would consider her. It wasn't until she discovered that Tracey was also applying to be a counselor that she reconsidered her decision. Her daughter didn't want to go to that camp to better herself, to work with children, or to gather credentials for her resume. She was going to party it up in the woods with Satan herself!

Biting her tongue about the camp was the hardest thing Dee had ever had to do, but her patience paid off. The Lord answered her many prayers when Bonnie told her that poor Tracey had been denied the position. Failed the background check. *Well, of course, she did.* Suddenly, the idea of Bonnie spending time at a summer camp didn't seem so tragic. At least she would be far away from Tracey Abernathy, hidden in the mountains of Tennessee.

I'm down on my knees to pray . . . Only You can wash my sins away . . .

And so, at the end of the freshman year, Bonnie packed her things to go to Camp *Whatchamadoozie*. Dee and Carl offered to drive her upstate, but Bonnie said Tracey would take her. Tracey had family in them there hills, family she hadn't seen in a while, so Bonnie would ride with her. *Well, glory*, thought Dee. *Isn't that convenient?*

Bonnie and Tracey loaded Tracey's car with everything Bonnie was taking: her clothes, toiletries, and Bonnie's CPR instructional doll, whom her brothers had named *Axel* for whatever reason. Dee waved goodbye as the girls drove away, and as she did so, she noticed that smile on Tracey's face, a smirk, this knowing grin that caused Dee's stomach to sour. *Whore of Babylon!*

The camp was nearly three and a half hours from Chattanooga, which would have placed Bonnie onsite by eleven o'clock that Thursday evening. But there was no phone call confirming her arrival. Carl forbade Dee from calling the camp in the middle of the night, demanding to know where her daughter was, but that didn't stop her from dialing some ignorant man named Drummond the following day at seven a.m. on the dot, who told her that Bonnie had yet to arrive. Dee paced the house for the better part of the morning and called that Drummond character every hour on the hour until he wouldn't pick up anymore. Then, she called the police, speaking to the sheriff, who said he'd check it out.

Finally, by four p.m., the phone rang. It was Bonnie (thank the angels), but there was something suspicious about her daughter. Bonnie sounded disconnected, distracted. *Busy* would be the term Dee would later use to comfort herself. Maybe Bonnie *had* been busy. She had just arrived, after all. Then again, perhaps she was angry, embarrassed even.

Over the next several days, communication was lax at best. One conversation. Dee had had only one conversation with her daughter. It was even worse than college. At least at the university, Dee and Bonnie spoke each day, at least for a moment. Suspicion kept Dee awake each night.

I used to think it took a giggly girl to win some fame in this mixed around world . . . but I know better now . . .

Dewalla thought it best not to mention her trip to Carl lest he found one of his soapboxes to stand on. She didn't care if her actions were right or wrong, and she didn't need her husband to point out the obvious flaws in her methodology. So, she slipped away after Carl left for work that morning and started on her way. She would find her daughter, look her in the eye, and then she'd know. Bonnie would be upset, yes. True, Bonnie may not speak to her for the rest of the summer. But Dee was convinced all she had to do was look into her daughter's eyes to know the truth.

Now, here she was in her BMW M5, the map unfolded in the passenger's seat, and Calvary 89.7 FM playing in the background. She was looking for a little off-ramp called 149-B to a place called Jasper Mill, Tennessee. From her calculations, the camp sat some fifteen miles from the exit. She looked at the digital clock on her dashboard. Eleven past noon. She should reach the campsite by around one o'clock if those calculations were correct. She would pull up to the camp, get out of the car, find Bonnie, and say . . . and say . . .

We'll play in the sunshine. We'll dance in the moonlight. We'll sing in the hard times. And find it on the wings . . . we'll find it on the wings of love . . .

Dee had no idea what to say or do when she arrived. She hadn't thought through it. Placing the car in reverse, she pulled from the driveway and made her way east toward the interstate on-ramp. Five minutes later, she sailed along US-27 S. *Maybe I'll fly off the handle*, she thought. *Maybe I'll just slap her right across the face! That'd bring her back to reality. Or . . . perhaps I can play innocent, act as if I just wanted to see the place Bonnie was staying and learn more about the people there. I could even say I was stopping by on my way . . . on my way . . . on my way to visit Sharon. Glory, that's perfect!*

Dee's sinning sister, Sharon, lived with a seventh husband in some doublewide trailer in Bristol, which had to be just a half hour away from the camp. Granted, Dee hadn't spoken to the woman in three years, ever since the disagreement over their mother's burial arrangements, but Bonnie didn't know that. Bonnie didn't know much about anything in Dee's life these days.

Exhausted and frazzled, Dee turned off the radio for the last two miles of her drive. She had to be sure she didn't miss the turnoff, and the radio was now only serving as a distraction. Just when she began to think she had gone the wrong direction, she spied a large archway made of polished twigs and branches with the words "Kamp Kromwell" fastened to the top. They had spelled "camp" with a "K." *How witty.*

Dewalla parked the car and walked to the long iron gate blocking the entrance. It was locked, but the bars were wide enough for her to slip through. She returned to the car, turned off the engine, and grabbed her purse. Then, she began to walk along the wide dirt road. She passed a parking lot on the right, where she spied Bonnie's car in plain sight. Stuffed animals littered the interior, and that damn Axel doll sat there ogling at her with his fake, glass eyes. And an odor. Oh, God, the smell! A stench hung low in the air around the parking area, the scent of rot. Dee was confident some dead animal lay rotting in the bushes nearby.

In the distance, Dee spied a young girl carrying armloads of what appeared to be vinyl targets for a shooting range. *It's Bonnie! There she is.* Dee waved her arms, but the girl didn't notice. Finally, Dee called out.

"Bonnie! Yoo-hoo!" The girl turned and paused. As she placed the targets onto the ground, Dee could see it wasn't Bonnie. The girl stared in Dee's direction with an uncertain gaze. "Can you help me?"

"Hello," said the girl as she approached Dee with a smile. "Maybe?"

"I hope so," chuckled Dee. "I'm looking for my daughter. I'm Dewalla Evans. My daughter, Bonnie, is supposed to be a counselor here."

The girl held out her hand. "Oh, yeah, yeah. Bonnie. I know her. I'm Beth."

Dewalla took her hand and shook it. "Oh, yes. We talked a few days ago. Sorry, I'm a bit winded. The gate down there is locked, so I had to walk."

"Sorry," said Beth. "Mr. Drummond keeps it locked except for Tuesday and Thursday mornings, when we get supplies in." Beth motioned to her. "Come with me. I think Bonnie was finishing up mopping the dining hall floor."

The two made their way up the path.

"Well, this sure is a lot nicer than I thought it'd be."

Beth laughed. "I know. I was surprised. It's really great, though."

"So, you're a counselor, too?"

"Yes. I work with Bonnie, actually. She manages the girls' cabins over on that hill with another girl named Rosetta."

"Well, how nice," said Dee as the two of them continued. "So, Mr. Drummond runs this place?"

"Yes," Beth replied. "Very nice man."

Dee looked back toward the parking lot. "You may want to tell him something is dead down there in the trees. I could smell it all around. He may want to check it out."

"Probably some bird or squirrel. I'll tell him."

"So, is it like the movies?"

"What?" Beth asked.

"I know you told me everything is on the up and up," said Dewalla. "But you know how you see camp counselors in movies all getting together, having a *good time.*"

Beth laughed. "It's pretty boring, actually. We just tend to the kids mostly, set up games, activities, keep the place clean—things like that."

"And do you have any Bible studies?" asked Dee, causing the girl to hesitate. "Prayer time?"

Beth shook her head. "Well, no. I'm afraid it's not that kind of camp, Mrs. Evans. We have kids of all different types of religions here, so we have to be careful to keep—"

"Well, that's too bad," said Dee with disappointment. "You can't find the Lord in too many places these days. Sad."

Beth didn't reply. Instead, she led Dewalla into the dark dining hall. The smell of overcooked beef stew, the evening dinner, mingled with the scent of the freshly mopped floors, creating an intriguing yet nauseating odor. Dee rubbed her offended nose.

"Bonnie?" called Beth to no reply. "Bonnie, are you still in here?" Silence.

"Knowing my daughter, she saw us coming and ran away," chuckled Dee.

"Oh, I'm sure it's nothing like that." Beth glanced around the hall. "Mr. Drummond is on an errand. Why don't you come with me to the office and have a seat? Then, I can go look for Bonnie. I'm sure she's probably over at the cabins." Dee nodded and followed the nice girl toward the rear of the hall, toward a row of doors. Beth opened the middle door and ushered her into the office. "I'll be right back."

"Thank you."

As Beth disappeared into the shadows, Dee examined the room. She wasn't sure how anyone would find a thing in the cluttered space. The two metal desks at either side of the room were overrun with unorganized papers and scattered supplies. It was enough to rattle her OCD like a cat in a cage.

Five minutes passed, then seven, and still no sign of Beth or her daughter. She reached forward and plucked a magazine from the desk in front of her. A brass plate that read *Mr. Earl Drummond, Director* sat on the edge. It was a copy of *Field & Stream*, hardly a favorite, but it would have to do.

Ten minutes. Fifteen. Twenty.

Dee huffed impatiently and grabbed another magazine from the desk. As she opened the cover, movement drew her eye. She turned to see the shadow of a face peering at her through the office door window. It vanished behind the glass, taking its shape along with it.

"Bonnie?" called Dee, but there was no reply.

She tossed the magazine onto the desk, rose to her feet, and walked toward the office door. Through the glass, she saw the figure of a girl disappear around the corner. She opened the door and carefully went down the dim hallway while the distant sounds of rambunctious children and splashing water echoed into the building. She called out for Bonnie once again but received no reply. As she turned the corner, she saw a short, petite figure slip through the

120

kitchen door at the edge of the dining hall.

"Bonnie, if that's you, I'm not in the mood, missy," warned Dee.

The kitchen appeared vacant. Waning sunlight oozed through the silvery screen of the open back door. The only sounds were the bubbling of a boiling pot clattering on the stove and music from a small radio sitting in the window.

"Bonnie?" Dee stepped deeper into the kitchen. "Bonnie Elizabeth Evans! You come here right this minute, or I'm going to take you home with me, counseling job or not!"

A shape emerged from the shadows of the pantry.

Dee jerked and grabbed her chest. It took a moment for her to realize it was Beth, the girl who had led her to the dining hall.

"Oh! Good Lord, Beth!" said Dee with a chuckle. "Woo! Did you find her?" But the girl didn't reply. She just stood there. She stood there staring at Dee with a strange yet slightly familiar smile. "Uh, maybe I . . . can go with you, and we can—"

The girl raised the iron skillet and banged it against Dee's brow, sending a loud *bong* reverberating off the tile walls. Dee's ears began to ring. She tumbled to the ground, unable to control her legs. Again, the girl raised the skillet and bashed it against the side of Dee's skull, and Dee heard the crack of bone in her ears. Several of Dee's teeth fell from her dangling jaw and scattered across the tile floor, leaving bloody trails behind them. Her nose began to fill with hot blood. She inhaled, and the salty fluid burned her crushed sinus passages.

Then there was laughter. Over the ringing in Dee's ears, she heard laughter. Maniacal cackling like a witch soaring on a broom in the moonlight. The girl was laughing, snickering with glee as she brought that skillet down repeatedly onto Dee's crumbling skull like a sledgehammer.

And ever since the day you put my heart in motion . . . Baby, I realize that there's just no getting over you . . .

Top 40 Pop trash, Dee thought.

Then Dee stopped thinking.

14

4:01 P.M.

I learned Nurse Conrad had many uses for the word "shit." For her, it was a universally flexible term, a magical phrase, complete with variable context to match her desired sentiment and connotation. It felt odd for "shit" to be the first thing Nurse Conrad said when I was brought to her office on Field Day.

Beth and Rosetta led me into the frigid nurse's cabin while I firmly held a cold, damp cloth against the back of my throbbing head. Conrad, who was busy tending to the badly scraped knee of Missy Jelesky, turned to us, adjusted her white paper nurse's hat, and furrowed her brow.

"Shit," Conrad spat. "Another one already? What is this—summer camp or the Thunderdome?"

"Sorry, Gina," said Beth. "We're trying to keep them safe out there. I swear."

Conrad gently took my wrist and stared into my eyes, glancing from pupil to pupil. "What happened to you, son?"

"He got hit with a coconut," Rosetta replied.

"No shit?" asked Conrad.

"No shit," I interjected.

Conrad pointed toward the exam room door to the left of her office. "You ladies take him back there, and I'll be there after I get Miss Jelesky's knee settled."

I had sunk into isolation after Chester's campfire exposé on Folklore Night. The general population seemed inclined to leave me to my own devices—even Kenny, who had trouble being alone for more than an hour. Occasionally, one of the Krew would hunt me down and check my status with a gentle "How are you?" or "How are you feeling?" They'd take note of my response and again leave me to my thoughts. Everyone was just as stunned to hear the name Sam Barnes as I had been. For the first time, I felt my horn was there for everyone to see, a glimmering swirl of jagged bone protruding from my forehead like a shameful beacon. It could no longer be concealed.

While sequestered in this solitude, Mr. Drummond found me hovering around the stable at the south end of camp the afternoon he had come to pick up supply orders from Ms. Brooks. I was at the rear of the barn next to the cellar doors, spending time with one of the horses named Daisy, when I saw Drummond enter the stable from the corner of my eye. I shrank away as he moved toward Ms. Brooks's office.

"Mr. Carpenter," called a bright voice. "There you are. I haven't seen you in days." I turned to see Drummond coming toward me. "See you've met Daisy."

"Yeah," I said uncomfortably. My brain prepared for social interaction.

Drummond stood beside me, hands on his hips, staring at the horse. He reached out and rubbed her neck. "She sure is pretty." I nodded without reply. We focused on the horse for a few silent moments before he continued. He nodded toward the metal doors just beyond where we stood. "You know, that used to be a bomb shelter."

"Really?" I said, feigning interest.

"Yep," he replied. "A few years ago, Beth got herself locked down there." He chuckled. "We liked to have never found her." I didn't add commentary. "Um, Beth told me what happened the other night." *Of course, she did.* I took a deep breath and sighed. "That Chester. He's a . . . well, he a character, alright."

"He's an asshat," I suggested.

Drummond pointed at me with the order forms in his hand. "Language." He paused and shuffled his feet. "But yes. He's an asshat." I smiled. He nudged me. "You know, I had myself a bully when I was in middle school. Darby Gillan. Talk about an asshat." A smile appeared under his bushy mustache. "He used to haunt me, that kid. We were both trying out for the football team, and he did everything he could to ensure I didn't get it. But you know what?"

"What?" I asked.

"I got picked, and he didn't. Oh, man. Was he pissed?! Not because I was better than him, really. I mean, I *sucked* at football. I'm a big guy, but I was never what you'd call an athlete. But the coach told me I had two things Darby didn't—brains and heart—and that's why he chose me over him." He glanced at me, awaiting some acknowledgment, but I was unsure where his conversation was leading us. "You know what I'm saying?"

"I think so," I replied.

I didn't.

Drummond must have sensed my confusion, because he added, "I'm saying I didn't have to be the best. I just had to be better than Darby." He tapped the top of my head with the bundle of order forms. "You got brains, kid. And heart. Don't forget that."

"I got something, alright," I skeptically replied.

Drummond chuckled and patted my shoulder. "Well, I'll leave you to it. Don't stay away too long, though. You'll miss all the fun." He turned and strolled toward the stable entrance. Then he paused and looked back. "You don't have to be the best, Joe. You just have to be better than the asshats."

I smiled and nodded, then watched as he disappeared into the sunlight. Daisy looked at me and tossed her head, flipping her mane from side to side. I took the brush in my hand and returned to stroking her head. And at first, Drummond's little tale was lost on me, but then it returned, word by word, line by line. It started to make sense.

The lesson stuck with me for the remainder of that morning. The more I thought about what Drummond had said, the more I realized he was right. I didn't have to be better than the population of the planet Earth; I just had to be better than Chester Henry, better than the asshats. That's when I had the novel idea: best Chester Henry at his own game.

Later that day, as the campers filed into the dining hall for dinner, I swept by the office to glance at the Field Day sign-up sheets. Each event had its own registration form, complete with time and location. As you can imagine, I was no athlete. I'm not now, and I wasn't then. That didn't mean there wasn't something out there, some challenge Chester had registered for, where I possessed some natural advantage.

I first saw Chester's name under basketball free throw, which was a no-go. I had only dribbled a basketball under extreme duress in gym class and was hardly good at it. Chester had also registered for the swim relay, which was out of the question. I could tread water just enough to keep from drowning. No, I needed to find something that didn't require overt physical exertion and would allow my heart rate to remain at that comfortable sixty-five-beat-per-minute rhythm to which it had grown accustomed. So, I started to look for less physically strenuous events.

I noticed Chester had signed up for archery, which didn't require a lot of perspiration. I could shoot a bow and arrow, but I doubted I could do so at a competitive level. Just as I was about to give up, I spied Chester's name scribbled under something I wasn't prepared to see. *Coconut bowling.* Well, I could undoubtedly bowl. I could bowl well, in fact. I wasn't the king of the lanes, but I had always held my own against my friend Leslie, even my brothers. My mind flashed to the countless hours spent at Fountain Lanes bowling alley, Leslie and I huddled into a lane of our own, locked in a game of one-on-one. Yeah, I could bowl, and I would bowl Chester's ass right off the map.

It was time to emerge from the shadows on the morning of Field Day. I wandered to the north end of camp, where the various competitors gathered for the contest. I lingered around the bushes just beyond the field. I spied the Krew in the distance and decided to join them.

"Well, hello, stranger," chimed Asia as I approached. I smiled.

"Oh, I'm so glad you're here," said Kenny, patting my shoulder. "This wouldn't be half as fun to watch without you here."

"Look at all of them," Lily said, nodding toward the group gathering for the Three-Legged Race. " 'bout to get out there and make fools of themselves in front of God and Jesus."

DJ nudged her. "You should've entered the swim meet. You'd have done good."

Lily shook her head. "I don't do well under pressure. I'd get out there and drown."

Susan, who had set aside her work at the stables for the day to help coordinate the events, stepped forward and tooted the whistle around her neck. Our eyes met, and she smiled at me. "Okay, welcome to Kromwell Field Day!" she called out. "Our first event is the Three-Legged Race. When I call your names, come to the starting line." She began to read off the names of the registered contestants, which, of course, included both Chester and Lynn.

126

The smirking asshats filed onto the field along with fourteen other contestants, all tied together in groups of two. Drummond stepped forward, fired the starter pistol, and they were off. Stacey Hanes and Linda Peters fell to the ground after taking three steps. Judd Brown and Harry Beals moved to first place, with Lindsey Rafferty and Tina Stevens *galloping* on their heels. Just to their right came Chester and Lynn, quickly gaining ground. With a sweep of his leg, Chester tripped Lindsey mid-gallop, causing her glasses to flop from her face and onto the grass. Some in the crowd noticed his move and began to boo, including the Krew.

"Cheater!" hissed Lily.

"He's cheating!" DJ added.

Asia scoffed. "Surprise, surprise."

It wasn't long before Chester and Lynn slipped into first place. A few feeble cheers echoed through the crowd as they crossed the finish line. Most of us were just disappointed. In a streak, Chester and Lynn took no less than second place in nearly every event for which they registered. Sometimes they won fair and square; most of the time, they didn't.

As with everything involving the pair, their cheating was implicit and cagy, hard to spy unless you were looking for it. During the Jet Ski Race, however, Lynn attempted to sideswipe David Something-Or-Other, scratching one of the new jet skis and nearly running David onto the bank. We did a celebratory dance when Drummond announced that Lynn would be disqualified from that race and his remaining events. It was a small taste of justice in a banquet of suck.

It was about two o'clock that afternoon when Danny stepped onto the field and tooted his whistle. Neil and Dennis began setting up oversized bowling pins for the Coconut Bowling event. I felt this surge of electric anxiety in my gut that seemed to energize me. Adrenaline flooded my brain, filling me with an unexpected sensation of excitement. I took a deep breath.

"What?" asked Kenny, who had noticed my fervor.

I shook my head dismissively.

Danny blew his whistle, and the crowd silenced. "Okay, now we'll have the Coconut Bowling contest. Each contestant will have three attempts to get three strikes. The top three who down the most pins in three throws will compete in a final roll." Danny glanced at the registration form in his hand. "When I call your name, line up behind me. Johnny Jerardo . . . Chester Henry . . . Lucy Turpin." As Danny continued to call names, I stepped from between

Asia and Kenny and slipped under the rope.

"Hey!" I heard Kenny call. "Joe! Joey, where you going?"

Danny paused and smiled. "Joe Carpenter."

There was a momentary rush of silence as I entered the field. I kept walking forward. I couldn't look back. If I did, I knew I might throw in the towel. My ears perked. Finally, I heard Kenny howl like a werewolf, and the crowd began to cheer. I couldn't help but smile. It was a good feeling, one I hadn't often experienced. I looked at Drummond, who nodded proudly. Chester paced among the other contestants. He looked at me and smirked. But hidden in that smirk, I saw a glint of apprehension, uneasiness. My presence seemed to set him on edge, and I *lived* for it.

Lucy Turpin was the first to bowl. She missed the pins on her first roll, and the crowd oozed with "oohs" and "awws." She got five of the ten pins with her second roll and seven on her third. David *Something-Or-Other* did a bit better. He got a strike on his first roll, but then he got eight on his second. He ended his run with five pins on his third attempt.

My mind wandered, leaving the field altogether, focusing on no one other than Chester Henry. It didn't matter if I did better than Lucy, David, or any other player on the field. I just had to do better than Chester.

At last, it was Chester's turn at the dirt lane. Neil stood up the ten pins and scurried away. Chester snatched the bulky coconut from the ground and ran his fingers over its surface.

"Get ready to see a pro," he announced to everyone.

I looked down and rolled my eyes. Chester hit a strike on his first throw. Lynn jumped up and down, barking like an idiot. I began to feel a little ill when Chester also struck on his second throw. Before his third throw, he turned to me and winked. He reared back and let go of the coconut. *Eight* out of ten. Not bad. But not perfect. As Chester spied the two pins standing, he turned toward Drummond.

"I need a different coconut. This one is uneven," Chester called.

"*All* coconuts are uneven, Mr. Reynolds," called Drummond.

At last, it was my turn. I stepped into the lane without looking in Chester's direction and plucked a sand-filled coconut. Dennis reset the pins. *This is no different than Fountain Lanes,* I told myself. *No one is here right now but you and Leslie. It's like any other bowling night.* On my first roll, I knocked down nine of the ten pins. I sighed with disappointment.

"Go, Joe!" screamed Lily.

"You can do it!" Asia added.

On my second roll, I managed a strike, and the crowd began to cheer. I glanced at Chester, whose concern had become harder to hide. I wasn't sure what caused him unease; the fact that I could bowl or that the crowd seemed behind me. Before my final roll, I paused, took a deep breath, and closed my eyes. I could hear Lynn coughing in the distance, some feeble attempt to distract me from the task. I let the coconut fly, knocking down all ten pins, and the campers roared. I saw Susan bounce up and down, clapping. Danny pumped his fist in the air and let out a yell. Neil patted my shoulder as he passed me to reset the pins.

Danny stepped forward and sounded his whistle. "Okay, okay. Our top three for the final roll will be Buddy Finn, Chester Henry, and Joe Carpenter."

Everyone cheered at the mention of my name, which filled me with confidence I didn't know existed. The three of us lined up beside Danny. Chester was sure to angrily nudge my arm as he took his place to my left. Buddy went first, knocking down nine of the ten pins. Then I stepped forward.

"Come on, Joe!" called DJ.

Again, I took a deep breath and knelt forward to snatch one of the coconuts from the ground. I stood there, staring down the dirt pathway toward the ten pins resting at the end of the lane. There had never been a moment of life more important than that moment. I could feel the muscles of my legs quiver with anticipation. At last, I let the coconut fly, and nine pins fell away, leaving a single pin wobbling in place. My throat seized. I held my breath as the tenth pin bobbed. For a moment, it seemed as if it would regain balance.

But at last, it wavered and fell to the right.

And the crowd went wild.

Our eyes met as I passed Chester.

"Fag," he quietly hissed at me.

Usually, such a taunt would anger me. This time, however, I smiled at Chester and returned that wink he had given me earlier. His face flushed with red anger. He was flustered, and that was good. I wanted him to be angry. Angry people make mistakes. He snatched one of the shells from the ground, evaluated it, and returned it to the ground. Then he selected another and smiled. He spit on the shell, and my face twisted with disgust.

"Okay, man," muttered Danny. "Just roll the ball."

"It's for luck," Chester said.

He turned, took a breath, and then threw the shell down the lane as if he was pitching a baseball instead of rolling a bowling ball. It smashed into the pins, scattering them across the field. Without hesitation, Chester began to jump up and down with elation.

"Woo!" he shouted. "That's how you do—"

"Wait," said Danny stepping forward. "Wait a minute, man. You can't *throw* the coconut at the pins. That's not bowling. You have to roll it."

"Who says?" Chester replied.

"I do," Drummond warned.

Dennis and Neil gathered the pins and set them up a final time. One of them had rolled so far away that Dennis had to jog to get it. Neil cautiously picked up Chester's mucous-ladened coconut and handed it to him.

"I think this is yours," Neil said.

"Whatever, man," barked Chester.

Once again, Chester wound up, reared back, and released the coconut. Time seemed to slip into slow motion as I watched the shell scamper down the path toward the oversized pins. It bounced lightly along the trail, sending plumes of dust into the sunlit air. It collided with the pins, splitting them down the middle. As with my turn, nine of the ten pins fell to the ground, and one was left twirling on its axis. When I thought the final pin would tumble to the ground, it balanced and stabilized. Chester's pride shattered like glass.

The crowd erupted into applause. The Krew ran onto the field and surrounded me. I could hear Chester's objections. He began going through a prepared list of reasons the contest hadn't been fair: the pins weren't set up correctly, the shells weren't balanced, the sun was in his eyes. The list went on. It didn't matter. No one cared. Least of all me.

My senses tingled as the Krew led me toward Drummond, who dangled my plastic winner's medal in his fingers. Something was approaching me. I saw Drummond's face sour with concern. Before I could turn around, something slammed into the back of my skull. I fell to the ground, ears ringing, head pounding. My hands wrapped around my head. As the whirring in my ears subsided, I could hear Chester yelling incoherently. It took a moment for me to realize that Chester had launched one of the coconut shells at my skull.

The next thing I knew, Chester was being reprimanded in the office, and I was staring at the CPR poster hanging in Nurse Conrad's office with that musty wet rag against my head, knowing that in two days, no one would remember any of this. I gazed at that cheap plastic gold medal in my hand, knowing I would remember. I'd never forget it. And neither would Chester.

That was the most important thing.

That was what it was all about.

I saw shadows move beyond the doorway as Nurse Conrad ushered the little Jelesky girl toward the exit. The girl limped as if she was walking on a compound fracture.

"Will I need to have a cast?"

Conrad sighed. "Let's see what that Band-Aid does for us first, Missy. We can get the chopper to medivac you out of here if it means saving that leg."

"Okay," moaned the girl, obviously missing the sarcasm in Conrad's voice.

With the girl gone, Conrad turned, shook her head, and marched toward my room. "Okay! Now that crisis is averted, let's see what we have here."

"Is she going to make it?" I asked.

"I swear . . . there are some kids who could break both arms and keep running around like nothing happened. Then there are those who get a splinter and act like we'll have to amputate." She carefully moved my hand and collected the damp rag from my fingers. I felt the warmth of her hand locate the throbbing bump on my head, and I winced at the pain. "That, sir, is an impressive knot. And you say this was caused by a coconut shell?"

"Well, they fill them with sand so they'll roll," I said.

"No shit. And who threw it?"

"Chester Henry."

"Henry, Henry, Henry . . . the lanky kid with the mullet?"

"No, I think you're talking about his friend, Lynn. Lynn Reynolds."

Conrad rounded the table and pointed at me. "Oh! The stocky fella with the droopy lips."

"That's him," I said with a smile.

Conrad pulled the penlight from her pocket and shined it into each of my eyes. "Any nausea?"

"A little. Not bad."

"Dizziness? Balance issues? Memory problems?"

"Not that I can tell."

She nodded and turned to the cabinet to her right. "I think you may have a slight concussion, Mr. Carpenter. But you'll live to coconut bowl another day." She grabbed several small white packets and handed them to me. "Take these. Ibuprofen. Should help with the swelling. And we'll need to get some ice from the dining hall to—"

"Conrad?" called a voice from the other room. I leaned over to see Drummond and Danny helping David Something-Or-Other into the office. David held a towel over his bloody nose.

"Shit! What now?" barked Conrad. She patted my knee and walked into the other room.

"We got a busted nose," Drummond said.

"Earl," warned Conrad, pointing a finger in his direction. "We either need to end Field Day, or you need to get me some temp help from the hospital."

"He just got popped with a baseball," Drummond added.

Conrad sat David in the chair, removing the towel from his crooked nose. She turned to Drummond. "Looks pretty *popped* to me!"

"Ith it bad?" asked David through swollen nostrils. Without another word, Conrad placed a thumb on either side of David's nose and *popped* it back into place. "*Thon- ova-bick*!" he howled.

"There you go," chimed Conrad proudly. David whined and stuffed his nose back into the bloody towel. She leaned into my room. "Joe, I think you're good. Stop by the dining hall and have Jack give you a bag of ice. Keep that on there for ten minutes at a time until it's melted. Ten on, ten off. Got it?"

I nodded and hopped off the table. While Conrad and Drummond entered a debate on the safety protocols of Field Day, I slipped through the front door and stepped onto the walkway. After acclimating to the icy coolness of Conrad's quarters, the hot summer wind stunned my senses so much it nearly took my breath. I walked down the pathway on the right toward the dining hall.

The spicy scent of Beth's chili lingered throughout the dining hall. My mouth watered with anticipation. All the excitement of the day had left me starving. I was just twenty feet from the kitchen when the pattering noise of footsteps drew my attention to the left.

Susan was leading Chester from the office. For a moment, Chester didn't even realize I was there. He had this look, an expression of sincere regret, an emotion I wasn't sure someone like Chester could even feel. He looked up and saw me on the other side of the room. I smiled and waved at him, allowing my medal to dangle from my fingers. His brow furrowed with anger, and he flipped his middle finger in my direction. Finally, he slid a finger across his throat just before Susan guided him out of the dining hall and into the campus square.

"Dickhead," I muttered. I paused at the kitchen door and knocked, but there was no reply. "Mr. Burns?" I knocked again. "Mr. Burns. Nurse Conrad sent me over to get some ice for my head." Still, there was only silence.

At last, I nudged the swinging door and peeked inside the kitchen. No one was there. The small radio beside the window played a song I didn't immediately recognize. The massive pot on the stove rattled from the blue heat churning underneath it. I opened my mouth to call out once again but hesitated. *Screw this. It's just ice.*

Taking one of the clear zip bags from the counter, I opened the door to the ice chest, scooped a mound of ice into the bag, and closed it tight. A glimmer of light caught my eye as I approached the chest lid. I turned toward the kitchen sink. Something shiny was on the floor, small and gold, hiding underneath the basin.

I stepped forward, knelt, and picked up the item with my index finger and thumb. It was a lump of gold. At first, I thought it was a charm, like those cheap gold nugget pendants that were so popular then. When I noticed blood-covered bone protruding from the top, I realized it was something else. *A tooth.* A gold crown.

I tossed the thing in the sink and wiped my hand against my shirt in disgust. For a moment, I thought I had to be mistaken. What would a loose tooth be doing on the floor of the kitchen? I crept forward and stared into the stainless-steel basin where it rested.

The water droplets in the sink had revived tiny specks of dried blood, creating a grotesque splatter. There was no doubt; it was a tooth. The meaty root stood in jagged peaks along the golden ridge. And it simply hadn't fallen out, either. No, this had been forced out, beaten from its socket by some hard blow, a . . .

"What are you doing in here?" barked a voice.

I jerked with a start and turned to see Jack's nephew, Dewayne, standing in the doorway. "Um . . . ice," I said uncertainly. "The nurse sent me for ice . . . for my head."

"And do you have it?" Dewayne asked. I held up the bag to show him. "Good. Now, fuck off."

15

CURSES

Shit dreams. Mossy hated shit dreams. She rose from the bed and wrapped the fuzzy robe across her shoulders. *Visions. . . hallucinations, more like it.* Most of the time, she awoke each morning not remembering anything she dreamt of. But sometimes her dreams were bizarre, horrific, real. Those would jerk her out of a sound sleep and slap her around like she owed them money.

The last time she had a dream that lucid was six years before, the morning her mother had passed. Mossy and her mother walked along a hillside, chatting about life, love, and beyond. The two of them came to a tall cliff, so tall you could see all of Jasper Mill and the world beyond. The deep valleys below lay hidden under a churning blanket of fog. Her mother turned to her.

"Well, honey," she said. "I think you know what to do from here." She kissed Mossy's forehead.

Before Mossy could clarify the woman's meaning, her mother leaned forward and spread her arms. Mossy screamed and ran to grab her, but she was gone. A petite house sparrow with white-and-brown feathers, the most beautiful little bird Mossy had ever seen, fluttered into the clouds.

Mossy awoke that morning knowing that her mother was gone. She called the ambulance before she even rose from the bed. Stepping into the hallway, she went to her mother's room and pushed open the door. There her mother lay, peaceful, content. Just outside her window perched a house sparrow. It wasn't as brilliantly colored as the one in her dream, but she knew who it was, all the same. If only all the dreams were that lovely.

Not like this one. This one was shit.

A shit dream.

Mossy snatched the cup of coffee from the kitchen counter and slid into the wobbly kitchen chair. *Need to tighten that leg bolt.* That notion crossed her mind whenever she sat at the table. It had for years, yet the bolt continued to loosen. Soon, she'd find herself on her ass.

She opened her notebook and took the pen into her hand. It was always best to write things down while they were fresh. She glanced at the clock. Four seventeen a.m.

Mossy had been in the forest, but not really. She was floating through the woods, suspended by some unseen wire. She was a bystander, a witness. Just below her, a figure in a tattered black dress led a child through the night. The boy, who must have been a teenager, clung to the woman's arm with one hand, and in the other hand, he held a human head—his *own* head—which had just been severed from his shoulders. Mossy drifted high above, watching the woman and the headless boy make their way through the thicket until they came to a clearing.

An enormous bonfire blazed ahead. Just beyond that fire stood the crooked tree at the Robinson farm. A horde of headless bodies danced merrily around the flames, each clinging tightly to their heads. The faces of each head twisted with manic glee, singing together in a discordant timbre that almost sounded like howling.

Rise to greet us, old John Tate. We have a job for you . . .

We call upon your wicked soul to do what we can't do . . .

The heads repeated this phrase, each round sounding more frenzied than the one before. The corpses paused and began to cheer as the woman neared them. They welcomed her and her headless guest into the fold. Mossy saw writing on his blood-spattered tee shirt as the boy's body stepped into the firelight. *Chester the Jester.* Written in airbrushed lettering above the hideous face of a cartoon clown holding a red balloon.

The young woman who accompanied the boy had short hair, spikey, dyed various shades of pink and blue. Wayward strands clung to her bloody face. There was something strange about her flesh, something Mossy couldn't quite see. It seemed rough, flaky, almost wooden, like tree bark. Mossy pulled herself closer to the woman, hoping to get a better look. As she edged closer, the horde began to toss their severed heads into the bonfire. After each screaming head was consumed in flames, its body would stagger forward and topple lifelessly to the ground.

As the corpses ambled forward, Mossy recognized faces, people she had known for years. Earl Drummond was there, clutching his head while it muttered babble and laughed manically. So was Jack Burns. The horse lady, the one called Susan, was there, too. In fact, it seemed like the entire population of Kamp Kromwell was there, each headless and happily sacrificing themselves. But to what?

The crooked tree began to quake. Its long, winding branches unfurled like the legs of a spider. The bark of its trunk shattered, spilling dark blood onto the ground. Smoke rose from its roots, filling the air with a noxious odor. At last, the hull spread like a womb and gave birth to a creature, a tall beast, half man, half tree. It stood over nine feet high and walked upon thick legs and root-covered feet. It held its massive arms wide, extending its muscular hands with long, vine-like fingers, each tipped with wooden talons. Upon its broad shoulders rested a head that almost reminded Mossy of a deer, with two long, winding branches that appeared much like crooked antlers. The beast marched forward, shaking the ground underneath its tread. It began to pluck the bodies from the ground and consume them.

Mossy felt eyes upon her. Now, not only the observer but the observed. This woman, this witch, had somehow seen her. She glared at Mossy with deep, black eyes and smiled. She snapped her fingers, summoning the attention of the tree beast. She pointed in Mossy's direction. As if on command, the creature dropped what remained of Drummond's tattered body to the ground and walked forward to claim Mossy. That's when Mossy knew what it was, *who* it was. It plucked Mossy out of the air like a falling leaf and pulled her close. It gazed at her with blue eyes, *human eyes*, familiar eyes.

"*Lit-tle Lo-is*," it rumbled to her with its wooden voice.

Mossy pushed herself away from the kitchen table and glanced at the notebook. The name *John Tate* was scratched into the middle of the page. *Son-of-a-bitch*, she thought. *That's all I fucking need.*

The name *Lois Greene* no longer meant anything to Mossy. She didn't even know who Lois Greene was anymore. She didn't give two shits what anyone in town called her, so long as they didn't call her Lois Greene. These days, she preferred "Floppy Mossy." It was fun, certainly memorable, and infamous.

Forget to wear a bra to the post office *just one time*, and this is what happens.

It was easier not to care, to disregard the trappings of beauty, and at one time, she had indeed been beautiful. Oh, yes, sir. But that was many years and many tears ago.

Regardless of what folks say, John Tate hadn't yanked her into his truck and beat the shit out of her. She would have them know that Tate had cordially asked if she wanted a ride from the library, and she had said yes. He exited the truck, walked to her side of the car, and opened the door for her like a gentleman. She couldn't help but notice how giant the beast was. He was . . . *unconventionally* handsome. One of his hands could have covered her entire face. Most everyone she knew was afraid of John Tate, but not Mossy.

Two days later, Tate saw her walking home from the market and offered another ride, which she accepted again. On their third encounter, Tate asked if she would like to return to his house to watch the fireflies, and she said yes to that, too. Lois didn't know why. She would rather have shoveled shit than deal with her alcoholic, self-righteous father, so if spending a little time with Tate kept her from seeing the man, she'd take it.

Tate drove them to his cabin, and the two sat on the big rock in the moonlight, watching the fireflies buzz and sparkle in the black trees. That night, she noticed his eyes, those big blue eyes. There was darkness behind those eyes, but that obscurity didn't shade her. No, sir. When Tate looked at her, the man shone.

She would also have folks know that John Tate hadn't lifted a finger to harm her in any way, and he certainly didn't assault her ladyhood. Hell no, she gave that to him freely three weeks after making his acquaintance. Then, Tate asked her to stay with him, and by God, she said yes to that, too. Lois would be free of her drunk daddy and timid, superstitious mother. She would be free, living in a cabin with a beast who hung on to her every word. There was only one rule: Lois had to stay clear of the barn. And she did. Sometimes, she would get curious about what was out there but didn't dare betray Tate's trust. If he trusted her, she maintained complete power over him. She suspected that breaking that trust could lead to disastrous consequences.

Lastly, and most importantly, she would have everyone know that she was not some fourteen-year-old child when she met John Tate. Her daddy loved to make that claim. It added a particular sickness to the events, a shame that no one could deny. She had turned eighteen over a month before speaking to the man. Tate would have never, ever harmed the hair on a child's head, and no one was going to tell her differently. Despite all his faults, and there were many, he pitied the small and weak, those unable to fend for themselves.

There were times, just before Tate had asked Lois to marry him, that he spoke of his "sickness," the darkness inside of him that sometimes came out, something he couldn't control. Naturally, she had thought he was talking about his addiction to alcohol, seeing that the man couldn't get through a day without Tennessee whiskey. But there was something much more sinister at hand.

Sometimes she would watch the barn from the upstairs bedroom window while Tate "worked," paying attention to the shadows that moved in the lamplight. Sometimes she thought she saw more than one shadow, frightened silhouettes. One night, just before the end, Mossy awoke to the sound of a scream, a blood-curdling cry that shivered her insides. She threw on her housecoat, rushed down the steps, and through the front door. Tate stopped her halfway to the barn. It was the closest she had ever come to disobeying him. He claimed one of the sheep had gotten sick, so he had to put it down, which was the cry she heard. She had no reason not to believe the man. But things began to crawl out of the soil.

Early the following spring, after Kromwell Industries hired Thompson Excavation to clear out a good bit of acreage in preparation for some big, hoity-toity campground, the bodies started springing up like weeds. That's when they came after Tate. The night the police arrived, Tate went to Lois to—as he put it—*clear* his *heart*. He told her the police were coming for him because they thought he had done "bad" things. Tate didn't mention what those things were precisely, but they were evidently bad enough to have twelve police cars on the property. To Tate, there was a monster inside of him that he couldn't control, and if he were to deny the beast, it would consume him entirely. Meeting Lois made him want to kill that beast, become something better, and free himself of the monster.

Could he have?

Maybe.

Tate told Lois it was important for the police to believe he had kept her there against her will. She had to say that he had forced himself onto her, that she had never consented to their relationship. It was crucial that when questioned by the police, Lois was to claim that John Tate was a hideous monster. She suspected in some way he was. But in another way, a way that no one would ever see, John Tate was an ill individual enslaved by gruesome acts of depravity, led to his destination by an abusive father and a deviant mother. This multi-layered life-form was capable of both sickening cruelty and tender kindness. Tate suspected that if Lois Greene showed the world for one fleeting moment that she held anything but disdain for him, her life would become hell. Little had either of them realized that her life would be a shitshow regardless of the path chosen.

The town found many ways to torment Lois. There were some of the so-called Christian community who looked down upon her for having "lain with the beast," whether Tate had forced it or not. There wasn't a man in town that would have her after the incident. It was as if Lois had a huge red "T" tattooed on her forehead, a brand that either stood for "Tate" or "trash." Depended upon the day. Some seemingly felt sorry for Lois. Of course, they weren't sorry enough to give her that job for which she had applied or accept her into their flock. Just sorry enough to feel better and fulfill their Christian obligation with thoughts and prayers.

Years continued to march forward, and the more time passed, the more people forgot about Tate. At least the precise details of his deeds. Tall tales and ghost stories consumed the rest. Lois was granted the nickname *Floppy Mossy*, a cruel title intended to instill shame and humility. Well, she'd be damned. Mossy embraced it, made it her own. By the time she was in her mid-forties, hardly a soul knew the name Lois Greene, and if they did, they certainly didn't relate the name to John Tate. But things have a way of coming full circle. The past—left to its own devices—will always come home. Had her dream, this nightmare, been prophetic? Was Tate rising from the bowels of the crooked tree to return home?

Ain't no fucking way.

Mossy pulled herself from the kitchen table to her living room bookcase. She began to dig through the piles of recipe books, photo albums, and knick-knacks. It was there somewhere, buried in those shelves of memories. At last, she paused. She plucked the small black book from the upper shelf and wiped away the dust from its cover. Returning to the kitchen table, she sat her glasses on the tip of her nose and thumbed through the book.

Her grandmother passed this alleged collection of folk magic and remedies to her mother when Mossy was young, back when Lois Greene was alive. It had been in the family for generations, but there was no way to know how long. Inside were handwritten notes on raising the best crops, recipes for herbal medicines, and, yes, *spells*. Mossy knew folk magic. Everyone in these parts knew. She was never so bold as to say she didn't believe in such things. She had seen firsthand what curses could do to one's family. However, a part of her, the logical part, was skeptical.

In the back of the book, scrawled in her great-grandmother's hillbilly English, were instructions titled *Dead Indetted* [Indebted]. Mossy had always heard if one knew of a soul—preferably a tortured soul that couldn't rest—they could call upon that entity to do them favors. It required a sacrifice, a life given so the dead could rise. Most only needed the gift of your garden variety farm animal—a slain pig or two, even a cow. Others required more energy. Human life was said to bring just about anyone from the ground. Several lives could raise a demon. And Tate was a demon.

But who would want to rip John Tate out of his shackles? Better yet, why?

Mossy rose to her feet and fished the vodka from the freezer. She dumped the lukewarm coffee into the sink and filled the cup. She drank it all at once. A kiss of sunlight popped through her gray windowpane, beaming into her eyes. She didn't know who wanted to call on Tate, but if such a thing were possible, she suspected that every one of those children at the camp was in danger.

As soon as the clock struck eight a.m., Mossy left the house and drove to the gates of Kamp Kromwell to speak to Drummond. She had to see them and ensure they were all alive. She parked at the lower entrance and started up the path toward the dining hall. Her heart felt relieved when she spied old Jack Burns skulking around the main parking lot, holding a rag over his nose and mouth. He glanced at her, shook his head, and returned to work.

"Jack," she called.

"Mossy, I ain't got no time for whatever you're about to go on about," he replied without looking up. "Something's dead out here. Smells godawful."

Mossy had smelled so much decay, she barely noticed. "I need to talk to Earl, Jack. I had—"

"Earl ain't worrying with you today, Mossy. He's up to his tits in crazy-ass kids."

Mossy reached out and took Jack gently by the arm. She did this so gently that it paused him. He turned to her with a stunned expression.

"Jack, I swear to God, it's important." His eyes remained hesitant. "Please!"

Jack's eyebrow rose with suspicion. "Fine. Let's go get him. But you better not start no stuff. Promise?"

"Swear," she assured.

Jack opened the gate. He slid into the passenger seat of Mossy's old pick-up, and they drove up the path toward the dining hall. Jack slipped into the building, and moments later, he emerged with Drummond and Beth. Drummond looked madder than a mosquito in a mannequin factory.

"Now, Earl, take a breath," pleaded Mossy, holding up her hands.

Drummond's hands went to his hips. "I'm in there trying to keep those kids civil enough to get through breakfast, so this better be—" Mossy took him by the hands, and he stopped talking.

"Do you have a boy in this camp named Chester?"

"What?" asked Drummond.

Mossy closed her eyes. "*A boy named Chester.* Is he at this camp? Chester the Jester."

"What did he do?" asked Beth curiously.

Mossy shook her head. "Is he okay?"

Drummond, who had noticed this wasn't one of Mossy's typical stunts, took her by the shoulders. "He's fine, Mossy. Just fine."

"Can I see him?"

Drummond and Beth exchanged glances. "Well, the thing is, Chester isn't here anymore."

"Did something happen to him?"

Drummond shook his head. "No, no. Nothing happened to him. He didn't have a great attitude, so we sent him home last night. His mother came to get him."

"And what does she look like?" asked Mossy. "Does she have brown hair? Shaved around the sides like some punker?"

Drummond looked at Beth with confusion. "No, Mossy, she was . . . blond, I think. Older lady." He saw tears fill Mossy's eyes. "Mossy, honey, I think you better tell me what's wrong."

"I dreamt . . . that boy was dead, Earl. All y'all were. And you were . . ." Finally, she smiled. She rubbed her hands down her tired face. "Apparently, I'm *really* just a crazy old heifer."

Drummond's irritation slipped away. He took a breath and squinted one eye. "Mossy, honey, are you okay?"

She shook her head. She turned to him with glistening eyes. "I don't know anymore, Earl. Sometimes I don't know."

142

Drummond glanced at Beth. "Here," he added. "Tell you what. Why don't you come on in for a minute? Get out of this heat. Have some breakfast with us. Then we can talk in my office, okay?"

Mossy nodded. She glanced at Beth. "Bethany, I am so sorry."

"No, no, no," said Beth as she rubbed Mossy's back. "It's fine, honey. It was just a dream. Don't let it upset you."

Drummond folded his arm around Mossy's shoulder and led her into the building, with Beth trailing close behind. "You need a little kiss?" he asked Mossy, who at last began to chuckle.

They stepped into the dining hall amid the flurry of campers busy with that morning's breakfast, and that's when Mossy froze. She stood there, legs locked, her horrified eyes glaring into the crowd of campers. Drummond paused with confusion, then attempted to lead her to the lunch line, but it was as if the woman had turned to stone.

Beth took hold of Mossy's hand. "This way, Mossy. We go in through that—"

"You *sonuvabitch!*" Mossy suddenly cried. "You goddamn sonuvabitch!" Silence swept through the hall as she raised an accusatory finger. But she wasn't pointing aimlessly into the crowd. She was pointing at one single individual.

Dewayne Burns stood at the edge of one of the long tables with an overflowing dish caddy in his arms. He glanced to his left and then to his right. He smirked with a perplexed grin and turned to see whom the woman was addressing. Dewyane realized he was the target when he saw the fury in her eyes. It was the crazy woman from the market whose cigarettes he had stolen.

"Mossy," said Drummond. "What's the—"

Mossy marched forward, stomping toward Dewayne like an angry rhinoceros, her arms pumping back and forth, nostrils flaring. Drummond reached forward to snare her, but she slipped through his fingers before he could take hold of her. Dewayne dropped the caddy to the floor with a crash and began to scurry away as Mossy pawed at his shirttail.

Jack rushed through the hall and snatched his nephew by the shoulder before Dewayne slipped into the kitchen. "Woah, woah, woah!" said Jack. "What is happening?"

Drummond seized Mossy from behind and held her in place.

"You little fucker!" she hissed.

"Okay! Someone needs to tell me what happened!" Jack announced as his nephew fought to escape.

"Get her away from me!" yelled Dewayne.

Mossy's finger snapped forward. "You! You murdered my cat!"

"What?" asked Dewayne, his voice raising an octave higher.

"I *told* Dunham it wasn't one of the Stevenson kids! Someone passing through. Horseshit! *You* killed my Rascal," Mossy added as tears streamed down her face. "Thief! You robbed me and then ran my cat down!" Drummond could feel Mossy's ribs catch with emotion. "And you didn't even stop. You didn't . . . even stop!"

"I did not!" yelled Dewayne.

Jack turned Dewayne around and glared into his eyes. "Explain."

"I didn't—"

"I said, explain, boy!" commanded Jack.

"I didn't steal anything, and I sure as hell didn't run over any cat."

"Liar!" Mossy bellowed. She looked at Jack. "You can ask Jody at the market, Jack. She saw the whole thing." Mossy began to cry. "And then, he ran my Rascal down and just . . . left us there." She slipped from Drummond's arms and melted into a weeping puddle on the floor.

Everyone's eyes moved to Dewayne, who gazed into the judgmental faces, unable to clarify or justify his actions. "I didn't know the cat was dead," was all he could manage.

Jack frowned at his nephew and pointed toward the kitchen. "Get in the kitchen."

"I didn't—" Dewayne attempted.

"*Get. In. The. Kitchen!*" Jack boomed, and Dewayne turned to leave.

Drummond bent down to help Mossy to her feet, and she shook him away. "Get off me!" she spat. She rustled to her feet, her face wet with tears. She straightened her ragged garments and raised her hand toward Dewayne. "You don't know it yet, *boy* . . . but retribution is coming."

"Mossy," said Drummond quietly. "We'll deal with him."

"Oh, he'll be dealt with, alright," she corrected as she wiped her face. "John will take care of him."

Drummond turned to face her. "Now, don't start that crap, Mossy. *Please.* I told you, we'll take care—"

"I'll call up old John." Mossy slowly stepped forward, eyes locked on Dewayne, who stood before her trembling like a newborn foal. "Rise to greet me, old John Tate. I have a job for you."

"Mossy, stop it," said Drummond.

She crept forward, indifferent to Drummond's plea, her eyes fixed on the boy. "I call upon your wicked soul to do what I can't do. Take your rusty bone axe and go hunt my enemies down."

"Mossy!" Drummond said as he took her by the arm.

"'cause the deal ain't done until they join you in the ground." She paused in front of Dewayne, who shied from her gaze. "Rise to greet me, old John Tate. You have some work to do." She raised a crooked finger to Dewayne's face. *"Old John Tate gonna rise on up. He's gonna rise on up . . . for you."*

16

4:55 P.M.

I'm unsure if it was Asia's flair for the dramatic or his determination to have his shining moment. Following the events of Field Day, he became obsessed with Kromwell Talent Night. For two solid days, it was literally all he talked about. He provided as much detail as possible without giving any specifics whatsoever. I had no idea what "talent" he planned to unveil at the event, but Asia intended it to be memorable. There was one small problem: whatever he planned to showcase couldn't be done without something from his home in Johnson City, the mysterious *red suitcase*.

Kamp Kromwell had a strict "no electronics" policy. No television sets were on site, and campers couldn't bring things like Nintendo Game Boys or portable CD players onto the campus. Mr. Drummond stated this was intended to "cultivate an environment of camaraderie" between the campers, who may otherwise isolate themselves.

While internal phones were scattered throughout the grounds for communication, there were only three accessible phones with external lines: one in the nurse's cabin, one at the stables, and Drummond's office phone. All campers were permitted two parental check-in phone calls each week, emergencies aside, all made from Drummond's phone. This presented a couple of problems for Asia. For one, his next phone call wasn't scheduled until the day after the talent event. Secondly, the call he wanted to make wasn't to his parents. It was to call his cousin, Lisa, the only living soul around who knew the mysteries of the red suitcase.

Asia pleaded with Beth to use the phone, but she wasn't going for it. She asked what was in the red suitcase. Asia wouldn't budge. Beth concluded it would be "unfair" to the other contestants, who would have to use whatever they could find on-site for their talent. Asia tried to convince Beth that the suitcase contained nothing magical, but she wouldn't bite. He'd simply have to make do with what he had access to on campus. But Asia had no intention of making do.

The phone at the stables was out of the question. Susan Brooks practically lived with those horses, and her office door had a deadbolt lock. And with the steady stream of patients flowing in and out of Nurse Conrad's cabin, the phone in her personal quarters was also inaccessible. Drummond's office, however, remained unlocked most of the time. The man wasn't a stickler for organization. Papers and invoices were always strewn around the desks. The only secure location in his office was the two file cabinets, which always remained locked tight.

Getting into Drummond's office would be no problem. Getting into it without *being seen*—well, that was another feat altogether. We had to pick a time when nearly everyone would be away from the square. The sunny afternoon seemed a good choice since everyone would be busy swimming at Lake Ellington or waiting for their turn at the jet skis. Unfortunately, this meant I would go without seeing Dan Thorogood in those loose swimming trunks of his, but it was a sacrifice I was willing to make for Asia.

With nearly everyone rushing to the water, Asia nodded to me, and the two of us casually slipped away from the group. To avoid suspicion, we navigated behind the buildings lining the square. Once at the dining hall, we crept around the left side of the building. Mr. Burns and Dewayne would likely be in the kitchen preparing for the evening's dinner, so we had to enter through the front. Ducking into the foyer, we tip-toed through the dining hall and pressed against the far wall. As we neared the hallway, Asia turned to me. We nodded in unison and turned into the hall.

Dewayne stepped from the men's restroom, and we froze. Quickly, Asia took me by the arm and pulled me into the women's room at the opposite end of the hallway. We held the door ajar and watched. Dewayne paused, glancing at his hands as if he had forgotten to wash them. For a moment, I thought he would turn around and return to the restroom. Finally, he shrugged, wiped his hands on his shorts, and walked away. Asia and I turned to one another with disgust.

With Dewayne no longer a threat, Asia reached toward the door. A toilet flushed behind us, and our eyes widened. The lock of the far stall popped open, and out stepped Nurse Conrad. She walked to the sink, washed her hands, and snatched a paper towel from the shelf. Finally, she turned toward us. Conrad stood without expression as we cowered before her like two wounded fowls looking at a starving wolf. Asia's mouth popped open to provide an explanation. Conrad raised her hand.

"I don't care," she whispered. The woman stepped past us and exited the restroom as though we weren't there.

Once Conrad disappeared around the corner, we rushed from the restroom and slipped into Drummond's office. Asia approached the desk as I gently closed the office door. He dialed the phone.

"Aunt Lulu," popped Asia. I nudged his side. "Aunt Lulu," he repeated in a whisper. "It's Alberto . . . No, no, everything's alright . . . I'm okay; Paul is okay . . . Where's Lisa?" A moment passed. "Lisa! . . . Listen, listen, listen; I need you to do me a favor. A *big, big* favor . . . Would you be a darling and bring my red suitcase up here?" I heard the voice on the other side of the line yell, and Asia's head began to weave like a cobra preparing to strike. "*Because I need it* . . . For a talent show . . . The one we're having at camp." His voice raised. "Because I didn't *know* we were having a talent show, now did I?"

"Hush!" I hissed.

He covered the phone and mouthed the word *sorry*. "Lisa!" Asia pleaded. "Come on! Please! I really, *really* need it . . . I didn't tell Lulu anything about Junior staying over, now did I?" There was a moment of silence, and Asia grinned. "And I didn't say anything about the joint in your car, now did I?" Still, there was silence. At last, I heard the voice on the line reply. Asia smiled. "*I love you*. Love, love, love you. Thank—"

Suddenly, a light scattered across the ceiling tiles in the hallway. I clutched Asia's wrist. "Shit!" I muttered.

"Gotta go," Asia said. "Love-ya-bye." He slipped the receiver back into the cradle and turned to me.

We heard footfalls coming down the hallway and the sound of muttering voices beyond the door. It was Drummond. My eyes searched the room, trying to find some means of escape. Taking Asia by the wrist, I pulled him behind Beth's vacant desk, and we wedged ourselves between the chair and the leg rest. The office light came on, filling the room with bright, fluorescent light.

". . . know why this is such a big deal," said the voice of Dewayne Burns.

"Because it's a big deal," Mr. Burns replied.

"You gentlemen have a seat," offered Drummond.

I peeked through the bars of Beth's desk to see three sets of legs entering the office, which, by their voices, I assumed to belong to Drummond, Mr. Burns, and Dewayne. There was the rustle of chairs, the grinding of rusty desk wheels, and a pause. Asia reached forward and took hold of my shoulder. He pointed at the toe of my shoe, where the light fell across the white leather. I pulled my knee upward against my chin.

"Dewayne," began Drummond. "Let me begin by saying you've done an excellent job here. For the most part, you've stayed out of trouble. Beyond the incident with Bonnie Evans and this *thing* with Mossy, you've kept your nose clean. You've done what's been asked of you."

Asia and I looked at each other and smiled. *What incident with Bonnie Evans?*

"I can understand the attraction that two young people have to each other," Drummond continued. "While it is against the rules for campus employees to date—"

"We're not dating," Dewayne corrected.

"You two were pawing all over each other in the pantry," spat Mr. Burns. "That's dating enough in my book."

Asia squeezed my arm so tightly that I thought it would detach.

"Whatever," Dewayne replied. "She came onto me."

Drummond sighed. "I hardly think that's the point, Dewayne."

"She did!" Dewayne added. "She may act all high-and-mighty, but she's a freak. She's into some weird stuff, man. Trust me. She wanted to—"

This level of information is what Asia referred to as "tea," and it was nearly too much for either of us to take, especially Asia, who I thought would spontaneously combust with glee at any moment.

"*Either way,*" Drummond interrupted. "Intimate relationships between employees, regardless of type, are frowned upon."

"We didn't do anything," Dewayne said. "And I can assure you, I'm not getting around that girl again, ever. Promise. And what about her? Are you doing anything about her?"

Drummond cleared his throat. "Bonnie is being dealt with. I can assure you. I could ignore the incident with Miss Evans; I can't ignore what happened with Mossy." Silence. "Why don't you tell me what happened?"

"It's not my fault," Dewayne immediately said.

"Just tell me what happened," Drummond urged.

Dewayne sighed. "I stopped at the market to get some smokes. The lady behind the counter gave me the last pack. I stepped from the counter to get a soda, and that Mossy lady got in line. The clerk let *her* buy *my* cigarettes, knowing that was the last pack of Marlboro."

"And you asked Mossy for them," Drummond said.

"Outside, yes. I offered to pay her twice what they were worth if she'd sell them. But she started being a smartass. She was going to charge me twenty-five dollars for them! That's crazy!"

Mr. Burns sighed. "That's how it works, son. She bought them, fair and square. They were hers to do with as she pleased. If she wanted to charge a hundred bucks for them, that was her prerogative. You had no right to take them from her and speak to her like you did."

"You ought to hear what she said to me!" Dewayne cried.

"Well . . . knowing Mossy, I could only imagine," Drummond said.

"You best be lucky the old bird didn't shoot you in the ass," said Mr. Burns. "She's about half crazy."

"Dewayne, continue," urged Drummond. "You were outside with Mossy. She was jacking up the price of the cigarettes. Then what?"

Dewayne hesitated. "I told her to shove them. Then I got in my car and peeled out of there." Silence filled the room. "I didn't see the cat," he added softly. "Uncle Jack, you know I'd pop just about anyone in the jaw for looking at me cross-eyed, but I would never, ever hurt some animal. Even some old mangy cat on its last leg, to begin with."

Again, an uneasy silence filled the room. I could hear this *tick-tick-tick* sound as if someone was tapping a pencil against wood in contemplation. My overextended knee was forcing my foot to run numb. I could feel the pricking tingle setting into my ankle.

"I didn't mean to hurt the cat," Dewayne said again.

"I don't think you did," Drummond conceded. "Sheriff Dunham called me this afternoon. He said that Mossy has agreed to drop all charges for the stolen cigarettes *and* the loss of her cat."

Just then, my leg jerked without provocation or expectation. The heel of my shoe bumped against the side of Beth's desk. Asia pulled me closer. I felt the heat of panic rise along my neck and flush my face.

"Well, awesome," said Dewayne, obviously not hearing the noise.

"*If* we let you go," Drummond finished.

"Man, you can't be serious," Dewayne chuckled. "She wants me fired?"

"Son, your record can't handle anything else," Mr. Burns added. "What other choice is there?"

"Dewayne, it's not the best solution, but it's the only one we got. You are more than welcome to come back next year. But I think to keep things calm and to keep Sheriff Dunham out of the mix, we need to act." Dewayne didn't reply. "It's for the best."

"What about Judge Harrison?" asked Dewayne.

The word "judge" caused Asia and I to exchange stunned glances.

"Let me talk to your uncle about that," said Drummond. "We'll think of something. Either way, it's better to be let go than to have some other charge added to your record."

Dewayne paused. "Guess that's that, then."

I heard the three of them rise to their feet. Footsteps moved toward the office door. The lights went dark, and the door closed with a click. I heard the key turn the lock. At last, I allowed my knee to slip forward. It unlocked like a rusty hinge. I felt the rush of blood returning to my foot, sending sparks of awareness along the flesh. Asia leaned forward as if he was going to crawl from our hiding place, but I held onto him.

"Not yet," I whispered.

He rolled his eyes and slithered back into place. After several minutes, I nodded, and we crawled from underneath Beth's desk. Asia placed his hands on the floor and smiled.

"I cannot *believe* Bonnie was into Dewayne," said Asia, rising to his feet. "I was sure that girl was going to be a *nun*. What if she's some S&M dominatrix or something? Ooh! What if she's starred in porn fli—"

"Why must you always go to the edge?" I huffed, crawling forward. "What do you think Dewayne did to—"

I turned to see Asia's mouth dangling open. Drummond stood just inside the doorway of the darkened room, twirling his keys on his finger. He smiled.

"I thought I heard a couple of rats running around the desks."

17

FREE BIRD

Crazy bitch. Dewayne trudged back and forth through the cabin, gathering his things and tossing them into his gym bag. He didn't know he had killed the fucking cat. No matter how nuts the old broad was, he would never have done something like that on purpose. No one would ever believe that, of course, but that didn't make it any less accurate. Hoodlum, yes. Opportunist, why not? Womanizer, absolutely! Killer? Mowing down animals with cars? No. Never. Though many could argue the point, Dewayne Burns was not heartless. He wasn't quite the prick everyone believed him to be. Or rather, the prick he *wanted* others to believe him to be. He knew what loss felt like. He knew.

In the summer of 1988, Dewayne noticed an old sheepdog wandering through the neighborhood, a thin, frail thing that would appear now and again in various places, sniffing through garbage, pilfering through parking lots, or lying in the cool shade of trees. One day, Dewayne's mother gave him a pot of stew she wanted him to throw out. Typically, he would take discarded food to the trees lining the back of his house and dump it, returning the container to his mother to wash. But on this day, he noticed that old dog lying by the bushes and decided there was someone who would enjoy the leftovers more than the bushes. From that moment, the dog was bound to Dewayne, who named the dog *Radar*.

The name just came to him, mainly because one of the dog's ears always stood to attention while the other flopped loosely about. That entire summer, Dewayne and Radar were inseparable. The two went everywhere together. Dewayne, who didn't have a good many friends, loved his new companion even though he smelled less than stellar and had more than his share of fleas. Dewayne's mother never allowed the dog into the house, but Radar seemed content to remain at his makeshift doghouse in the backyard, where he would retire each night, waiting on the morning sun to bring his little friend out to play.

Dewayne's stepfather hated the dog, loathed it. Dewayne never knew why. The only reason he could think of was that the dog brought Dewayne joy, and things that brought Dewayne joy seemed to infuriate his stepfather, who was a bastard of biblical proportions. Richard Midkiff, known as Richie by his drinking buddies, was a vile alcoholic with an unparalleled talent for verbal abuse. The man delighted in tormenting Dewayne and took every opportunity to do just that. Richie was smart enough to know that laying a hand directly on Dewayne would have gotten his ass thrown out on the street. So, instead, he found other ways to torment Dewayne. Most of the time, it was name-calling, yelling, and threats, and that was enough.

One summer afternoon, Richie was in rare form. He hunted Dewayne down and demanded that he clear his afternoon to mow the grass. As usual, Dewayne complied. Halfway through the task, the mower ran dry of gas. Noticing the gas can also was empty, Dewayne went to find Richie, who by noon was already six beers into a case of Michelob. Ritchie mumbled he would get gas, so Dewayne continued his day until he could finish his chore. Oddly enough, Ritchie didn't inquire about the yard for the remainder of the day, and Dewayne was okay with that. Until the next morning.

As usual, Dewayne awoke and filled a bowl with dog food to take to Radar. But as he neared the doghouse, he could sense something was terribly wrong. The dog, who would typically wag his whole body at the mere sight of Dewayne, now lay on his side motionless. Stepping closer, Dewayne could see Radar wasn't breathing. He stood there for nearly ten minutes, staring at the dead animal beside the bowl of watery green liquid. Infuriated, Dewayne burst into the house, demanding to know what happened to his dog. Ritchie was pleased to inform Dewayne that he had fed the dog antifreeze.

"Maybe without that fucking dog to distract you, you can get the yard done," Ritchie said with a smirk of satisfaction.

Dewayne stood there, stunned, disbelieving anyone could be so callous and heartless that they would murder a defenseless animal. The only positive thing from Radar's passing was that it gave Dewayne's mother the final push she needed to toss Ritchie out in the street. Dewayne believed that Radar knew his death would be the last straw, that the dog sacrificed his own life to rid Dewayne of Richard Midkiff's odious presence. It felt better that way.

Dewayne tossed his jeans into his bag. *I wouldn't have killed your cat on purpose, lady. You? Maybe. But your mangy ass cat?* And now he had to return home and face the consequences, his mother, and most of all, Judge Harrison, who would want to know how Dewayne had lost such a cushy service job. Drummond said he would handle it, but what could Drummond do? Dewayne would have to finish his service some other way, picking up trash, cleaning graffiti, or scooping dead animals off the road. *Animals like Radar.*

The cabin door opened, and Dewayne paused. His Uncle Jack poked his head into the room. "Better hurry it up," said Jack coldly. "Gonna start the campfires. I'll come down and unlock the gate for you in a few minutes."

Dewayne nodded. "Uncle Jack," he said just as Jack was about to leave. Jack looked at him and sighed. "I took her cigarettes. I did. She was being a nutty bitch, and I took them. It was a dick move, and I can't change it. But I didn't . . . I would've never run over her cat on purpose. You know I wouldn't have killed her cat."

At last, Jack's face softened, and he sighed. "I know, kid," he said. "The woman's crazier than hell, dammit."

"What am I gonna tell Mom?"

Jack shrugged. "The truth wouldn't hurt. Tell her the truth. And don't worry about the community service thing. We'll find something else." Dewayne looked to the floor, and Jack could feel the shame emanating from his nephew. He sighed again and entered the cabin. Walking up to Dewayne, he put his arms around the boy's shoulders and hugged him. "You just need to make better decisions, kid. Think. Okay?"

"Okay," said Dewayne.

Jack patted Dewayne's back. "Now, you be careful going home. Call the office when you get there and let me know you made it."

"Okay."

With that, Jack turned and left the cabin. Dewayne tossed his Converse shoes into his bag, zipped it, and yanked it from his bed. He took one last look at the bunk and stepped into the dusk. He looked up into the cloudy sky, searching for the fabric of sparkling stars. That was one thing he hadn't really appreciated at Kromwell. Looking at the stars. Somehow, they appeared different in the mountains, closer, more brilliant. That night, unfortunately, clouds hung low in the sky, shielding the stars from view. Even so, the crickets sang a wanting tune, and the cicadas whirred high in the tree branches. There were still things in nature to appreciate.

As he made his way down the main road, he could hear the bustle and laughter ringing through the surrounding trees, and suddenly he found himself filled with regret. Kromwell hadn't been such a shit job. In fact, it had been kind of fun, sometimes entertaining. He'd even go so far as to say he'd miss it. He'd miss working with his uncle each day. He'd miss being out in nature's elements. And he would undoubtedly miss Bonnie. *Yeah, Bonnie.* She had been the most fun of all. She had been fun at least *three* times, though he'd never tell a soul.

Bonnie had immediately liked Dewayne; he could sense it. He didn't care how *holier-than-thou* the girl claimed to be; she wanted him. It was clear she liked the bad boys, and Dewayne's jerk persona, exaggerated though it may have been, had been enough to bring the virgin to the villain. Behaving like a gentleman certainly hadn't gotten him any attention from girls throughout his life. But the second he turned himself into a punk, ladies seemed to crawl out of the woodwork like termites of temptation.

Bonnie wasn't what Dewayne would have called "girlfriend material," though. Sure, she was hot. And, oh, yes, she knew how to have fun. However, there was something off about the girl, something he couldn't pinpoint. It was as if she was two different people, a good girl in the light of day and a ravenous temptress in the darkness of night. Most guys would have found that hot, and Dewayne did, but her total commitment to each persona made him ill at ease. When Bonnie was good, she was perfect. And when she was bad, she was fucking awful. It was light and dark, yin and yang. Good and evil? Maybe. Still, he would miss Bonnie most of all.

By the time Dewayne reached the parking lot, night had fallen upon the grounds, casting dark, moonlit shadows that stretched along the grass like murky hands clawing into the earth. He removed his keys from his pocket, unlocked his car, and tossed his satchel into the trunk. Then he closed it and hoisted himself onto the car's hood to await his uncle. And he waited. And he waited some more. After nearly forty-five minutes, Dewayne's patience was running thin.

"Sonuvabitch," he muttered. "Hello!" he called out. "Could whoever's going to unlock this damn gate come on? I'd like to make it home before midnight." There was no reply. He chuckled. "Mr. Drummond sucks ass!" he added with a laugh. He looked up at the clouds again, wishing they would dissipate so he could see the stars. Sure, you could see stars in the city, but they always looked so much brighter in the freedom of nature. They looked like—

Pop!

The crack of breaking twigs under footfalls caught Dewayne's attention. He turned to peer into the darkness. His ears perked, amplifying the amphibious murmur of toads nesting in the lake. Yet, there was no movement. Only sound. A warm breeze crept forward, wrapping around him like a warm blanket. Suddenly, Dewayne sensed he wasn't alone.

"Hello?" he called out. "Alright, I'm in no mood for this shit, guys. Just open the gate, and I'll get the fuck out of your hair."

Pop!

In the dark shadows, someone was there watching him, *hunting* him. Slowly, Dewayne slid from the hood of his car and fished his keys from his pocket. He unlocked the front door and slipped inside, slamming the door behind him. With a bang, his fist came down on the lock, and he took a deep, relaxing breath.

"Motherfuckers," he whispered.

He slipped the keys into the ignition and switched on the battery. Without warning, the radio illuminated with that Guns & Roses' *Welcome To The Jungle* scream. Dewayne gasped and nearly busted through the roof of the car. Covering an ear with one hand, he fought for the volume knob and silenced the blaring music.

"God!" he whispered as his racing heartbeat began to stabilize. "I gotta start listening to Barry Manilow or some shit."

Bam!

"P-p-p-piss! F-f-fuckface!" screamed Dewayne with an unconscious stutter as he spun toward the driver's side window. Jack stood there with a smile on his face. Dewayne rolled down the window. "Dammit, Jack!"

"Listen to the mouth on you, boy," chuckled Jack. "Okay, let me unlock this. Now, call when you get home."

"I will, I will," said Dewayne with a nod.

Dewayne exited the gates and waved to Jack as he turned down that long, winding road leading him to the interstate. He reached for the radio and turned the dial to E-Z 97.5, the Adult Contemporary station. The soothing sounds of Lynyrd Skynyrd sang Free Bird over the hissing speakers. *Yeah, that's better. That's the mood tonight.*

Ahead he spied the on-ramp to the highway. He glanced in his passenger's side mirror and merged right.

"*But if I stay here with you, girl,*" he sang in his off-key dribble. "*Things just couldn't be the same. 'cause I'm as free as a bird now.*"

Dewayne reached for the rearview mirror. When he noticed the dark figure creeping forward from the backseat of his car, it was too late. He jerked the wheel to the right, veering from the road and burrowing into the row of bushes lining the street.

"Fuck! Fuck!" he hissed as he reached for the door.

A hand jutted forward and wrapped around Dewayne's forehead. The other hand began to push something cold and sharp against his neck. As the jagged metal sank through his flesh and into the spine at the base of his skull, he felt his legs disconnect from the rest of his body and turn limp, like useless logs of meat. The instrument sank deeper into his flesh, burrowing through the muscles and arteries. He opened his mouth to scream as the steel slipped into his larynx, silencing his cry. A red glimmer caught his eye. His horrified eyes rolled downward, peering at the blood-drenched arrowhead protruding through his torn esophagus. As the warm blood poured down his chest, Dewayne's head fell limply against his door, and his eyes rolled upward. The clouds had gone, leaving only the heavens in his view.

The stars.

They looked like . . . diamonds. Diamonds set against black satin cloth.

18

5:38 P.M.

"I have one thing to say: you betta work!"
—Supermodel (You Better Work): RuPaul—

Asia and I managed to forgo harsh punishment for breaking into Drummond's office. With Dewayne gone, Drummond placed Asia and me on kitchen duty with Mr. Burns, which Rosetta would oversee. The two of us assumed rotating schedules throughout our stay at Kromwell, and Rosetta would be sure we were present for every shift. Asia would help Jack prepare breakfast and clean up each morning, and I would do the same for each dinner run. After opening my third tub of freeze-dried onions that smelled like my brother's feet, I would rather have been buggy whipped.

Drummond forbade Asia and me from speaking about anything we had overheard while cowering in his office, a simple request we readily ignored. I had never "served the tea" before. Having that level of gossip at my disposal led to a feeling of enormous power I had never known. I wasn't the only knight wielding this sword, of course. But Asia didn't serve tea at all. Not even a leaf. He was too preoccupied with the red suitcase to have time for idle scandal.

I didn't see much of the suitcase's contents. Asia seemed very protective of it. Occasionally, I would spy a wandering glimmer of sequins or a shine of glitter, all of which left me wanting. When I would ask what it contained, Asia would only say, "You'll have to wait for her." I had no idea who *she* was, but she was apparently getting ready to wow the campers during the talent event.

The closest I came to knowing what Asia had in store was when Paul mentioned a word I had only heard on rare occasions: *Drag*. I had heard the term in my youth and thought it meant a man in women's clothes. It represented nothing more than a ten-dollar Halloween wig, a cheap thrift store dress, and gaudy blue Cover Girl eyeshadow. The antics of Benny Hill, Bugs Bunny, and Klinger from *M*A*S*H* reinforced this ideology. Of course, in those days, I had no idea that "drag queen" was an art form, something far removed from typical transvestism. Oddly enough, that realization would come to me later through MTV.

In the crisp autumn of 1993, well before my encounter with Sam Barnes, I remember sitting in the living room with my older brother Bruno as my mother and sister prepared for the following day's Thanksgiving festivities. I was thumbing through the Sears holiday catalog. MTV was playing because it was a time when MTV aired music videos in regular rotation instead of soundbites heavily seasoned with reality television.

I was pulled from the pages filled with that year's hottest toys when I heard a sassy voice exclaim, "You betta work!" On the screen was a very tall blonde woman parading to an up-tempo club rhythm. By the tone and tenor of the voice, it didn't take long for me to realize that it was a man wrapped in women's designer fashion. I sat there enamored by the sight, captivated by it, stunned that this wasn't some campy charade intended to garner laughs from the audience, but a flair, a showcase, a vehicle of elegance capable only by a species as unique as the unicorn. I didn't realize it at the time, but I was *proud*.

Seeing that RuPaul only had "one thing to say," I informed Bruno that the blonde woman dancing on the screen was a dude. I watched my brother stare vacantly at the screen, intently studying RuPaul for any signs of apparent masculinity and finding none. For a moment, I thought his head was going to cave in. He appeared attracted to and terrified by the fascinating figure singing on the screen, and I loved it. To this day, I don't know why I said anything to my brother. My mother would later call it "being a smartass," and maybe she was right. Bruno, who was often clueless about the world around him, would have gone the rest of his life not knowing RuPaul's actual name was *RuPaul Andre Charles*. I think there was this particular flavor of satisfaction in my knowing something that Bruno did not, something related to this *"wondermous"* world of unicorns, which both fascinated and frightened him.

While my involvement with drag would remain detached for some years, my first glimpse at seeing a drag queen in person would take place that evening during the Kromwell Talent Show. We all gathered in the auditorium next to the dining hall for what was sure to be a grand gala extravaganza that would rival even the most overly produced Oscar ceremony. Nurse Conrad, Mr. Burns, and Beth Hawkins were judging the competition.

The camp counselors opened the show that evening with a raucous rendition of *Let's Hear It For The Boy* by Deniece Williams. A girl from Rosetta's cabin played the piano while Bonnie and Rosetta sang an off-key duet dedicated to a manly supporting cast.

First up was Dennis, dressed as a very unamused policeman. I don't think Dennis moved his feet while the girls pranced and sang around him. Next came Danny, who wore a sailor's uniform—a rather tight-fitting sailor's uniform, I might add. He walked to each end of the small stage, posing for the audience while they cheered him on. Last but certainly not least was Mr. Drummond in a *fireman's outfit*, of all things. At first, we could sense that Drummond was very uncomfortable being on stage, but the more we applauded and cheered him on, the more into it he became. By the end of the number, Drummond was flexing in manly poses and smiling brightly.

Next to the stage was this chick named Judy Satterfield from Rosetta's cabins, who I think performed some kind of sign-language/ballet montage to the song *Somewhere Over The Rainbow* by Patti Labelle. At least, I think it was sign language. She pirouetted so much it was hard to tell at times. There was a moment where I believed she would twirl so that she would summon a funnel cloud that would whisk away the entire camp to the merry old land of Oz.

Of course, as with any authentic talent showcase at summer camp, there had to be at least one disqualification, which Drummond awarded to David *Something-Or-Other* for his humorous rendition of *Do-Wah-Diddy* by 2 Live Crew. Since the melody sounded familiar to everyone, it took Drummond a moment to realize that David was singing verses teeming with obscenities instead of the classic upbeat tale of love performed initially by Manfred Mann in the sixties. David wasn't on stage long but sang enough to complete at least one perverse verse before Drummond chased him off the stage.

Following this lurid display came a handful of mediocre performances, including a magic act with an overzealous rabbit, a dramatic reading of Hamlet, and a baton/hula-hoop combo performed to Michael Jackson's *PYT*. Beyond this, the show was primarily forgettable translations of top forty pop hits, boiled down to their most elemental chord progressions against caterwauling vocals.

Oddly enough, not one of these numbers featured Asia Demarco. The Krew and I wondered if Asia had decided to back out of the show entirely until, at last, we heard a muffled bass drum rumbling through the dark hall. The heavily sampled drumbeat continued to build for over a minute while lights surrounding the stage flickered and pulsed, leading the audience to clap in rhythm. A muffled voice on the track suddenly echoed, "*See, what we're gonna do right here is go back,*" and the curious audience began to stand. At last, the voices started to sing.

All over my body, I wanna feel your body all over my body . . .

At that moment, Asia Demarco stepped through the curtains and onto the stage, greeted by stunned faces. He, or rather *she*, wore a black robe that hung down to her shiny boots with six-inch heels. Her face was without flaw. In fact, if not for his trademark smile, I wouldn't have known who was underneath the makeup. Asia ripped away the robe as the music exploded, revealing a one-piece outfit covered in sequins and glittering tassels. He kicked his leg up, grabbed his ankle, and fell into an impressive vertical split without missing a beat. The entire auditorium erupted.

As the song played on, Asia danced like I had seen no one dance before. It was choreographed perfection, not unlike those performed by the likes of Janet Jackson or Madonna, but something more, something fiercer, unhinged. The song broke down, and she leaped from the stage onto the floor, kicking her left leg higher than any Rockette had dared kick and falling into yet another split. She mouthed the song with perfection, never missing a syllable, so much so that sometimes it seemed as if she was the one singing.

She paraded through the audience, stopping momentarily to grace some with her presence, especially Lynn Reynolds, who appeared like a lost puppy without his partner in crime. She paused in front of Lynn and gave us a seductive wink. Instantly, I spied that familiar confusion in Lynn's eyes, that same bewilderment that had been in my brother's eyes years before when he wasn't sure if he should find RuPaul attractive or repulsive. She blew Lynn a kiss before returning to the stage, and he *smiled*. I realized then that Lynn Reynolds had no idea who this person was. But this was not Alberto Deleno Demarco.

This was *Asia*.

And Asia was a star.

Once Asia's number came to its riotous conclusion, Mr. Drummond spent nearly two minutes trying to quieten the auditorium. Asia had managed to whip the campers into a feverish fervor. We had all just attended a concert, an unexpected presentation from a brand-new artist who had taken the music industry by storm, and everyone was enraptured, even the few boys who were confused by the feelings they were having.

"Okay, okay," said Drummond as he took the stage. He raised his hands. "Everyone . . . calm down, please." The cheering began to subside. "Could we have each contestant back on stage, please?" The competitors gathered onto the stage, and Drummond turned to the judge's table. "Beth, are we ready?"

Beth, Mr. Burns, and Nurse Conrad huddled together. After a moment of hushed conversation, Beth marked down the evening's winners on a piece of paper and walked toward the stage. Drummond took the form from her hand and turned toward the contestants.

Drummond cleared his throat. "Here we go. Now, for the third-place ribbon and one large pizza from Gondolier Pizzeria, we have . . . Judy Satterfield for her rendition of *Over The Rainbow*." The audience lightly applauded. Judy smiled with excitement and took the ribbon from Mr. Drummond. "Congratulations, Judy," he added. "For the second-place ribbon and fifty dollars cash, we have . . . Keith Marks and his rabbit, Hocus." Keith bowed and stepped to Drummond as the crowd offered applause. Incidentally, Hocus disappeared some three minutes into Keith's act, never to be seen again. Drummond stepped to the edge of the stage. "And now, for the first-prize trophy and one hundred dollars cash, we have—"

"*You're all gonna die!*" cried a voice from the rear of the auditorium.

Stunned, everyone spun to see Mossy standing in the auditorium doorway, covered in mud and leaves. A wild expression of panicked horror was on her face. Before another sound was heard, a flood of ravens poured through the open doors like a black fog of feathers.

Everyone began to scream.

19

DEAD MAN'S PARTY

Suzanne Dunham dropped the phone onto the cradle and rolled her eyes. She glanced at the cuckoo clock hanging on the living room wall. Eight thirty-seven p.m. Rising from the recliner, she moaned and entered the kitchen to prepare the evening coffee. She wasn't going to wake Fred one minute before nine; she didn't give a damn what Earl Drummond claimed Mossy allegedly found. *Crazy old bat.*

As sheriff of Jasper Mill, Fred had to sleep in shifts. If things were going to go awry—and they did at least twice each week—problems began around two a.m., when the local watering holes bolted their doors for the night. Things were rarely violent or uncontrolled, mind you. Local law enforcement primarily served as the arbiter of disputes, called to settle disagreements on anything from property lines to unreciprocated favors. There was always someone somewhere who wasn't happy with their situation, and Suzanne knew Mossy was the least satisfied of all.

The population seemed to drift into an unconscious state of peace from six to eleven a.m., before noontime tempers flared. This gave her husband a split shift of slumber. Fred could usually rest his head in the morning from six until ten and then again in the evening from around six until nine. Outside of those meager hours, duty called. It wasn't a perfect, undisturbed sleep, but it was sleep, and Suzanne wouldn't steal a minute of it.

Contrary to popular belief, the problem wasn't Mossy. The problem was people like Earl Drummond, who entertained dramatics from Mossy more than anyone should. If it were up to Suzanne—and it wasn't—she would have thrown the nutjob in jail for trespassing, disturbing the peace, or just being one outlandishly ridiculous heifer. But not Drummond. Obviously, the man held some unspoken sympathy for Mossy, compassion for this isolated woman who had only herself in the world. But, just like Suzanne's grannie would say, if someone is all alone, there's usually a good reason for it. And Suzanne could see plenty enough reason to stay clear of Mossy.

The Dunhams had moved to Jasper Mill with hopeful hearts twelve years before. A seven-year veteran of the Knoxville Police Department, Fred had heard of a small-town job that offered the opportunity for advancement without the noise of city life. At first, Suzanne was apprehensive about such a move. Then she saw the house. The area seemed so peaceful and serene that it called to her, beckoning her to become one with its tranquil solitude. The place they would eventually call home sat at the lower edge of Lake Ellington, a two-story rancher boasting over two thousand square feet of living space, which would have quickly gone for twice the price in a town like Knoxville. The move would also place them two hours away from Suzanne's in-laws, which was glorious. It would be so lovely to live in a place where Fred's opinionated mother couldn't just "pop by" whenever the woman was in the mood to berate Suzanne on anything, from Suzanne's approach to housekeeping to her biological inability to bear children. The latter of these subjects filled Suzanne with the desire to toss hot soup on the old crone. In a way, albeit a small way, Mossy reminded Suzanne of her mother-in-law.

Suzanne had first laid eyes on Mossy at Simmons Grocery, nestled some thirty minutes away in the more urban part of town where temptations were plentiful and sinners were in abundance. Simmons was the only place where one could find everything one needed, and on that day, Mossy apparently needed birdseed, lots and lots of birdseed. No one quite knew the reason.

Suzanne spied the oddly dressed figure in aisle ten, piling seed bags into her wobbly cart. The woman, who Suzanne suspected to be homeless, was having great difficulty fetching the last sack of grain from the upper shelf. Eager to be neighborly, Suzanne left her cart parked on the side of the aisle and joined the woman.

"That's my seed," the woman barked as Suzanne approached the bag.

"Just about to grab it."

Suzanne turned to her. "Yes, I was just going to help get it for you."

"I can get it *myself*." The woman's tone made Suzanne pause. The lady stepped forward, raised her leg, and kicked the lower shelf with the heel of her boot, causing the seed bag to slip from the shelf and into her arms. "See?"

Suzanne nodded without a word and returned to her shopping. Ten minutes later, in the checkout line, the cashier told Suzanne that the woman was known as Floppy Mossy and was "crazier than a soup sandwich." Truer words were never spoken.

In the parking lot, Suzanne watched in awe as Mossy argued with herself all the way to a rusty truck with a section of brown tarp duct-taped over its passenger's side window. As Mossy piled seed into the creaky truck bed, she stopped and pointed at someone who wasn't there, wagging her finger and telling the phantom that they "by God knew better." Sensing eyes upon her, Mossy paused and glanced in Suzanne's direction, who quickly slipped into her SUV and roused the engine. *I wonder how many bodies she has in that truck*, Suzanne thought.

Suzanne next heard the words *Floppy Mossy* when Fred said them aloud three weeks later. She was reorganizing the filing cabinet at the station house when he stomped into the space and barked, "Who in *the* hell names their child 'Floppy Mossy'?"

There had been an altercation at the Smoky Mountain Flea Market, which visited the local convention hall monthly. Mossy, who had been in attendance most of the day, was haggling with a booth owner over the listed price of a rice cooker. *Well, maybe she needed a rice cooker*, thought Suzanne. When Mossy couldn't persuade the merchant down from the asking price of ten dollars down to five, Mossy decided to exhibit her frustrations by breaking the hand grip on the pot. The market organizers called Fred to the scene, who became so aggravated by the altercation that he gave the seller ten dollars to settle the dispute.

"I would've given fifty to shut them up," he sighed.

Confrontations involving Mossy continued to unfold. It seemed at least once per month, Fred was dealing with the woman in one manner or the other. Granted, her transgressions never involved matters that were necessarily law worthy. Mossy wasn't one to break and enter, steal, deal in narcotics, or physically assault someone. Usually, the confrontation arose because Mossy considered something to be unfair or unreasonable in some way. It could be a store owner's rule within their establishment or the price they were charging for whatever Mossy needed at the time. When the spirit hit her, she would ostentatiously declare her objection and refuse to leave until the other party altered their opinion to suit her. Most did if only to shut her up, which only encouraged such behavior. Others did not, and that's when they would call Fred to the scene.

Though Fred would never admit it to Suzanne, there was a part of him, too, that felt pity for Mossy. He had dealt with the woman enough to know her, at least in some manner, and he had come to know her life, how empty it appeared to be, joyless. While Suzanne could undoubtedly appreciate the woman's lonely existence, she conducted herself as if she couldn't give two shits less about Mossy's misfortune. Mossy knew this, and she knew that Suzanne wasn't one with which to trifle. To that effect, Mossy tended to stay clear of Suzanne when they happened to appear together in public. She would get no sympathy from Suzanne Dunham, and she knew it.

Suzanne wouldn't go so far as to say she *hated* Mossy. On the contrary, over the years, she had grown not to mind the woman, really. And there was a sense of sorrow for the life Mossy had chosen, though Suzanne would have walked on her lips before confessing such a thing. Her compassion, while modest, was enough to pay Mossy little mind, to excuse those arguments over expired coupons, and ignore the rants concerning the subpar quality of day-old bread at Simmons Grocery. Sympathy or not, Suzanne didn't care if Earl Drummond had told her that Mossy was being held captive by a cargo ship of space aliens; she wasn't waking her husband one second before nine o'clock.

Fred was a creature of habit. Suzanne could literally set her watch by his behaviors. The morning nap proceeded as follows. At six in the a.m. precisely, Fred would wander into bed alongside her, rousing her from her sleep. As she sat up, he would mutter in that gruff, tiresome voice, "Wake me at ten," before falling over and drifting to sleep in less than thirty seconds. Suzanne would slip her feet into her slippers and walk downstairs to the kitchen, where she would make eggs, bacon, and toast for herself. She set aside four pieces of bacon for Fred, which she would reheat in the microwave for him at precisely nine fifty-five a.m. At nine fifty-seven a.m., she would slide two pieces of white bread into the toaster, slice two rounds of tomato, and pull a cool leaf of lettuce from the crisper. At ten, the browned bread would pop from the toaster, and Suzanne would yell, "Fred . . . come get your BLT." She would immediately hear his feet slip to the floor.

The evening shift was a little different. Unless delayed by some emergency, Fred would meander into the house between five thirty and five forty-five each afternoon. Suzanne would have dinner waiting for his arrival. At approximately six, with dinner concluded, Fred would push himself back from the table and announce, "Wake me at nine." Then, he would wander upstairs to the bed, which Suzanne kept straightened but unmade for such an occasion.

While he slept, she washed the dishes, did the laundry waiting in the hampers, and watched her stories. Around eight thirty p.m., Suzanne would start the coffee pot and watch the clock. Most of the time, she didn't have to call Fred in the evenings. She usually heard those big feet of his creak on the floorboards between eight thirty and nine. They would continue to groan underneath his toes as he walked to the washroom and ran cold water over his warm face. Then, he would slowly march down the steps, as if stepping into a firing line. He would always pause once he reached the ground floor and stretch his back before going to the hot coffee mug Suzanne had prepared.

"Well, did you dream anything good?" she always asked.

"Just you with no clothes on," he'd always reply with a wink.

And if the evening was calm, that would be the extent of it. Fred would finish his coffee, snatch his keys from the bowl on the counter, kiss Suzanne on the forehead, and walk out the door to await whatever adventures the town would bring in the night. She would watch David Letterman before taking herself to bed, and the whole thing would begin again the following morning.

The coffee pot chimed its conclusion, and Suzanne glanced again at the clock on the wall. Eight fifty-seven. When she thought she would have to call for Fred, she heard the floorboards creaking underneath his feet. She dreaded telling him he must attend to another Mossy matter that evening. Dead people at Robinson's farm? It was the most ridiculous thing yet. The most likely explanation was that someone had shot and dressed a deer by the crooked tree in the field. Deer wasn't in season, but that hadn't stopped anyone before. And Drummond had sounded very skeptical when relaying the details to Suzanne.

As Suzanne heard Fred's footfalls on the staircase, she poured a mug of hot coffee and placed it on the countertop next to the yellow bowl that held the keys to Fred's cruiser. She saw his shadow wobbling back and forth on the hardwood floor at the base of the stairs. Taking a seat at the counter, she took a deep breath and sighed.

"I hate to be the bearer of bad news, darling, but Earl Drummond just called," she began. "He's got Mossy up there at the camp in an awful fit." Fred reached the ground floor, and Suzanne noticed his bare feet. "She claims she found dead bodies up around Rob—"

A wave of icy fright poured down Suzanne's frame like someone had turned a bucket of frigid water over her head. Her teeth clenched. Her mouth ran dry. The trembling lids of her eyes pulled back, allowing her pupils to wax into full dilation. She clutched the countertop with her fingers, digging her nails deep into the compound wood underneath.

Her husband stood at the base of the stairs gaping at her with one lonely eye. Blood soaked his blue shirt, running in long, sticky streams down his right pant leg. The upper-right side of his skull was gone, exposing chunks of ragged brain and fragments of loose bone. Splinters of wood and bark protruded from the wound like someone had pummeled Fred with a tree branch. He raised his hands and ran them over his sticky face.

"Just you with no clothes on," he muttered in a raspy, bubbly voice as if she had asked about his dreams.

Suzanne slipped from the stool and backed against the wall behind her as Fred continued forward, hobbling unsteadily on his feet. He reached forward mechanically, slipping a trembling finger through the coffee cup handle and raising it to his lips. He tilted the cup, allowing the hot coffee to enter his mouth and pour through the side of his jagged jaw. *My God—he's dead*, she thought. *He's dead . . . but he doesn't know it.* Fred reached forward to place the cup back onto the counter but dropped it to the floor with a clatter. Shoving his hand into the yellow bowl, he fished out his keys and turned toward the front door.

"Fred?" Suzanne mumbled.

He began to move toward her, walking forward in jittering, unsteady steps, his one remaining eye fixed on her position. *He's coming to kiss me goodbye,* she thought. *Oh, God. God, please don't let him kiss me.* These actions, unconscious in nature, continued to churn in what remained of the dead man's mind, a robotic map of motions that he took at that particular time of the evening, motivating his body to instinctively proceed.

Once Fred reached Suzanne, his eye gazed upon her with realization, recognition that he no longer belonged to the world of the living. Fred Dunham collapsed to the floor as if this final understanding was enough. An ominous shadow caught Suzanne's attention, and she turned to see a tree just outside the kitchen window, one she had never noticed before. It raised its bloody branches to the windowpane and peered at her with one ghostly white, inhuman eye.

At last, Suzanne Dunham began to scream.

20

6:13 P.M.

"Seasons don't fear the reaper. Nor do the wind, the sun, or the rain. We can be like they are."
—*Don't Fear the Reaper*: Blue Oyster Cult—

At some point, we all encounter surreal terror, an event so bizarre we're unsure if we're awake or dreaming. This imminent terror triggers an electrified sensation like a swarm of insects skittering over the flesh. An inexplicable warmth extends along the extremities, immediately followed by a frigid rush that impales the heart, spreading outward, upward, forcing the fine hair along the body to stand on end. The pulse quickens. Then fades. The pupils dilate. And at last, the brain gives the body a direct command: *run*.

I first felt that sensation when I saw that black cloud of crows burst through the doors of the Kromwell Auditorium. The hysteria of the moment has been weakened by time, leaving me with only snapshots, vintage photos bleached by the sun. The main thing I recall is standing there amid the chaos of screaming campers, staring at that freaky Mossy lady, feeling that somehow, she had summoned the animals into the threshold and commanded them to attack. The birds swooped toward us with intention. I didn't think I could will my muscles into action until I heard Drummond's voice booming above the chaos.

He called the lucid among us to help wrangle the children, who were petrified with fear. Drummond called out again as the masses flowed through the rear exit, directing everyone next door to the dining hall. We began pouring through the open door en masse, nearly tripping over one another. Once everyone was inside the dining hall, he bolted the doors, leaving the auditorium to the mercy of the crows. Groups of campers gathered about the empty space. Some huddled together in sobbing clusters, while others stood motionless, muted by stunned disbelief, just as I had been moments before. I was roused from my bewildered thoughts when Mossy stepped beside me and shrieked like a banshee.

"He's coming!" I jerked and turned toward her, seeing her eyes wide with panic. "They've set him free!"

"Mossy—" began Drummond as he stepped toward her.

"He's coming!" she repeated.

Drummond snatched the woman by her arms and gave her a single firm shake. "Stop it! Stop it, Mossy! You're scaring everyone to death! We have children in here!"

Mossy's large eyes peered around the room and recognized small faces wet with tears. This revelation appeared to calm her—at least to a degree. She turned back to Drummond. "Earl. Listen to me. I know what I'm talking about."

Drummond then seemed to lean in my direction. "Take her back to the office while we get everyone calmed down out here. I'll be back there in a minute."

Confused, I gently took Mossy by her shivering arm and led her toward the main hall. It wasn't until I saw Beth to my left that I realized Drummond had been speaking to her, not me. Too horrified for either of us to care, Beth and I led Mossy through the dim hallway toward the office door. As we entered, I heard the light switch click, and the room was illuminated by a wispy fluorescent glow. Beth sat Mossy in the chair in front of Drummond's desk.

"Joe, would you get her some water?" asked Beth calmly. I turned to the container at the back of the room, quickly filled one of the paper cups with cold water from the tap, and handed it to Beth. She nodded and took the cup from me. "Here, Mossy, drink this."

Mossy took the cup, drank the water in one gulp, and returned the empty cup to Beth. "I'm not crazy," she managed.

"No one's saying you are, honey," Beth offered.

I saw Mossy's eyes drift to someplace far away, and they began to glisten with tears. "Those poor people."

Beth took a seat next to her. "What people?"

Mossy reached toward the water cooler, and I handed her another cup. "They're dead, just like in my dream. They're all dead," she muttered.

"Who?" Beth urged. "How many?"

"I don't know how many," Mossy replied as tears tumbled down her dirty cheeks, leaving thin lines of pink flesh in their wake. "Too many pieces to count. Five . . . maybe six."

Mossy was interrupted by Drummond, who slipped quietly into the room and shut the door behind him. Beth turned to him.

"How is everyone?" she asked, knowing the answer.

"Shaken, not stirred," said Drummond as he dropped into his chair. "We're missing a handful, but they haven't gone far. Rosetta and the others are checking the cabins. I'm sure they're hiding there." His eyes fixed upon Mossy, who returned a defiant look. "Mossy, now, what is going on?"

"They're dead," she replied. "Just like in my dream. Just like it!" Drummond opened his mouth, but Mossy raised her hand before he could speak. "*And before you ask*—like I told her—I don't know who. I don't know how many." She raised a finger. "But I do know *by who*."

Drummond sighed. "And just where are all these dead people?"

"Up the ridge. Around the crooked tree. Just like my dream," said Mossy, taking another sip of water. "The boy; he's there, too."

"What boy?" asked Drummond.

"The *thief*. The one who killed my Rascal."

This revelation forced Drummond forward. "Dewayne?" Mossy nodded and took another sip of water. Drummond turned to Beth and snatched the phone from the cradle. Pressing the intercom button, Drummond spoke into the receiver. "Hey, um, Jack, when you get everyone settled, grab Danny and come back to the office, would you?" He dropped the phone into the cradle and turned back to Mossy. "Did you recognize anyone else?"

Tears filled her twitching eyes. Her lips quivered. "The boy. Chester the Jester." My eyes widened. Drummond and Beth looked at each other. Mossy began to weep. "Just like in my dream."

Feeling I had to move, I turned to the cooler and fetched Mossy another cup of water. She took it with a quivering hand and sat it on Drummond's desk.

Drummond slipped deeper into his chair and rubbed his face. I could sense that he was mentally thumbing through the facts.

"It can't," he muttered before trailing off. He leaned forward. "And what about the *by who?*"

Mossy glanced at Drummond with a fearful gaze. "Somebody called him, Earl. *Old John.* He's come back."

Drummond scoffed and fell back into his chair. "Oh, shit, Mossy."

"I'm telling you!" she declared with a conviction that caused me to shudder. She pounded the table with her fist, and Beth and I jumped with fright. "That goddamn tree looked like something hacked it open! Whoever killed those people laid them out there for a purpose. We got to get out of this place!"

Earl raised his hand. "Mossy, calm down. Tell me what happened. What were you even doing around the Robinson place?"

Mossy paused, took a deep breath, and lowered her head. "I had that dream again—the one I told you about. I didn't want to show up here again and rouse any trouble, so I thought it best to just go check it out myself, make sure nothing was out there but a tree, settle my mind." She looked at Drummond. "But when I got there, it was a nightmare come true. That fire was there, just blazing high as you ever did see. Beeswax candles across the ground. And there they were . . . sprawled out there as an offering to him." She raised a finger at Drummond. "I don't know who did it, how they know the old ways, but they've called Tate up. And he's coming for us. He's coming for *all* of us."

Earl raised his hand. "Mossy, even if such a thing were possible—I'm not saying it is—and if I believed in such nonsense—which I don't—what business would John Tate have here?"

Mossy's tears stopped. Her brow furrowed. "Well, I'm sure I don't know, Earl," she spat as she began to ramble through her sack-like purse. "But somebody sure the hell has camping on their mind." She tossed a tattered, bloodstained Kromwell tee shirt onto Drummond's desk, and I felt Beth's hand clutch my wrist.

"What the—?" coughed Drummond as he slid backward.

"Oh, that got your attention, did it?" Mossy chuckled. She looked at me and shook her bag. "I got everything in this bastard."

"Where did you get that?" Drummond asked with disbelief.

Mossy gaped. "Ain't y'all been listening to shit I say? This here is old magic. This here belongs to the folk ways, the ways my grannie and momma used to talk about when they thought they were alone in the kitchen. Talk of raising the dead, getting even. Revenge."

I felt my mouth slip open before I could stop it. "Revenge?"

"Joe?" said Drummond as if he hadn't noticed my presence before I spoke. "What are—?"

"Revenge," confirmed Mossy before Drummond could have me ushered out of the room. "*Vengeful* things."

"Mossy," began Drummond. "I appreciate your beliefs, but why in God's name would anyone want revenge—"

Mossy began to chuckle. "My beliefs?" She picked up the cup from Drummond's desk and took another sip of water. I saw that faraway gaze return to her eyes. "My grannie, she used to tell a story about a friend of hers named Betty Varnes. Betty had a husband named Charlie, an old drunk who'd been catting around with one of the town floosies, Edna Johnson. One day—'round about August, I think—Edna proclaimed to the world that she was pregnant, that she was going to settle down, get married . . . all that shit. Wasn't five days later she was on the wrong side of a headstone. Got hit by a car while crossing Main Street. *Death by Misadventure*, they said. Well, no one bought that. Everybody knew it was Charlie's baby, and everyone knew that Charlie had been the very person to run Edna down."

"And what does that have to do with Tate?" asked Drummond.

"Nothing," Mossy clarified. "It's the *magic* that's the important part. Some four weeks after Edna was laid to rest, Charlie was up on Dawson Ridge just over the hill from Lake Ellington, drinking and carrying on with Dan Green, Butch Billings, and a bunch of other drunks, like always. And they see this figure come stumbling out of the woods, some woman wearing a dirty blue dress. At first, the men thought one of the town hobos was coming to ask for a beer, like they sometimes did. It didn't take long for them to realize that it was Edna Johnson, risen from the grave."

"Oh, dammit, Mossy," chided Drummond. "You can't be serious."

"Go ask old Dan Green," Mossy replied. "Dan will tell ya. They were all piled in the back of Dan's pick-up. Said they could smell her from fifty paces; the stench of death. She was covered in dirt and mud, clutching the flower brick from her tombstone. All her fingernails were ripped off from where she had clawed her way out of the ground. Said she had ripped the stitches in her lips open and was calling out, '*Charlie . . . Charlie, why did you run me down, Charlie?*'" Mossy paused and glanced at Drummond. "Don't act like you ain't heard the story."

"This town is full of stories," Drummond conceded.

"What happened then?" asked Beth, unable to stop herself.

Mossy nodded. "Those boys scattered like rats. All except Charlie, who was too scared and confused to move. As Dan was running away, he said he only looked back once. Charlie never made a sound, not even when Edna beat him to death with the flower brick from her headstone."

The door creaked open, and Mr. Burns peered into the office, with Danny hovering over his shoulder. "You call us, boss?"

Drummond cleared his throat and sat forward in his seat, allowing the chill of Mossy's tale to thaw. "Uh . . . have we found any of the others?"

The men entered the room, and Danny closed the door behind him. Danny cleared his throat. "Rosetta and Bonnie found several kids up in Cabin Three. Neil and I found another few huddled under the beds in Cabin Six. Dennis is on his way back with another group. They're just a few unaccounted for. We'll keep looking."

Mr. Burns smirked. "They're probably taking advantage of the situation to be up to no good." He noticed the odd look on Drummond's face. "Everything okay?"

"Jack, when was the last time you saw Dewayne?" Drummond asked.

Mr. Burns's eyes moved to each of us, and then he shrugged. "Don't know. About seven yesterday evening, I'd say. It was just starting to get dusk when he left."

"And you watched him leave?" Drummond added.

"Well, I didn't hold his hand all the way to the gate, if that's what you're asking, but I watched him drive off," Mr. Burns replied.

Drummond plucked the phone from the base again and dialed a number. After a moment, he said, "Suzie? Yeah, it's Earl up here at Kromwell . . . Oh, no, it's nothing, I'm sure, but I think we're going to need Fred to meet us up at the Robinson place as soon as he can get there . . . Well, Mossy's here, and . . . yes, Mossy. She's said there's been some goings-on at the tree." His eyes locked with Mossy's. "Well, that's the thing. We're not exactly sure yet. But have Fred bring the ambulance just in case." He dropped the phone back onto the cradle.

Mr. Burns's eyes moved to the tattered shirt on Drummond's desk. "Did Dewayne do something?"

Drummond rose to his feet. "I don't think so, Jack." He looked at Danny. "Danny, we need to take the shuttle out to meet the sheriff."

"Sounds good to me," Danny said, stepping forward.

Jack raised his arm, blocking Danny's chest. "Oh, now, wait a minute.

If Dewayne is involved in something, I think I'll need to tag along."

Drummond reached out and patted Mr. Burns's shoulder. "I need you to stay here, Jack. I need my senior staff members here with the kids; folks who know this place well. Okay?" I could sense that veiled compliment did little to calm Mr. Burns, but he nodded in agreement. Drummond motioned for Danny, and Mossy rose to her feet. "Beth, you look after Mossy here while we're gone."

Mossy placed a hand on her hip and snickered. "You don't think I'm just gonna sit here, do you?"

"I think that's *precisely* what you're going to do, dear," confirmed Drummond. "I need you—"

"Out of the way," Mossy finished.

"*Safe*," Drummond corrected. "I need as many adults as I can muster here with these kids." He nodded to Beth. "Tend to her, Beth, and radio me the second we have everyone accounted for. Dan and I will get back here quick."

As Drummond and Danny left the office, Mossy's head rolled toward Beth. "Ain't nobody safe here, missy."

21

IT'S ALIVE

An unsettling silence hung between Drummond and Danny as they drove along McKinney Road to the Robinson Farm. The night felt thick, heavy, and curiously moist, though within that swelter dwelled a coolness that churned a dense fog into the air. Danny turned and peered through the passenger side door of the shuttle into the darkness, watching the peculiar mist rise from the black waters of Lake Ellington and assume curious shapes, like smoky apparitions. There was something else out there in the night; a vibration that, to Danny, felt almost palpable.

"Sir," said Danny at last. "Why are we going out to visit a tree again?"

Drummond sighed. "Well, because Mossy said to check it out, and if I don't, she'll never be quiet. And I make it a point to keep Mossy quiet." He could tell this statement did little to quell Danny's curiosity. "Listen, son, I know you've heard about some goings-on in this town. All you kids have, I'm sure. Those things—those stories—they just come with the territory. They tend to get folks like Mossy riled up from time to time."

Danny nodded. "Stories about John Tate?" Drummond nodded. "So

. . . did they really find him tied to this tree we're going to?"

"Eh, that's what everybody says, anyway. Can't say it's true. But I do know that those legends have led to all kinds of craziness on the stretch of land. Kids partying, vandalizing, *séances*. People come from all over just to get a look at that damned tree. I've heard more stories about that thing than I could ever tell in a lifetime."

"What did Mossy think she saw?" asked Danny.

Drummond sighed. "I'm not sure what Mossy saw. You never know with her. It's always hard to tell what's real and what's only real in the woman's head. I'd bet anything that she stumbled upon some kids up there having a time and carrying on. Maybe they saw the town kook coming and wanted to give her a scare. They do that to her from time to time."

Danny shrugged. "So, Mossy's the town kook."

"The town *joke*, more like it. People . . . well, people aren't too nice to Mossy." Drummond could sense the empathy this elicited from Danny and smiled. "Don't get me wrong—Mossy is about as sweet as a salt lick in lye. Nobody has the nerve to step on her land without invitation. That'll get you a heart full of regret and an ass full of buckshot."

Danny chuckled. "She seems like she's not dealing with a full deck."

Drummond winked and raised a finger. "Ah, and that's the genius of it all. The thing is—and most folks don't know it—Mossy ain't half as crazy as she acts like she is. I can see through her . . . *eccentricities*. Just like her house. On the outside of that place, it looks like some Tobe Hooper horror flick. But on the inside, spotless. Everything in its place, clean, not a speck of dust in the house. I bet you I could eat off that kitchen floor."

"Well, why does she look so—"

"Cracked?" laughed Drummond. "She figures the crazier she acts, the more folks will just leave her alone. And, God knows, they leave her alone." He sighed and gripped the steering wheel.

"She likes you, alright," posed Danny.

"That woman hasn't had an easy life, but she's lived it all the same. She does the best she knows how to get through day by day. I guess I feel a bit sorry for her."

"What about her family?" asked Danny. "Doesn't have anybody to come to check in on her?"

"Not that I know of," Drummond replied. "It was always just her and her folks on that land, from what I hear. They passed long ago, I think. After that, Mossy just kept to herself. Sure, she'll come up to the camp bitching about something every so often. Most of the time, I think she just gets a hankering to see the living, is all. So, she makes up troubles. But in no time flat, she's on to poking fun at me." As they turned onto a narrow dirt road, Drummond squinted his eyes and peered into the distance. "And what do we have there?"

Danny glanced out of the window and saw flames dancing in the distance. "Look like a bonfire."

"Where in hell is Fred?" posed Drummond. "He should have been here by now."

They drove up the road, tossing plumes of dirt in their wake. Suddenly, something caused Drummond to slow their approach. No one was near the battered tree, which looked like someone had torn its middle through. A jagged hollow stretched upward from the roots for what seemed to be at least ten feet.

"God, what happened to that tree? Did a car hit it?" asked Danny as he began to roll down the window.

"No," muttered Drummond, taking Danny by the shoulder. "Think it's best to leave that window closed, son." Danny returned the window to its closed position. Drummond placed the shuttle into Park.

"Are we getting out?" whispered Danny. Drummond didn't answer. Danny noticed Drummond's eyes were fixed, not on the wounded tree, but on something that stood just past its damaged hull. "What?" Through the dying flicker of firelight, it appeared to be just another tree standing some five yards away from the smoldering fire. "What is it?"

"That tree," said Drummond. "The other one."

"Yeah."

Drummond reached up and wiped the sweat from his lip. "It wasn't there last week."

Danny's head snapped around, and his eyes attempted to focus through the veil of night. To him, it was nothing more than a tree. Young, yes, not nearly as tall as its maimed father, but it was still only a tree.

"Sir, it's a tree." Still, Drummond's eyes didn't move. "Are we going to get out? Or are we going—"

Crash!

The abrupt jolt caused Danny's chest to seize. His eyes moved to Drummond, whose lips drew back from his teeth in an expression of horror. It was then that Danny realized someone had thrown something heavy at the shuttle, an object that had rolled to a stop upon the hood. Through the cracked windshield, Danny saw eyes peering back at him, lifeless eyes, the sticky eyes of Dewayne Burns. His severed head lay wobbling on the lid of the Kromwell shuttle.

"*Holy Mary, Mother of God!*" screeched Drummond as he wrestled with the gear shift. His foot began to unconsciously pump the gas pedal, causing the shuttle to roar and tussle in place.

A rumble caught Danny's attention, and his eyes fixed upon the second tree, which began to unwind from around itself. The branches folded into thick, muscular arm-like appendages, and its roots stomped the ground like two stout legs. As it raised its head, Danny saw a tattered cloth mask covering its face like a hood made from a dingy potato sack. The blood-spattered heads of other unfortunate corpses dangled in each of its bark-covered hands. It glared at Danny with one foggy eye and screamed into the night with a roar so fierce that it rattled the shuttle's windows. It rushed toward the vehicle, swinging the severed heads like medieval maces.

"*It's alive!*" cried Danny.

The beast collided with the vehicle before Drummond could fight the shuttle into gear, sending it spinning ninety degrees. One of the heads slipped from the monster's grip. Danny saw Dewayne's head flip to the right and bounce along the hood like a gore-covered basketball. The creature stomped forward and threw another head toward the rear window. With a crash, the head barreled through the back window of the shuttle, cracked against the windshield, and landed between Danny's legs. The bloody eyes of Chester Henry rolled upward and peered at him with silent anguish. Danny shrieked and began to judder around in his seat, struggling to wriggle the head from his lap.

"*Son* of a *bitch!*" screeched Drummond. He threw the car into Drive and slammed his foot onto the gas. Just as relief began to envelop him, he noticed the shuttle wasn't moving. The motor was roaring like a wild bear, and the tires were spinning out of control, but they weren't gaining ground. Drummond glanced into the rearview mirror to see the tree clutching its last severed head in one hand and holding the tailgate of the shuttle with the other. For a moment, it almost seemed as if the thing realized Drummond was watching it, because it winked at him with its one vacant eye.

"Hold this, and step on the gas?"

"What?" cried Danny.

"Hold the wheel and step on the gas!" Drummond shouted.

Danny scooted in his seat, being sure to step over the head of Chester Henry wobbling in the floorboard, and took hold of the steering wheel. He grasped the wheel with his left hand and saw Drummond dig into the floor behind the driver's seat. Drummond removed a dusty twelve-gauge shotgun from under the seat. He flipped open the barrel, noted the single shell resting in the chamber, and spun around, nearly slapping Danny in the face with the barrel.

"Try this on, *you fuckin' fern!*" yelled Drummond.

The boom of the shotgun rattled the windows. A loud, painful hum filled Danny's ears, and they began to ring with a high-pitched squeal. The buckshot connected with the creature's wooden hand, shattering it into splinters. It howled into the night. The rear wheels of the shuttle bounced to the ground, and Danny's head snapped back as the vehicle lurched forward. The truck careened off the main road as Drummond struggled to turn around and regain control.

"Watch out!" called Danny as Drummond jerked the wheel to the right, barely missing the metal fence post ahead.

"Get that thing outta here!" Drummond nodded toward Chester's head, which continued to roll aimlessly along the floor.

Danny's brow furrowed. "What? *I'm* not fucking touching it!"

Drummond yanked the shuttle back onto the road and reached across Danny's stomach. He opened the door and jerked the steering wheel to the left, allowing Chester's head to topple out of the cab. As Drummond shut the door, Danny glanced into the passenger side mirror and saw the boy's head bouncing and spinning along the pavement. The monster bent forward and plucked the head from the road, reclaiming its prize.

22

7:05 P.M.

I remember sitting in that dining hall with the rest of the Krew, studying this strange creature called Mossy, wondering what tragedies must have befallen a person for them to devolve into such a lowly state. She stood near the hallway with Rosetta, deep in discussion. One could sense that in a time long since passed, this Mossy character had been a lovely young woman. I could still see those traces of fiery amber woven into her graying hair. And her eyes, now riddled with crow's feet and concern, sparkled with the emerald green of youth. There was something more to the woman; I could feel it. I still didn't know what to make of her crazy-ass stories. She had spun them with such sincerity, it was difficult not to believe every word.

Rosetta turned, and Mossy followed her back into the dark hallway. Asia slithered around the corner of the table and plopped down next to Kenny with a smirk on his face. He leaned toward me. "So, spill it. What was all that about?" asked Asia with curiosity.

"She said she found bodies."

"Bodies?" muttered Kenny. "Like *dead* bodies?"

I nodded. "Several, I think. She found the bodies around that tree that everyone talks about."

"No shit," whispered Asia.

I glanced to either side and leaned forward to ensure I'd remain unheard by those around us. The Krew leaned in. "She said one of them was Chester."

"Chester!?" exclaimed Lily, covering her mouth. I raised my hands to quieten her. "*Asshole* Chester?" she reiterated in a hushed whisper.

"And Dewyane," I added.

DJ's eyes widened. "That fool who works in the kitchen?"

I nodded once again. "Not anymore. He was let go because of all that mess with Mossy and her cat."

Paul's eyebrow raised. "Ooh, you don't think she . . . you know . . . went all Jason Vorhees on his ass, do you?" he whispered.

"No, no," I dismissed. My eyes moved toward Mossy as she and Rosetta reentered the dining hall. My eyebrow arched. "Don't get me wrong. She's definitely giving me some Michael Myers vibes, but I don't think she killed anyone."

Rosetta and Mossy headed toward the kitchen. Asia glared at the woman and smirked. "Are you sure? She was just in here the other day, casting some hooroo on Dewayne."

Rosetta peered at us warningly, and Asia waved with a grin. I did my best to avoid eye contact. As the two women disappeared through the kitchen doorway, the six of us leaned into one another again.

"Okay. If she did it, why did she flip out and come tell everyone about the bodies?" I posed.

"To throw us off," hissed Lily. "Ain't you ever read Agatha Christie?"

"Well, then, who are the other dead people?" I asked. "Did she kill them, too?"

"Probably," said Paul.

"Why?" I asked. "What's the motive?" They paused at my query. "Ain't you ever read any Agatha Christie?" I retorted.

Lily rolled her eyes. "Maybe they pissed in her grits. Who knows why crazy bitches kill?"

Rosetta and Mossy walked through the kitchen doorway and stood at the wall. Mossy proceeded toward the main doors. Once she reached the entryway, she removed a jar containing a strange white powder from her satchel. She unscrewed the lid, poured a pile of powder into her palm, and began peppering it along the base of the doors.

"What's that? She treating for roaches?" Kenny whispered.

I rolled my eyes. "Maybe it's—" At that moment, Mossy's eyes locked with mine. My mouth forgot how to move for reasons I still cannot explain. Mossy eyed me for a moment. Then she casually strolled across the dining room floor toward where we were seated. Without question or gesture, Mossy hiked her leg over the bench where I sat and took a seat next to me. She took turns eyeing each of us, then smiled at Asia.

"You're pretty," said Mossy.

Until then, I hadn't noticed that most of Asia's makeup remained on his face.

Asia's eyes filled with apprehension. Then he smiled. "Aww . . . thank you, girl." My foot connected with Asia's shin, and he winced.

"So," Mossy continued as she hiked that bag onto her shoulder. "Are you gonna keep it, or are you one of those who's planning to . . . you know." The woman grasped an imaginary object in one hand. She snipped it with the other hand like a pair of invisible scissors, which I could only assume translated into a query concerning Asia's penis and his intention to retain its services.

Asia glanced at me and cleared his throat. "I think I'll hang onto it for now, honey. I'm kinda partial to it."

Mossy nodded. "Hmm. Comes in handy." She slipped her fingers into her bushy hair and grated at her scalp. "There's been many a day I wish I had me a *wang-danger*. Less trouble. Easy maintenance. Just shake it off and go." She nodded toward Paul. "This your boyfriend?"

"No," spat Paul. "No, we're brothers. *Adopted* brothers." He grabbed his can of orange juice and took a sip to avoid saying anything further.

Mossy nodded at Kenny. "What about this one?"

Kenny immediately flushed red. "Uh, no. No."

Asia cocked his eyebrow and peered at Kenny. "As if."

Mossy turned to me. "What about this one? He's kinda cute."

"Just another friend," said Asia.

Mossy nodded and elbowed Lily. "One can never have too many friends, I suppose." She dug into her bag, fished out a silver flask, and unscrewed the lid. She took a heavy sip, quaked, and patted her bag. "I got everything in this fucker."

Lily leaned forward. "Why do they call you Floppy Mossy?"

Mossy shrugged. "Don't know. I guess I look a little mossy sometimes. And—" She reached down, lifted her rather ample left breast, and let it fall lifeless back to her chest. "These days, these things are about as floppy as you can get." Immediately, DJ snorted, forcing orange juice through his nose like an uncapped water hose.

"What's that powder?" I interjected, hoping to steer the conversation away from penises and breasts. Mossy turned to me with a quizzical expression. I pointed at her bag. "That powder you were putting at the door."

"Oh!" she said, rummaging for the jar from her purse. "This is my *no-go* powder. My grannie's recipe."

"No-go powder?" asked Asia.

"If I put this down somewhere I don't want you to go, *you no go there*," Mossy chuckled.

Asia turned to us with a raised brow and placed a hand on Mossy's shoulder. "I *adore* this woman." She turned to Mossy. "Will you adopt me?"

Mossy giggled. "I'd be happy to, baby. I'm just not sure I'd provide the type of lifestyle you're accustomed to. You seem more like a caviar girl, and I'm strictly grits and gravy."

"He'd manage," Lily added.

The rustling sound of feathers began to claw its way over the muttering voices of the dining hall, drawing Mossy's attention. She turned toward the darkness in the windows. With a bang, a large black bird collided with the glass of one of the entryway doors and fell to the pavement, dead. Seconds later, another followed its suicidal descent. Bewildered silence swept the room as everyone turned toward the doors.

"They're testing it, you see," muttered Mossy. "Trying to find a weak point."

I felt goose-pimples dance along the nape of my neck because I realized she was right. But how? Why?

Rosetta and Beth approached the table, with Neil following close behind. They looked at Mossy. "Mossy," Beth began. "We still can't find Lindsey or Janie. Everyone else is accounted for. Rosetta, Neil, and I are going to—"

"You're not going out there, are you?" said Mossy.

"Mossy, we can't just leave those kids wandering out there in the dark," Beth explained.

Mossy looked at her with pleading eyes but said nothing.

Neil smirked. "Don't worry. I won't let anything happen to them."

Mossy turned to Neil, glanced him up and down, and sighed. "I'm sure you won't, *stud*." She reached into her bag and retrieved a metal cigarette case.

Dumping the loose cigarettes into her purse, she took the jar and filled the metal container with powder. She closed the lid and handed it to Beth. "You see anything . . . *anything* that looks like it ought not to, you use this. It's like acid to things that mean you harm."

Neil snickered. "Maybe I can try some of it on my mother-in-law." A joke that fell flat to those around him.

Beth nodded. "We will, Mossy."

Mossy took Beth by her hand. "Promise."

Beth placed her other hand on Mossy's trembling fingers. "I promise. Cross my heart."

Mossy tried to manage a smile. She nodded. "Go out the back. Be sure to step over the powder I put down there. Mind it, now. Don't cut the line."

"We will," Beth added. She turned to the group of us. "Will you all keep Mossy company until we get back?"

Asia was the first one to nod. "She's my new best friend."

Mossy smiled.

23
THE TREEHOUSE

Beth, Rosetta, and Neil slipped through the dim kitchen and moved toward the backdoor. Beth reached for the doorknob. Her eyes spied the jagged line of white powder that marked the exit.

"Looks like coke," Neil muttered. Rosetta rolled her eyes and turned to him. A silly grin stretched over his face. He placed a thumb to his nostril to snort Mossy's powder from the tile.

"What's wrong with you?" Rosetta asked.

"Sorry," Neil replied. "I get silly when I'm nervous."

Rosetta turned around. "You're nervous a lot."

Beth carefully opened the door, mindful of the powder at her feet. She pushed the screen door forward and slowly stepped onto the paved walkway beside the garbage cans.

"You really don't believe that stuff will do anything, do you?" asked Rosetta.

"I don't know whether it will or won't." Beth held the door open for them. "I *do* know that Mossy will come to check that line in two minutes, and if it's scuffed, she'll lose her shit."

Rosetta nodded and stepped over the powder. "Ooh, we don't want that."

Once outside, Beth couldn't help but notice how cool the night air felt on her skin, heavy and damp, like a chilly, moist blanket retrieved from the snow. Everything seemed peaceful—too peaceful. There was no noise. No crickets singing, no frogs croaking in the distance. It was as if the world waited, anxious to see what would unfold.

They entered the shadows behind the dining hall, slipping into the wildly grown hedges that wound there like an earthy labyrinth.

"Where do you think they could be?" asked Neil. "They weren't in the cabins, and I know they didn't run back to the auditorium."

Beth reached forward and parted a line of thin branches in her path. "Well, I always find Lindsey in one of two places: either galloping by the lake or crouched in the treehouse by the rope bridges. I think we'll start with the treehouse first."

"She could be at the stables," posed Neil.

Beth shook her head. "Susan won't allow her to be there by herself. She doesn't need another horse." Neil giggled nervously.

"The kids aren't supposed to be in the treehouse after dark," Rosetta added.

"And when have they done *anything* we've asked them to do? Especially Lindsey?" Beth stated.

"I suppose you're right," Rosetta admitted.

As the trio ventured into the towering trees, Neil cleared his throat. "You really think that half-crazed mountain lady found dead people?"

Beth sighed. "You know, Mossy is many things. Sure, she's a little eccentric. Maybe even a little crazy. She may even stretch the truth now and again to suit her liking. But in the years I've known her, she's never been a liar."

Rosetta chuckled. "Maybe Dewayne decided to stick around."

Beth brushed branches away from her face. "Yeah, my guess is that Dewayne was pretty p-o'ed at Mossy for getting him fired. So, he decided to get her back. I think Earl and Danny will find Dewayne up at the Robinson place, laughing his ass off."

"You really think Dewayne could have pulled off something that elaborate?" Neil posed.

Beth pondered. "I don't know. But there must be some logical explanation for it."

"Maybe Chester met up with Dewayne and—" Neil began.

Beth raised a hand, and Neil paused. The old treehouse stood ahead, nestled high among tattered rope bridges in the darkness. A faint glow of flickering candlelight shone through its dusty windows. They stepped toward the tree trunk, and Beth gazed into the moonlight. The roped ladder to the treehouse floor had been pulled into the cabin.

"Lindsey?" Beth called. "Janie? Are you two up there?" There was no reply. Beth turned to Rosetta and Neil with a look of concern. "Lindsey."

Suddenly, a face appeared at the opening of the treehouse floor. Lindsey Rafferty held up the end of the treehouse ladder. "We can't get down. The ladder came loose, and we can't put it back."

Beth sighed. "There are two bolts on the floor. You just have to slide the end of the ladder into each of those."

"It won't work," whispered another voice. Janie Peterson looked down at them. "I think it's broken."

"It's not broken," assured Beth. "You just have to make sure you're fitting it in the right bolt."

The two girls disappeared into the shadows of the treehouse. Beth could hear discussion and debate, phrases such as "No, you do it like this" and "It goes the other way." She shook her head in aggravation and stepped to the neighboring tree.

"What are you doing?" Neil asked.

"Well, we have to get up there one way or another," Beth said. She examined the rope bridges dangling above. "If I can get up to that rope bridge, it runs right over the support beam to the treehouse. I can . . ." She took a deep breath. ". . . walk across there and get to the treehouse."

Neil chuckled. "You're not serious." Beth didn't reply. "My God, you're serious. That's about twenty-five, thirty feet off the ground. Are you insane?"

Beth snapped toward him. "And what else would you have us do? We can't leave them there."

Neil shook his head. "That's not what I'm saying. Let's go back and tell the others. Maybe there's—"

"I can do it," Rosetta said. Beth and Neil looked at her. "I can do it." Rosetta looked up at the trails of rope bridges and wooden beams. "It's the balance beam, just like in gymnastics."

Neil scoffed. "Sorry, but aren't those like four feet off the ground and surrounded by cushions?"

Beth stepped back. "Rosetta, you don't have to—"

"I can do it," Rosetta confirmed. "Trust me."

Rosetta stepped toward the tree on her right, which had the lowest branches. *Girl, you're going to kill yourself*, a part of her thought. *No, no, you're not. You've done this . . . hundreds of times. You know this.* But the truth was she hadn't done this, not in a long time. Neil was right. It wasn't the same. The balance beam was tricky, but it was four inches wide and surrounded by safety mats, and even then, it could be troublesome. The wooden two-by-four above her was just under two inches wide and over twenty feet from the hard ground. Still, she had to try.

She pulled herself onto the first branch of the tree, feeling the titanium rod in her thigh tighten. *Just look up. Like on the uneven bars. Just look up.* Carefully, she continued to scale the tree, her eyes fixed on the support beam that stretched from the midsection of the tree to the bottom of the treehouse.

"If it's any consolation, Rosetta, you look really sexy right now," Neil whispered.

Rosetta snickered. "Good, because *sexy* is exactly what I'm going for."

As she searched for her next secure step, something caught her eye, something swaying in the shadows to her left. At first, she thought it was just another tree standing amongst the others.

Then it moved.

Not in a breezy swaying manner but in a thoughtful, intent way.

Rosetta stepped onto the upper branch and placed her foot on the support beam extending to the treehouse. She turned back to the trees. A figure lingered in the distance, a large, brooding shape that seemed curiously human. It was tall, very tall. So tall, Rosetta could nearly see a face from where she stood among the branches. The electrified static of fear danced along her arms. She felt the tiny hairs on the nape of her neck rise with apprehension.

"What?" asked Beth. "What's the matter?"

Rosetta didn't reply. She couldn't pry her eyes from the figure, the hulking shape in the distance. The muscles in her chest seized with the realization that it watched her in return. "Someone's out there."

"What?" asked Beth.

"Someone is—"

Beth turned toward the distant trees to locate what held Rosetta's attention. She, too, saw the brooding shadow. It took a step forward, and Beth felt her breath catch in her throat. It was a person, she thought, a man. But at the same time, it wasn't. It was something else. It clung to something in its hand, a round object dangling from its fingertips. Beth's eyes widened with horror as the shape entered the haze of moonlight. It held a woman's severed head by the scalp, bloody blonde curls drooping around the twisted face.

"Oh . . . my God," whispered Beth. She looked up at Rosetta. "Hurry," she managed. "Hurry!"

Rosetta turned to the wooden plank underneath her foot. Scattered visions flooded her mind, those early days of gymnastics. The raspy voice of Ruth Charles, her youth instructor, echoed in her ears.

Now, two of the most fundamental moves you can learn for the balance beam are the Front Walkover and the Back Walkover.

Rosetta grasped the tree branch on her right and took a deep breath.

One would think that a Back Walkover would be the most difficult, but that's not necessarily true.

She closed her eyes and turned away from the wooden board.

Remember that with the Front Walkover, you must spring up out of a full bridge.

She let go of the tree branch, allowing her left foot to slip just behind her right.

"Rosetta, what are you doing?" called Neil. "You're going to fall!"

With the Back Walkover, you can rise naturally as long as your foot finds its landing point.

"Rosetta!" screamed Beth. "Don't!"

Rosetta closed her eyes. With a quick lurch upward, she began to gracefully flip head over feet across the narrow wood. *Stay focused.* She lost her balance only once but quickly regained her footing. *Breathe.* As she tumbled backward, her eyes focused on the corner of the treehouse ahead. All she had to do was reach the edge. *Just one more turn.* Her head slid backward. She grasped for the two-by-four for what would be her last turn. Pain radiated through her arm as the jagged splinter of wood sank into her palm. She stumbled.

"Rosetta!" Beth and Neil yelled.

Just before she slipped from the beam, Rosetta's bloody hand caught the corner of the treehouse. Her balance returned. She evened her weight and breathed a sigh of relief.

"What is it?!" cried Lindsey.

Rosetta spun toward the thicket of trees. The shape marched forward, trudging through the tall grass. She ducked into the treehouse as the two girls shrieked with ear-rattling squeals. Rosetta fumbled with the bolts and smoothly slid the left side into the socket. Then she turned it to the right. Broken. The socket was missing. The girls couldn't have gotten it to latch.

"*The tree is coming!*" cried Janie.

Rosetta spied a gap in the floorboard behind her. She stuffed the rusty bolt into the opening and began to furiously beat it into place with her fist. Once in place, she jerked on the ladder to test its tether. Feeling it was solid enough, Rosetta tossed the ladder through the open floor. It unfurled with a clatter, the wooden teeth chomping against one another. Beth and Neil took hold of the ladder from below to steady it.

"Come on!" Beth exclaimed.

Rosetta turned to the girls. "Go, go, go!"

Lindsey slid forward and started down the rickety ladder. Janie followed.

As Rosetta stepped onto the ladder, Beth turned toward the forest. She saw the creature approaching them, swinging a human head with long, blonde hair. The thing paused in the moonlight, heaving jagged breaths as if it wanted them to be utterly aware of its presence. It wanted to frighten them.

It was shaped like a human, but it was unlike any man they had ever seen. It stood nearly eight feet tall and had thick, broad shoulders. The flesh that covered its body wasn't soft or plump like human skin but dry and enclosed in bark like the trunk of an old oak tree. Dirty burlap draped the head perched upon his pronounced neck. A single pale eye glared from the hole cut in the cloth. It turned toward the screams echoing from the treehouse above and then toward Beth and Neil. Two branch-like horns protruded from its temples, like the spiky antlers of a demonic deer. It raised the woman's head toward them, dangling in its twisted fingers like a lantern. It was a middle-aged woman Beth did not recognize. The skull had been burrowed out. Two candles sat in the woman's gaping jaw. The flames blazed through her hollow eye sockets like a garish jack-o'-lantern.

"Come! The fuck! On!" yelled Neil to the girls overhead.

"Go," shouted Beth to Rosetta. "Go, go, go!"

"What is it?" cried Rosetta. "What is it?!"

Beth glanced at the ladder and then back to the creature in the distance. It was clear that it would be upon them before the girls could make it securely to the ground. She released the ladder and took a step back.

"What are you doing?" called Neil. "Come on! Come on!"

"We won't make it," Beth said. "We all can't make it."

"What?" cried Rosetta, pausing just underneath the treehouse. "What are you talking about?"

The beast dropped its gory lantern to the ground and rushed forward.

"No!" cried Beth. "Hey, you!" But it didn't hear her. She plucked a chunk of branch from the group and hurled it at the monster. The limb crunched against its shoulder and shattered into bits. The thing stopped and gazed in Beth's direction. "Yeah, that's right, you piece of shit. Come on!"

It raised a withered hand and brushed the dust from its shoulder.

"Beth, run!" shrieked Rosetta.

Instantly, Beth lunged into a sprint with the monstrous tree close behind. She could hear its heavy footfalls crunching in the dried leaves and debris scattered along the forest floor. *Oh, God*, she thought. *Oh, God, help me!*

Leading the creature to the campground was not an option. Beth had no choice but to race deeper into the dark trees and the abysmal unknown. For each step in her stride, the creature took at least four. It was fast approaching from behind. It was so close she could almost feel the heat from its body, energy from a form that could not possess life, breath from an object without lungs.

Beth spied a toppled tree ahead in the distance. Dark moss covered its trunk, which stretched across a shallow gully. It was her chance to gain ground. She took a deep breath and slid effortlessly underneath the fallen tree. At that moment, she realized the gully below was no mere hill but a gulch at least thirty feet deep. Her fingernails clawed at the vines winding along the fallen trunk. At last, she clutched onto a protruding root and abruptly stopped.

Boom, boom, boom!

The massive feet of the creature approached, and she closed her eyes. With the fallen trunk camouflaged by overgrowth and darkness, it snared the thing's foot. The beast lunged forward, soaring into the air. With a howl, it plummeted into the darkness below.

As Beth's muscles relaxed, the mossy trunk creaked and rolled forward. It followed the monster toward the shadows as Beth scratched at the weeds and roots to avoid being pulled into the darkness. She heaved herself onto the soft, moist ground. A crash rang out when the trunk smashed into the rocks below.

Beth rolled onto her back, heaving and gasping. As she exhaled with relief, she felt something slithering along her legs. Thorny boughs crawled along the ground around her. She spun onto her stomach and tried to scramble away from their grip.

"No, no, no!" she hissed.

Suddenly, the creature rose from the gulch. Vines wriggled from its form like the tentacles of an octopus, winding around Beth's body and holding her in place. It leaned toward her, pulling her closer. Her fingers clawed at her front pocket for the silver cigarette case. The beast reached forward with a thick, rough hand and wrapped its crooked fingers around her neck. She winced as it pulled upward, intent on ripping her head from her body.

Jerking her right arm free, Beth showered the monster with the white powder from Mossy's silver case. It shrieked and threw her to the ground. The powder began to smoke and bubble like she had tossed acid into the creature's face. It howled with agony, releasing Beth and plunging into the darkness below.

24
7:22 P.M.

There was a vibration in the dining hall. I remember that. A restless buzz so soft, it couldn't be heard by the human ear but strong enough to be felt on the skin. We did our best to occupy ourselves at the table. Lily and Paul played a hand of Crazy Eights with a deck of cards from the game bin. Kenny sat to my left, repeatedly tying and untying his right shoe with different knots. DJ and Asia focused on a game of tic-tac-toe. And I focused on Mossy.

I watched her as she paced back and forth like an expectant father. She would wring her tanned, wrinkled hands and glance at the clock on the wall. Occasionally, she would peer in my direction, and I would quickly avert my gaze, turning my attention to other happenings in the dining hall. Bonnie, Dennis, and Nurse Conrad tried to keep the younger children calm and occupied. Dennis had started a board game with one group of kids while Nurse Conrad finished placing band-aids on various scrapes and scuffs. Mr. Burns emerged from the kitchen with another box of juices, which Bonnie began distributing to everyone who wanted one.

Asia dropped his pencil to the table. "Oh, my God," he moaned.

"Someone play some music. *Say* something." Silence. He turned to Mossy. "So, how long have you lived here in Jasper Hill, Miss Mossy?"

"Mill," I whispered.

"*Mill*," Asia corrected.

Mossy paused. "What?"

"How long have you lived here?" Asia repeated.

"Always," Mossy grumbled and then resumed her pacing.

Asia glanced at me with an arched eyebrow. I shrugged. He nodded in my direction. Confused, I shrugged again. He motioned toward Mossy. I rolled my eyes.

"Um," I interjected. "Mossy, you do magic?"

I promise you I had no idea why I posed such an asinine query in such a simplistic manner. I might as well have asked the woman if she polished the stripper poles before she swung from them. She turned to me and smiled.

"Magic?" she said. "Like pull a rabbit out of a hat and shit?"

"Oh, not really *that* magic," I struggled. She strolled to the table and took a seat in front of me. "That powder, for example. The *no-go* stuff. That's, like, magic, right?"

She reached forward and patted my hand. "Thank God you're pretty," she sighed, prompting snickers from Asia and Lily. She sat her bag on the table. "To be honest, son, no such thing as magic. Nobody who knows the old ways goes 'round waving magic wands or staring into crystal balls. All that's horseshit." She leaned onto the table. "But some folks, some wise folks—wiser than you or me—they know how to use things, even everyday things, to . . . *see* the unseen." Mossy reached over and plucked the playing cards out of Paul's hand.

"Hey! What are you doing?" Paul said. "I was winning!"

"No, you weren't," Lily chuckled.

Mossy scooped up the cards and jumbled them around in her hands.

Bonnie paused at our table. "Would anyone like a juice?"

Lily raised a hand. "Got any apple?"

Bonnie scanned the tray. "Hmm . . . all out. Just orange and grape. I saw some apple, though. I'll be back."

With the cards organized, Mossy split them and shuffled them like we were about to play a hand of poker.

"Take these cards right here. Now, you can play some Solitaire with them, yeah. But if you treat 'em right, they can tell you things." She handed them to me. "Now you shuffle those cards, and you ask anything you want to know about your future."

"Really?" I asked with a smile. "Just shuffle and ask a question?"

"Anything you want. But," she said, raising a finger. "Make it specific. None of this—*Oh, will there ever be a time when I'm rich*—bullshit. Think of a timeframe. The next week, month, season. Something like that."

I began to shuffle the deck. As I did so, my mind filled with simple, two-dimensional questions. Would I fall in love in the next year? Would I be successful by the time I was thirty years old? Mossy grabbed my hands and looked into my eyes.

"What does your heart want to know?"

Out of the darkness of my subconscious arose a name: *Sam*.

Mossy snatched the cards from me, leaving the stench of Sam Barnes laced within them. I hadn't been thinking about Sam Barnes. The man hadn't been in my thoughts at all. But when Mossy had interrupted my thoughts so suddenly, his bloated form floated to the surface like a corpse. I knew Mossy could sense my apprehension. But still, she pressed forward, laying out the cards in a scattered pattern upon the table before us. Once she had dealt around eleven cards, she sat the remainder of the deck beside her and examined the spread.

"*Ap-ple*," sang Bonnie as she neared the table. She handed the juice to Lily, who thanked her. Her eyes moved to the cards on the table. "What are you guys pl—"

"Shhh," urged Mossy.

Mossy's eyes scanned the cards and then glanced at me. She continued this back-and-forth analysis for a solid minute. Then her face softened with empathy. Bonnie slid onto the bench beside me as if invited to join us. Mossy's mouth fell open to speak, and I felt my gut tighten. I knew she had seen Sam Barnes in those playing cards. I didn't know how precisely, but she had seen him there, lurking in the spades.

"Oh!" chimed Bonnie. "Is it like a memory game or something?"

Without another word, Mossy scooped up the cards and returned them to the deck. "Yep, it's a little game I like to call *Mind Your Business*."

"Ooh, fun," said Bonnie vapidly.

"We were telling fortunes," Lily clarified.

Bonnie's face twisted. "Oh, my God! Really?" She looked at Mossy. "You can do that? With regular old poker cards and stuff?" She plucked the cards from the table and thumbed through them.

"Would you like for me to tell you about *your* future?" asked Mossy with a shivery tone.

"Oh, goodness, no," said Bonnie. "My mother would have herself a hissy if she thought I was playing those kinds—"

Mossy slammed her hand down onto Bonnie's fingers, locking the cards in her grip. "Tell me about Bonnie Evans."

Bonnie made an odd face, shook her head wistfully, and laid the cards on the table. "Well, let's see . . . what do you want to know?" Mossy carefully slid the cards from underneath Bonnie's fingers. "Let's see, let's see. Well, I was born in Chattanooga. I have an older brother and younger sister."

As Bonnie continued to prattle about her favorite subject—herself—Mossy drew playing cards from the deck and dealt them onto the table. While she did so, I began to understand what had just happened. Mossy hadn't asked Bonnie to regale us with aspects of her personal life; she had asked the cards about Bonnie.

"I . . . had a puppy named Peanut." Bonnie leaned into DJ. "Whom I loved, by the way. I love dogs. Um . . . I attend the University of Tennessee Chattanooga studying Social Work. I'd really like to be a therapist, a licensed clinical social worker. But you know . . . the more time that goes by, I'm wondering if I should change my major to—"

"When did your brother pass?" asked Mossy, seemingly from nowhere.

Bonnie paused and gaped at Mossy. "Beg pardon?"

"Your brother," Mossy repeated. "I don't see a sister. Two brothers. And it was the older . . ." Mossy turned another card from the deck onto the table. The Eight of Spades. "No . . . no, the younger one. Tragic. When did he die?"

Bonnie chuckled. "I have two siblings. A brother and sister, and I can assure you they are alive."

"And your mother. She had a bit of a . . . *sipping* issue, right? Problem with the liquor?" She turned another card. "Oh, and at least a passing acquaintance with the odd narcotic, I see. Heroin, maybe? Or something a little cheaper?"

Bonnie squirmed uncomfortably. Her face flushed red. "My mother is a pillar of the—" She hesitated. Then she smiled. "Wait a minute," Bonnie giggled. "Are you reading my fortune? Or, sorry, *trying* to read my fortune?"

"Well," Mossy replied. "I'm reading *somebody's* fortune." She raised an eyebrow. "But it sure ain't yours, darlin'."

Bonnie scoffed. She ran her tongue across her lower teeth like a snake. "Well, this has all been lovely, but I need to get juice—"

In a flash, Mossy lunged across the table and seized Bonnie by the wrists. "*You think I can't see it, huh?*" hissed Mossy.

"Wh-what?!" mumbled Bonnie as fear filled her eyes.

"Mossy!" Asia said. "Let her go, Mossy."

Asia, Paul, and Lily jumped and took hold of Mossy's shoulders, attempting to pry her away from Bonnie, who was now overcome with disbelief and horror.

"You ain't who you claim you are. Are you, missy?" Mossy continued. "There's no *God* in these cards, no righteousness, no holy. No! Oh, but there's plenty of darkness. *Plenty!*"

"Let go of me!" shouted Bonnie. "You're hurting me!"

Dennis rushed to us. He linked his arms around Bonnie's chest and tried to separate her from Mossy. Jack ran from the kitchen, nearly dropping the case of juice in his hands. But Mossy maintained her grip on Bonnie's arms, glaring at her with furious anger.

"Shadow is everywhere on you, girl. I can see it! I can see it right now! Lust, greed. Lies! Blood! *Murder!*"

I watched something dark enter Bonnie's eyes, an eclipse of innocence, something wicked, something true. It was as if another entity clawed through the dainty façade that was Bonnie Evans. Her brow furrowed with fury. Blood rushed to her swollen cheeks. Her mouth twisted with hatred. She pried herself away from Mossy, nearly tumbling backward. A stream of vulgarities poured from Bonnie's mouth that would have caused the most seasoned sailor to blush with shame.

"*Yooouuu bitch!*" Bonnie hissed in a raspy voice I did not recognize. "You stupid mountain trash from hell! Who *the fuck* do you think you are?! Huh? You don't *know* me! You don't know who you're fuckin' with! I'll rip out those rotten motherfuckin' teeth with pliers, and fuckin' feed them to you! You hillbilly whore!"

A stunned silence swept through the dining hall. Time crawled. Though I was frozen in place, my eyes darted back and forth, taking note of the horrified expressions of everyone who witnessed this collapse. Mr. Burns had rooted to the floor, eyeing Bonnie as if she was some alien creature that had descended from a flying saucer. Even Dennis, who had swiftly come to Bonnie's aid, backed against the wall in shock.

It wasn't only that Bonnie—the girl who had corrected herself in front of me when she said words like "shoot"—had gone on a violent, obscenity-laced tirade. She had done so in front of everyone, including dozens of young children.

My eyes found Mossy. I expected to see her sitting there like the rest of us, stunned, overwhelmed. But that old bird just sat there, arms crossed, chuckling like Bonnie had just told a colossal joke.

"*There* you are," Mossy said.

Those three words snatched Bonnie back to reality. She suddenly seemed painfully aware of what had transpired. She was also aware of how strangely we looked at her.

"Oh, gal," whispered Asia, pointing to Bonnie's head. "I think you've got . . ."

A thin strand of faded pink hair had worked its way from underneath a blonde wig. Bonnie reached up and returned the loose hair under the cap. Fear returned to her face. Her eyes widened and began to glisten with tears.

The distant crunch of gravel shook us from our trance. Light poured through the glass doorway of the dining hall. We heard the screech of brakes and the slamming of car doors. Earl and Danny sprinted from the shuttle toward the front of the building, both covered in sweat and panic. Earl burst through the door, an empty shotgun in his fist. Jack rushed toward him.

"Jack!" heaved Earl. "We have to get everyone out of here. Something is out there."

"What?" asked Mr. Burns. "What? What's out there."

"We don't know," breathed Danny as he locked the doors behind him. He bent over to catch his breath. "But it's huge."

Earl pointed toward the crowd. "We got to get everyone out of here." His eyes began to scan the room. "Where's Beth?"

"Her, Rosetta, and Neil went out to fetch Lindsey and Janie," Mr. Burns said. "But they haven't got back yet."

"Damn it! Damn it," Earl boomed.

Mr. Burns took Earl by the shoulders. "Earl, what's going on?"

Earl moved through the dining hall, searching the faces of those present. "Where is Bonnie?"

I turned to see that the girl we had known as Bonnie Evans had disappeared.

Bam!

Something pounded against the glass of the front doors, causing us all to quake with fright. I saw Beth leaning wearily against the doors. Rosetta, Neil, and the two girls paced behind her. Beth was covered in dirt and muck. Again, she pounded the glass.

"Let us in!" Beth screamed.

Danny rushed to the door and flipped the lock. Beth and the others ran into the hall, and Beth locked the doors behind them.

"Something . . . is out there," Beth heaved.

Nurse Conrad grabbed her medical bag and rushed to Beth's side. She was covered in cuts and scratches. Specks of dried blood ran down her arms like something had clawed them.

"We know," Danny said. "Earl and I saw it, too."

"What is it?" Lily asked.

"We don't know. A tree," Rosetta said. "A man. A monster?"

"Whatever it is, it's bigger than hell," Lindsey added. Beth was too tired to correct her.

Mossy stood, walked toward Earl, and took him by the hand.

"I'm not going to ask if you believe me now, because I know you do." She turned toward the children. "We have to get these kids out of here, Earl. We have to get as far away from this place as possible. I don't know what Tate was called for, but I know he won't stop until he gets it. There's no stopping it once it's started."

Drummond didn't argue. He just nodded in acceptance.

"We got the bus . . . in the shed. That'll hold most of us. The shuttle will take the—"

A shrill scream shook the room. I turned to see Mr. Burns standing before the doors, shaking, shuddering like he was having some kind of seizure. Tears rolled from his red, bulging eyes, and he looked toward the ceiling with this piteous expression like he was asking God or whoever was listening to save him. Two thorny vines protruded from underneath each of his pant legs, running along the tile floor and through the broken line of Mossy's powder that Drummond had inadvertently stepped through when entering the building. Pink foam began to bubble from his lips.

Just beyond the glass stood a creature I could only describe as an oaky behemoth. A dirty cloth shrouded its massive head. It scratched at the glass with two branch-like horns protruding from its temples. A white eye peered at us through the hole in its mask. Shrieks filled the dining hall. The adults began to shepherd the children toward the back of the room.

As we rushed toward the office hallway, I glanced at Mr. Burns again before the vines ruptured through his flesh, wriggling like thorny, blood-soaked tentacles. He fell to his knees with a groan. The vines yanked him backward, his limp body shattering through the glass doors.

25

MISS BROOKS REGRETS

"And so it was that later, as the miller told his tale, that her face at first just ghostly turned a whiter shade of pale."
—*Whiter Shade of Pale*: Procol Harum—

Drummond watched helplessly as the frantic crowd poured through the rear exit. He had to do something, take control, and lead the situation, or the children would scatter. They would disappear into the forest, which was the worst thing that could happen. They would never find deserters; there would be no time. The children would be alone, in the dark, ready victims for whatever had clawed its way from hell to consume them.

He bounced in the air, waving the spent shotgun over his head, doing his best to direct the flow of frightened youngsters.

"This way!" Drummond called out. "Stay with the group! Stay with the group!"

It was working. The herd merged in his direction. He led them around the dining hall toward the parking shed where the campus bus was housed.

"Where are we going?" cried one of the campers.

"Danny," Drummond called out. Danny pushed through the others. "Help me get this shed opened. I think Jack had the keys."

He reached down and snatched a large rock from the ground. Danny did the same. The two men pummeled the bulky padlock that secured the shed doors like two lumberjacks chopping at a log. A meek voice called from the rear of the group.

"Um, guys? That's not going to make a difference," said Rosetta.

"We have to get this door opened!" said Drummond.

Finally, the latch of the lock ripped loose. Drummond and Danny pulled the doors wide to find Rosetta standing in the middle of the shed with a look of defeat, pointing at the bus. The aluminum siding in the back of the shed had been pried open like a rusty can of sardines. The hood of the bus had been ripped wide, and the engine inside had been demolished. Pieces of bark and wood clung to the metal gears.

"It knew we'd try to leave," Beth uttered.

Drummond turned to her, unsure of how to respond. His eyes wandered over their surroundings, his mind spinning, calculating what their next step could possibly be. Finally, he shoved his hand into the front pocket and retrieved the keys to the shuttle.

"Come on! This way. Stay with the group!" boomed Drummond.

The crowd turned and scampered behind Drummond as he rushed toward the shuttle. Once they reached the battered vehicle, he slid open the cargo door. Beth and Dennis lifted the smaller children inside.

"Be careful, now," whispered Beth. "Everyone inside. Find a seat and duck down."

Drummond turned to Danny and took him by the shoulder.

"Here," Drummond said, handing over the keys. He took Beth by the wrist and motioned for Dennis. "We have to get as many of the kids as we can into that shuttle. You three take them to the stables. The phone lines and power are separate from the rest of the campus."

Dennis shook his head. "But, man—"

"Get down to the stables and call 911."

"What?" asked Beth. "What do you want us to tell them?"

"Tell them there's a fire. Tell them the gas ignited, and the whole damn place is up in flames. Everyone comes when you yell 'fire.' Then call Sheriff Dunham again and Butch at the fire department. They can get here the fastest. All the numbers are listed near the phone."

"Earl—" Danny attempted.

"Then get in that shuttle, and you drive until the damned thing runs out of gas . . . in *any* direction. We'll find you." Beth looked at Drummond with panic. He set down the rifle and took her by the shoulders. "I promise." Danny,

Beth, and Dennis looked at each other, trying to process what he had said. Drummond grabbed the rifle and nudged Danny's shoulder. "Let's go, son!"

A rumble shook the grassy floor underneath their feet. The shattering of glass. The crumbling of concrete. The creature barreled through the back of the dining hall, sending a shower of wood and stone into the air. It paused, searching its surroundings, hunting for its victims. Spying the campers with one pale eye, it charged toward them like a wooden bull. Dennis jumped through the cargo door into the shuttle floor. Danny and Beth rounded the vehicle, jumped inside, and roared the engine.

"Wait!" cried a voice. "Wait! We can't leave them behind!"

"Go, go, go!" cried Drummond as he pounded the side of the shuttle. The group separated.

Drummond, Mossy, Nurse Conrad, and the remaining campers rushed into the square. Danny did his best to maintain control of the shuttle as it fishtailed through the field toward the stables. The creature stopped. It looked at the group led by Drummond, and then it glared at the taillights of the shuttle it had battled earlier.

"Hey!" screamed Drummond. "Hey, you bastard! This way!" The creature looked at Drummond. It turned and charged forward in pursuit of the shuttle. "No, no!" Drummond cried. "This way, you sonuvabitch!"

Danny gripped the steering wheel of the shuttle, his knuckles gleaming white. He leaned into the driveshaft, doing his best to keep the truck from slipping into the soft soil of the field. They were gaining distance from the creature that ambled behind them. The panicked screams of the children rose above the heartbeat pounding in his ears, growing louder, shrill, almost deafening.

"Danny, watch out!" yelled Beth.

"I'm doing my best!" he replied.

"We have to go back!" Kenny shouted.

"We have to go back and get Asia, Joey, and Paul!" DJ added.

Beth turned to them. "We can't. They'll be okay. Mr. Drummond will take care of them. I swear."

The shuttle bounced toward the paved road ahead.

"Everybody! Hold on!" screamed Beth.

The shuttle jerked into alignment as the rubber tires connected with the dry cement. Beth grasped tightly to the dashboard and passenger door. Just ahead, the floodlights surrounding the stable shone like the beacon of a lighthouse on a rocky shore. Danny pressed the gas pedal to the floor. He glanced in the rearview mirror. There was no sign of the creature. No shadows. No movement.

Danny stomped the brakes with both feet near the stable entrance. The shuttle squealed to a halt, its tail wavering. Beth grabbed Danny's arm and looked at him and Dennis.

"You two stay here with the kids," she said. "And leave the motor running. I'll make the calls."

"I'm coming with you," Danny said. "You don't need to go in there alone."

"No," she replied. "They need you more. I know where everything is at. It'll just take a second."

Beth jumped from the shuttle and rounded the front of the vehicle. She paused as she entered the main stable, where the office was located. Deep indentions were carved into the soft soil of the ground just inside the doors. The horses had vanished. Some cubicles lay ransacked and tattered, as if the animal had broken itself free of its confines and run into the night. To escape something. *Escape what?*

"Miss Brooks?" called Beth softly as she approached the damaged office door.

The lights within the office flickered and faded, creating an eerie strobe effect for the dancing shadows along the walls. Beth slipped into the dark entryway, feeling something crunch underneath her feet.

"Susan?" Beth called again.

She placed her shaking palm against the main office door. The glass pane of the door had been shattered. Bloody shards of glass clung desperately to the wooden frame. Moving inside, Beth clasped her hands to her mouth when she saw blood and blackness spread across the office floor.

Hundreds of dead hornets lay strewn around the room. Nearly all the office windows were broken, devastated by the onslaught of mutant wasps that somehow forced themselves through the thick glass panes.

Beth turned. A muffled shriek escaped her mouth. She clasped her hands over her lips to contain it. A plump body was suspended against the far wall of the office in a ghastly crucifixion. The woman had been nailed to the drywall with thick wooden shards protruding from her wrists, neck, and torso like stakes in a vampire's heart. Her swollen head sat upon the folds of her engorged neck. The face was so distorted by pus and fluid, Beth couldn't tell who it was at first. The keys to the horse cubicles dangled from the broken leather belt hanging around the corpse's waist: Susan's keys. A few remaining hornets fumbled wearily across Susan's bloody face, plucking at the oozing flesh. The woman had been stung to death, impaled by the venomous stingers of thousands of hornets.

A buzzing sound whirred to Beth's left. One of the wasps, still half alive, swooped toward her. She ducked, and the bug collided with the hanging light fixture. It dropped to the desk. Grabbing the desk calendar from the table, Beth turned to crush the insect. She had never seen a wasp so strange.

Its wings buzzed one last time, and then it ceased, legs winding slowly, stinger pulsing. It had to be at least four inches long, if not five. But upon closer look, she could see the wasp wasn't covered in a shiny exoskeleton. It was bark. *Tree bark*. The thing was made of wood.

Beth's face twisted with disgust. She brought the desk calendar down upon the insect with a crunch. She pummeled it again, then again. At last, nothing remained of the creature except grisly sawdust.

The horn of the shuttle beeped, centering Beth's thoughts. She turned back toward the wall, rushed to the phone, and yanked the receiver from the cradle. Her finger traveled down the dry-erase board and found the numbers to the sheriff's office and the fire department. First, she dialed 9-1-1. *Fire*, she rehearsed in her mind. *There's a fire.*

"Emergency Services," said the voice. "What's your emerg—"

The line clicked, hummed, and went silent.

Outside, Danny beeped the horn once again. "I'm going to get her."

"No, man, just wait, like she said," Dennis urged.

The cries of the children had faded into pale whimpers.

"Shh," Danny said as he turned to them. "It's alright. It's alright."

"We gotta go," pleaded a little girl's voice.

"I know. I know," Danny assured. "We'll be on our way in just a second."

A flutter of black passed before the bright headlights and took shape on the shuttle's hood. The stout crow perched there like a feathered hood ornament. It looked at Danny, head curiously twisting from side to side. Soon, another joined it. Then another.

Beth lunged through the doors of the stables. She rushed toward them and paused, her eyes drawn toward the full moon above. Danny rolled down the window.

"Come on!" he yelled.

"Get out," she said. She looked at him. "Get out! Get out! Get out now!"

A thump caused Danny to jerk with a start. The children cried out.

"Hurry!" Beth screamed.

Another crow rushed toward the passenger window of the shuttle and hurled itself against the glass next to Dennis.

"Woah! What the f—?"

One by one, the blackbirds surfaced from the veil of night, throwing themselves at the shuttle windows. The glass of the shuttle door began to splinter in glittering lines like a spider's web.

"Come on!" cried Beth again.

As the crows descended upon the shuttle like an army of night, Danny and Dennis slipped through the driver's side door and jerked the cargo door open.

"Come!" yelled Dennis. "Hurry!"

Children began to pour from the shuttle as a funnel cloud of black wings formed above them.

"Go to the cellar," Beth said as she guided the children toward the open metal doors on the floor. "We'll be safe there. The cellar!"

As they guided the last children into the stable, a massive fist made of black feathers slammed down onto the shuttle, crushing the roof like a tin can. Beth and Danny closed the stable doors and dropped the wooden bar across them. Several crows had made it inside, flying madly around the rafters. One dove at one of the boys climbing into the barn's cellar, clipping the soft flesh of his cheek. Danny removed his overshirt and snatched the bird from the boy's face. He tossed it to the floor and stomped it with his foot, leaving only bloody sawdust.

Danny's eyes gaped. "What the . . .?"

"Where are we going?" howled Dennis.

"The cellar," said Beth as she helped the last of the children along.

"But we have to get out of here!" Dennis muttered. "I'm not supposed to be here!"

Beth took his face in her hands. "It's *not* going to let us leave." Dennis looked into her eyes. For a moment, she suspected he would try and refute her statement, but he nodded in agreement. "Now, let's go."

The three counselors descended into the darkness with the children, closing the heavy door behind them.

26

ACTS OF CONTRITION/
8:00 P.M.

"For thou art the Kingdom and the Power and the Glory. Forever and ever, amen."
—*Act of Contrition*: Madonna—

I huddled there in the dark of the auditorium, Asia and Paul at my side. My mind swirled with snapshots of Kenny, that plump face plastered against that shuttle window, the sheer panic in his eyes as Drummond slammed the door closed before the rest of us could enter. Kenny beat on the window, calling our names as they drove away with the thing in pursuit.

I hoped it would not be the last image the two of us would have of each other.

Drummond crouched by the stage with us. He dropped the empty shotgun at his feet. Mossy sat cross-legged to my left. Rosetta clutched her bloodied hand, sweat and tears glistening on her face. Nurse Conrad knelt beside her.

"Are you okay?" I heard Conrad ask.

Rosetta raised her wounded hand into the sparse blue light. "It's a splinter, I think."

Conrad raised an eyebrow. "Good God, honey, more like a *branch*."

She looked around the floor. "*Shit*," she hissed. "I dropped my bag."

"The girls' room," whispered Drummond.

Conrad nodded. She stood and darted toward the restrooms toward the front of the building. She emerged from the girl's room seconds later armed with a fistful of tampons and panty shields.

"Lookie here," she said with a smile. "Who else is bleeding? I've got you covered."

She stepped toward us and then paused at the front doors of the auditorium. She glanced through the windows.

"What?" Drummond muttered.

Conrad shook her head. "Nothing." One last step.

Thwip!

I heard the sharp clink of cracking glass, followed by a familiar *thwipping* sound. I remember discovering that sound in my backyard when I was nine, flinging around a thin branch from my mother's rose bush like a rapier. It made this slicing sound as it cleaved the air around me, the kind you hear during swordfights in movies. This was the same sound.

Conrad's eyes widened. She jerked stiffly, muscles locking. Her body teetered forward and toppled to the hardwood floor with a resounding thud. The cotton pads scattered across the floor like dominos. A thin rod tipped with coarse feathers protruded from the back of Conrad's skull like a marionette pole. The arrow had slipped through the night, entering the small window of the right-hand door, and buried itself into Nurse Conrad's head. We began to cry out. Drummond dove forward, urging us to remain quiet. We pressed ourselves into the shadows, cowering in the darkness by the lockers next to the auditorium stage.

Footsteps were tramping along the wooden auditorium stoop. I heard a sound, a melodic whistle, a happy tune I couldn't place. Scraping at the doors. The jingle of keys. I saw Drummond reach down to his side, searching for keys he no longer had. He closed his eyes and winced. The left-hand door of the auditorium creaked open. A shadow holding a bow stood at the threshold.

Bonnie Evans entered the auditorium, except this girl looked nothing like Bonnie Evans. Absent that blonde wig, I could see the light shimmering through her pink and purple hair. Her Kamp Kromwell shirt hung from one shoulder. One of the bows from the archery yard was clutched in her fist.

"Now, don't tell me that old Conrad is the only one in here," she said. She paused at Conrad's body and took hold of the arrow's shaft. She sighed. "See, this shit was supposed to be easy." She kicked the loose tampons around the floor and chuckled. "Gonna take more than Tampax to fix that, sister," she added, prying the arrow from Conrad's head with a wet crunch.

She strolled down the aisle, her eyes whirling around the left of the auditorium, where the storage room was.

"Come on out! No use prolonging the inevitable. Either I'll get you or my friend will. You're dead either way. You're *all* dead." She kicked one of the chairs out of her way. "Beth? You in here? I think you and I need to talk about my interview. I *know* it didn't have anything in the application about background checks."

I saw Drummond's eyes widen with surprise. Had something triggered a memory? He leaned forward and stared at the girl through the shadows. Neil turned to see what Drummond was looking at, and the plank of hardwood underneath him groaned, sounding like the dead rising from the grave. My gut seized.

The girl's eyes flickered like a snake spying a mouse, and she spun toward where we huddled in the shadows. She slipped the bloody arrow into the bow and drew it. Without a word, Drummond rose to his feet and stepped out of the darkness.

"Tracey?" he asked. Her eyes moved to the rifle in his fist. "It's empty. It's empty." He tossed the spent shotgun across the floor and raised his hands. "Tracey . . . *Abernathy*, right?" She stretched the string of the bow tighter. "You're the one Beth interviewed. I don't quite know what's going on or how you got here, but you need to come with us. Surely, by now, you know there's something hunting us out—"

Tracey began to laugh. "Oh, don't worry about me, Earl. I'll be just fine."

"Tracey, you *have* to listen to me. You don't understand what's out there," pleaded Drummond.

"I know very well what's out there. And it won't listen to nobody but me."

I saw Drummond's hands fall to his sides.

"What?" He seemed confused, unsure of what to say next. "How . . . why?"

Tracey wiped the sweat from her face with her elbow. "The name David Abrams mean anything to you?"

At the time, I didn't know the name, least of all what it meant to Tracey. But it was apparent from the look on Drummond's face that he knew it well.

"The one you all just left to die."

"Tracey—" Drummond tried.

"No!" she boomed, stretching the bow tighter. "Don't try that shit now. I've had about all the *thoughts and prayers* I can fucking handle." She kicked another chair out of her way. "I told Momma. I told her not to let Davey come here, but she wouldn't listen. You were supposed to be watching him. You *all* were supposed to be watching him. But none of y'all cared."

"That's not true," Drummond said.

"Hell, yes, it is! Don't pretend. We tried, you know. We tried to do something. To find *justice*. First, Momma tried to get your dumbass sheriff to do something. He was useless. Probably on Kromwell's payroll. When that failed, she called one of those highfalutin Nashville lawyers. That bitch was no good. Said she met with Kromwell's legal team, and after reviewing the reports, it was merely *death by misadventure*. Death by misadventure. Can you believe that shit?"

"Tracey, I don't know what the company did," said Drummond. "I'm sorry they wronged you. But that has nothing to do with anyone at this camp."

"It has *everything* to do with it," she hissed. "Finally, we went to the papers, thinking that publicity would scare Kromwell."

"David's death was in the papers," Drummond said.

"Two inches," Tracey barked. "That fuckin' reporter talked to us for three hours. We gave him plenty of dirt on Kromwell. And all he wrote was a two-inch article that appeared underneath the Coca-Cola ad." She shrugged her shoulders. "Guess we didn't have the kind of money he needed to tell the whole story. Certainly not the kind Kromwell Industries paid to bury it."

I saw her lower the bow. Her eyes began to wander.

"Well . . . after that, Momma just gave up. Started drinking again. Drugs. Four months later, we came home to find her face down on the living room floor. She just couldn't bear it any longer." Tracey shook her head. "Next thing I knew, I was in the home, some fucking psycho ward. I had nothing but time. Time that I used to think about things. I knew I had to do something. Something big. Something so big, so loud, so horrible, the world would have to listen. Kromwell Industries would be ruined. But I had to get inside. Become part of the team. All was going according to plan until Beth shot me down. I sure as hell wasn't going to let Bonnie come without—"

"The real Bonnie Evans. You killed her," said Drummond.

"Well . . . yeah!" Tracey raised her arms. "What else was I going to do?

It would've been so much easier if I hadn't had to lug the bitch along with me. But I needed her. Left her in that trunk for days. She about stunk up the whole campus." She shrugged. "Pretending to be her was simple. I mean, you all had never met a damn one of us. You didn't know who was who. All it took was a blonde wig, a little righteousness. No one batted an eye."

"But why all that?" Drummond pleaded.

Tracey tilted her head to the side like a dog hearing a whistle. "For a little *magic*. But it didn't work. Not with one. Then Bonnie's loud-mouthed mother had to show up and almost ruin everything." She chuckled to herself. "The woman didn't even recognize me. Told her I was Beth, and she didn't bat an eye. After I crowned her with a frying pan, I added her to the pile. I thought two would do it. Two would be more than enough. But no, it was going to take more. I thought, 'Who the hell is this fella, Satan himself?'" Tracey gawked at Drummond as if expecting him to respond. "Then I got Chester and his fat momma just down the road. You ought to have seen him. 'Bonnie, don't kill me! What'd I do to you?'"

"He was just a kid, Tracey," Drummond said.

"Oh, please! He was a dipshit. Nobody is going to miss Chester." She slipped the arrow back into the bow. "After that, I had a taste for killing, a talent for it. Old Dewayne was just for fun. And—let's face it—you need to thank me for that one. *Five*. Five brought that son-of-a-bitch right out of hell. Five did the trick."

Drummond shook his head. "What trick?"

Mossy rose to her feet and left us. When she did, I felt a subconscious frost flood my stomach.

"To call our friend up to play," barked Mossy, stepping from the shadows. Tracey jerked with a start and pointed the arrow at Mossy's head. "So, *you* called him up, did ya?" she added in that artless tone of hers. She meandered over to one of the auditorium chairs and plopped herself down. "Oh, honey, you can shoot that poker at any time. Talk about a mercy killing. Before you do me in, though, you have to tell me where you—"

"Learned it?" asked Tracey. "I grew up with the stories, just like everyone else around here. You just have to listen. I thought why not? Might as well give it a try. People here have a bad habit of talking too much about . . . *superstitions*. Nothing gets the old wives' teeth chattering like tales of black magic and the devil."

Mossy giggled. "You got that right." She crossed her legs like she was talking to a neighbor at a bus stop. "I never thought it was real."

"That's why it would've never worked for you," Tracey said. "You have to believe it. Want it. And I wanted it. Oh, I wanted it so, so bad."

"So, what was your plan if it didn't work? If Tate didn't show up?" asked Mossy. "You just going to keep on plucking us off one by one?"

Tracey shrugged. "Well, it wouldn't have been the utter destruction of the camp and *everyone* in it, no. Not as shocking. If it didn't work, I figured I could at least take out a few of you. Drum up as much bad news as possible. It'd be worth going to jail."

I saw Mossy's brow raise. She stretched out her hand, fanned her fingers, and examined her fingernails. "Oh, you ain't going to jail, sweetie. After Tate finishes with you, you'll have a one-way ticket to hell."

"Don't try that shit," Tracey warned. "I'm protected. The caller controls—"

Mossy burst into laughter. "Protected? You . . . you think you called up some *butler* from the ground? Something to heed your beck and call? What you made was a *bargain*, darling. Fair market price. Blood for a soul." She chuckled again. "Or did them old wives not tell you that part?"

I thought I saw doubt enter Tracey's eyes for the first time.

Mossy nodded. "Oh, whatever you've called Tate up to do, he'll get done, all right. Won't stop till it's through. You can bet your ass on that. But then the final price will be paid." She pointed a crooked finger at the girl. "That's *you*, hon. Because the real treasure, the real gem, is the soul. He can go on slaughtering all of us, burn this place right to the ground, but he can't take our souls. Those belong to us. But yours? Yours he can do with what he damn well pleases." Tracey's bow lowered. "*And once the caller's laid to rest and buried in that hole, the demon claims its final prize and takes the caller's soul.*"

Tracey pulled the bow tighter. "That's . . ."

* * *

". . . bullshit," whispered Dennis. "This can't be happening, man." The sound of fluttering black wings rumbled overhead. The birds battered themselves against the steel doors of the cellar.

Boom! Boom!

Blood from the crows crushed in the onslaught trickled through the seams of the doors, puddling onto the stairs.

Beth crossed the concrete floor and pulled the string on the light overhead. A faint glow poured through the space, illuminating little faces damp with tears. "Well, something is happening. We better be ready to deal with it."

As Beth's eyes adjusted to the light, she scanned the room, taking a mental inventory of everyone present. Danny huddled with the children, doing his best to keep them calm. He urged them back, deeper into the cellar against the cinderblock walls.

"We have to get out of here," rattled Dennis frantically. "We have to—"

Danny lunged forward and gripped Dennis by the shoulders. "Dude!" he spat. "You're going to need to pull it together, man. We'll get out of this. But we have to stay calm. It won't do us any good to upset these kids."

Dennis took a deep breath. He looked at the tiny faces staring at him and nodded. "Right, man. Right." He wiped his face. Another deep breath. "What is this place?"

Beth stepped forward and handed Dennis one of the long, black metal flashlights she had found. "It used to be a bomb shelter. Now, it's just Jack's storage garage." She handed another flashlight to Danny.

"I want to go home!" cried Lindsey.

Beth turned toward her. "I know. I know." She walked toward the huddle of children. "It'll all be over soon. And then we'll get everyone home. I promise. Nothing can get us in here. We're safe."

A heavy stomp came down upon the floor above them.

Thud.

The flurry of birds faded.

Thud.

Another footstep fell. Beth turned on her flashlight above them as a plume of dusty smoke floated from the ceiling. It had arrived. It was looking for them. One of the children whimpered. Beth turned to them and held a finger over her lips, urging silence. She motioned for Danny and Dennis to join her at the far side of the cellar. Danny tiptoed toward them. Dennis didn't move. He was frozen, eyes locked on the ceiling, watching it vibrate under the creature above.

"Psst," whispered Danny. Dennis turned to him, eyes filled with fear. Danny scuttled forward, grabbed Dennis by the collar, and dragged him toward Beth.

"Fuck, fuck, fuck," whispered Dennis.

"Shut up, dumbass," Danny hissed.

Again, the cellar door quaked.

"It wasn't supposed to go like this, man," said Dennis.

"Shut up!" Danny said.

Bang!

A heavy fist came down upon the doors overhead, rattling the walls around them. The children cried out. Beth hurried toward the shelves to the room's left and began to rifle through the contents. A soil-covered hand axe lay behind the brake fluid bottles and matchboxes. Above that lay a rusty crowbar. She tossed the crowbar to Danny and clutched the axe in her right hand. The two took flanking positions in front of Dennis and the children.

Suddenly, the metal door above began to pound and tremble. Screams filled the cellar. Beth felt her fingers tighten around the axe handle in her grip. *Come on*, she thought. *Come the fuck on.*

The seam of the left-hand door began to buckle, allowing florescent light from the stable above to seep into the cellar. A thorn-covered vine poked through the opening. It slithered down the steps, feeling its way around. Beth charged forward. She raised the axe into the air and descended upon the vine, splitting it in two. A howl filled the stable.

Bam! Bam! Bam!

The creature pummeled the doors above them.

Bam! Bang!

At last, the weakened doors burst open, and a mass of slinking vines poured into the cellar like a bundle of serpents.

Dennis cried out. He dropped his flashlight and grabbed the bottle of lantern fluid from the cellar shelf. Opening the lid, he sprayed the fuel throughout the space, soaking the writhing vines and the cellar floor.

"What are you doing?" shrieked Beth. "Stop it, Dennis!"

Danny rushed forward, jerking Dennis backward. "Fuck, man! Stop! We can't set the thing on fire! There's nowhere for us to go!"

Dennis fell backward onto the floor, tears flowing down his face.

The vines rose into the air. They began to weave into themselves and take shape. Beth watched in horror as ragged burlap slithered up the creature's frame and wrapped around its newly formed head. It glared through the mask at them with that pale eye she had seen so clearly at the treehouse. The monster lurched forward, shoving Danny backward into the shelves. They crumbled, their contents clambering to the floor. The thing reached out to Beth. She reared back and swung the axe with all her might, sinking the blade deep into the creature's forearm. It pivoted and took her by the throat with its other oaky hand. It lifted her into the air. Her legs flailed wildly about, searching for ground.

Danny charged forward, crowbar in hand. He sank the steel teeth into the midsection of the monster. Stunned, it dropped Beth to the ground. It stomped one foot forward, bared its chest, and roared at them like a lion, shaking the brick walls around them. Danny took hold of Beth and pulled her to her feet. Instead of retreating, however, Beth snatched the axe from the ground and held it forward.

"Come on, you son-of-a-bitch!" she wailed.

Then, as if stunned by her words, the monster silenced. It peered around the room, unsure of where it was. Without warning, it melted into thorny slivers, digging through the concrete floor into the soft ground underneath like a mass of worms escaping into the earth.

Beth stood there, breath labored, mouth ajar. Danny stepped beside her. The two of them peered at the gaping hole in the floor before them. They turned to each other in disbelief.

Danny snickered. "Damn," he said. "Remind me not to piss you—"

The crack of the flashlight sounded with a *pop*. Danny's eyes rolled into his head, and he slumped to the floor. Dennis stood behind him, flashlight in hand, a maniacal expression on his face.

Beth gasped.

* * *

I saw fury twist Tracey's face. Her brow furrowed. She slipped the arrow from the bow and took the blade in her fist.

"We'll see about that, bitch!"

She jerked the arrow through her closed hand, slicing the flesh. Fresh blood trickled onto the ground.

Mossy lunged from her seat, head down, shoulders out, looking like a petite linebacker. She tackled Tracey's midsection, knocking the girl off her feet. Suddenly, I was filled with a mixture of rage and panic. With Tracey down, I leaped to my feet, and the others followed. We rushed out of the shadows— Asia, Paul, Rosetta, Neil—pouring into the auditorium like a tribe of Spartans charging to battle, intending to ensure the girl remained down.

Before we could reach where the women were locked in their struggle, an eruption from below knocked us off our feet. Snake-like vines scattered across the floor, writhing in the air like the arms of a giant squid. The creature rose from the depths below us, ascending into the air, carried upward by its climbing appendages. As its feet touched the floor, it lunged forward and snatched Mossy off Tracey. It hoisted Mossy into the air and turned her to face it, glaring at her with one vacant eye. I expected to see her fight, wriggle in its grip, and try to escape.

Instead, old Mossy just smiled.

"Hey there, you big ole bear," she said softly. The creature stopped. It began to recoil into itself. "Yeah, you know me, don't you?" It placed her gently on the floor and stood before her, its chest heaving with rattling breaths.

"What in the literal hell?" Rosetta murmured beside me.

Mossy reached up and placed a hand on its burlap-covered face.

"I'm sorry, honey . . . for everything. I'd say you didn't deserve all this, but I think we both know you sort of did." The thing didn't care for that statement. A low growl rumbled in its throat. "Now, *don't you start that* with me. You know it's the truth."

My mind was suddenly engulfed with folklore tales and crackling campfires. I watched the two figures standing before us—the massive tree-like monster and the old woman—as they transformed. The creature became a hulking man with thick arms and tender eyes, and Mossy, a young girl with amber hair and soft skin. I realized that the tale of John Tate was true. Mossy knew it was true. She had been there. In another life. Back in the days when people called her Lois.

Lois Greene.

Mossy had been the girl abducted by Tate those many years ago, held hostage. Or had she? Had she seen through the monster to a kind heart buried underneath the horrific exterior?

Suddenly, Mossy's head jerked backward. She cried out and began to paw wildly at her back. As she slipped to the floor, I saw Tracey standing behind her, a bloody arrow in her grip. The creature's head snapped forward. It lurched at Tracey, intending to snatch the girl from where she stood, and I wanted it to. I wanted it to rip her to pieces.

Tracey held out her bloody hand. "Ah, ah, ah," she cooed, forcing the creature to pause. "Not yet. We made a deal."

With the thing's attention turned to Tracey, Drummond rushed to Mossy. He took her by the arms and pulled her across the floor toward us. From the corner of my eye, I saw the tree turn and peer at us.

"My purse," Mossy muttered.

"What?" Drummond asked.

"Give me my purse," Mossy whispered. "I need it."

I handed Mossy her bag, and she slipped her hand into it.

"Are you ready?" called Tracey from the stage. The monster stood before her, waiting for the command. "Stand up. All of you." I glanced at Mossy. "Leave the old bitch there. Let her bleed out. It's not going to matter in a few minutes, anyway." Mossy nodded, and I rose to my feet along with the others. "So, here's what's gonna happen now. I'm going to stand here on this stage and watch Tate tear each of you apart. And I'm gonna like it. Then we're going to burn this place to the ground."

"But didn't she say it'll kill you, too?" Rosetta asked. "That's kind of fucking stupid, isn't it?"

Tracey pondered for a moment. She shrugged.

"Sure, I have regrets! My momma used to say hindsight is always twenty-twenty," Tracey spit blood onto the stage. "What's done is done. I'll go out knowing Kromwell Industries will be over. Maybe, just maybe, my family will get some peace."

My ears were drawn to a clicking sound behind me, but I dared not turn around. I felt cool steel slip between my fingers. I wondered for a moment what it could be. My fingertips brushed along the metal, and I realized it was Drummond's shotgun. Mossy was trying to hand me Drummond's rifle. *But why.* The damn thing was empty. Useless.

Tracey clapped her hands together. "Now, the *really* fun part is choosing which of you gets to die first. Let's see." She eyed the group of us like she was selecting who would be part of her dodgeball team. "Maybe, maybe we could start with the hapless hero, Neil. The guy who only pretends to have a spine."

The barrel of the shotgun slid further into my hand. And just what was I to do with it once I had it? Throw it at Tracey? Swing it at the creature? A helpless feeling overwhelmed me, that same feeling that overtook me while staring into the face of Sam Barnes.

Victim.

I was again a victim.

"Or maybe we could go with Rosetta. The bitch who needs to quit peeping into windows and mind her own business. Yeah, I saw you that night. I should've just jumped you right then."

"Why don't you come jump me now?" hissed Rosetta.

Tracey patted the creature's shoulder. "That's what he's for." She looked at Asia. "Or! Or, we could go for the little queen. The boy . . . or girl . . . or whatever the hell you are. You've confused me since you got here, freak."

Then her eyes moved to me. "Or poor Joey. You know, the moment I saw you get off that bus, I knew I recognized you. I just didn't know from where at first."

God, I know you don't care for people like me . . .

"Until Chester found you out. Boy, he got your ass good. I mean, *everybody* in the whole state heard about the kid who got raped up at Landers by some perv. Nobody knew who it was."

. . . and that answering my prayer is the last thing on your mind . . .

"But *I knew* who you were. Me and my little brother were at Landers the day it all went down. I was front and center when they walked that gross bastard out in handcuffs."

But please . . . please give me just one last thing. Let me die quick.

"Then they brought you out, all beat up and shit. And I remember thinking, 'God if a fat bastard like that screwed me blue, I'd just want to be dead." She chuckled and clapped her hands. "You know he told the papers that you came onto him. Right?"

I felt my fingers tighten around the barrel of the shotgun resting in my fingers. Flashes flared in my mind, transparencies, snapshots in time. I saw those faces: Principal Harold, Vice Principal Pikes, Chester, Lynn, and, yes, *Sam.*

My thugs.

My villains.

My very own monsters.

Tracey snapped her fingers and pointed toward me. The creature stepped forward. "Don't worry, though. No one's going to remember Landers after you're—"

Blam!

I instinctively flipped the rifle forward, placed it against my shoulder, and pulled the trigger, firing buckshot shrapnel into Tracey Abernathy's face. The force was so great, I stumbled backward two steps. Pain surged through my shoulder from the kick of the barrel. I remember Tracey gaping at me with this incredulous look, her face and shoulders peppered with buckshot pellets. Blood poured down her chest. She turned to me as if to say, *You little fucker— you shot me.*

The creature made of trees stopped and teetered on its thick legs.

224

Then, together, Tracey and her monster crumbled to the ground.

I stood there, shaking. I raised the rifle again and pulled the trigger. *Click.* It was empty. Tears of relief ran down my face while I repeatedly pulled that trigger. *Click. Click.* Drummond reached forward and tried to slip the rifle out of my hands, but I couldn't let it go. I just kept firing, blasting each of my monsters away.

"It's okay, Joe. Shhh. It's okay. Let go."

I glanced at Mossy, who winked at me. She coughed a raspy cough.

"I told you," she said, shaking that big ass bag. "I got *everything* in this fucker."

"You had buckshot and didn't say anything to me?" asked Drummond.

"Did you *ask me* if I had buckshot? No, I don't think so," Mossy moaned as she sat up.

Asia took me by the arm. "How did you learn to shoot that good?"

Rosetta slipped her arm around my shoulders. "Bitch was just thirty feet away. He didn't have to shoot good. He just had to shoot."

One of the creature's wooden fingers twisted.

* * *

"Are you crazy?" screamed Beth at Dennis.

Dennis held the bloody flashlight toward her. "Nothing's wrong with me. I'm getting the hell outta here. If Tracey thinks I'm gonna sit here and wait on that thing to rip *me* to pieces after everything I did for her, that bitch is mistaken."

"Tracey?" shouted Lily. "Who is Tracey?"

"Dennis—" Beth began.

"Shut up!" he shouted. He backed toward the steps. "It was just supposed to be a fling, man. A romp with a freaky chick. That was it. I didn't want to get caught up in all this black magic bullshit." He raised his bandaged hand. "But she made me a part of it—fucking bitch—and now it's going to kill me, too!" He looked at the floor. "But not if I kill you first."

He snatched the can of lamp fluid from the floor and began peppering it along the ground, trailing it up the steps as he ascended.

"What are you doing?" Beth declared. "Are you fucking crazy!?"

"I'll tell you what I'm doing. I'm getting the hell out of here! Forget this folklore shit. If you're gonna kill people, kill 'em!"

Emptying the last of the fuel, he tossed the spent bottle to the ground.

* * *

The pile of vines began to tremble. Then they rose.

"Um . . . what's happening?" asked Neil.

"Wait, I thought this was over?" added Rosetta.

I turned to Mossy, who pulled herself to her feet, cradling her bloody back.

"It's not supposed to happen like this," she mumbled. "If the caller dies, the demon dies. That's how it's always been. Always."

The vines wrapped around themselves as Tate was reborn.

"Well, it looks pretty alive to me, lady!" shouted Paul.

Mossy seemed bewildered, confused. She turned to Drummond. "There's another one. Someone else. Somebody besides the girl. We have to get out of here."

Drummond wrapped Mossy's arm around his shoulder, and we rushed toward the auditorium door together.

The tree began to roar.

* * *

Beth saw the lamplight glisten against Dennis's damp arm. His shirt and shorts were doused with oil. She turned to Lily.

"Get back. Get everyone back."

Beth fell to her knees and began to pummel the cement ground with the rusty axe. The clanging of the blade reverberated off the cinderblock walls around them.

Clang! Clang! Clang!

Confused, Dennis chuckled. "What the hell are you doing?" He reached into his pocket and retrieved his silver Zippo lighter. "Digging your way—"

Beth raised the axe high above her and came down upon the floor with the blade one final time with everything in her. A tiny blue spark glimmered in the puddle of fluid that trailed to where Dennis stood. The flames spread quickly, scurrying along the floor and slipping up both of his legs like radiant centipedes. He began to scream and flail about as the fire thickened, burning with a yellow-red glow. He tumbled down the stairs, shimmering red, smoke rising from his blistering flesh. In his panic, he slipped into the burrow left by the creature, screaming and wailing as he plunged into the darkness.

"Come on!" shouted Beth.

Lily and DJ hurriedly ushered the children forward and up the stairs, while Beth and Kenny carried Danny. The smoke began to rise as the fire spread throughout the cellar, consuming all in its wake. Once in the stable, Beth spun toward the open cellar doors. A flaming form lunged through the smoke toward her, clawing up the steps, shrieking and moaning. Beth tossed the steel doors closed and wedged the axe into the handles, leaving the man she knew as Dennis Fern to smolder in the darkness.

* * *

We rushed into the night as the creature burst through the front of the auditorium. Mossy collapsed in the middle of the courtyard, unable to go on.

"Mossy, come on. Help me out," Drummond called out.

"Just leave me, Earl," Mossy breathed.

I flanked Mossy's left side and helped Drummond hoist her to her feet.

"We're not leaving you anywhere," he replied.

I felt the rough sensation of foliage around my ankle. Something had snared me. I fell to the ground, losing my grip on Mossy. She and Drummond tumbled beside me. The others stopped and returned to us, but it was too late.

We gathered together, waiting for Tate to finish his task, when inexplicable flames enveloped the monster. It burst into a fiery inferno before our eyes. I don't know how or why. None of us had set the blaze. But it had arrived like an answer to an unspoken prayer.

The creature fell to its knees. As smoldering black ash began to overtake its shape. I thought I saw it look at Mossy, a glimmering tear in that one pale eye.

It was over.

It was finally over.

27

10:00 P.M.

"Honey, I know . . . times are changing. It's time we all reach out for something new.
That means you, too."
—*Purple Rain*: Prince & the Revolution—

It was just another bonfire, watching that thing burn. I sat in the grass, my eyes transfixed on the crackling flames. As they danced, my mind melted into idle thoughts. I've never felt a sensation like it before or since. It was as if my brain had run a million-mile marathon, and it was now collapsing with exhaustion.

The next thing I knew, I was sitting in the back of an ambulance. The EMTs wiped soot from my face and patched my cuts and scratches. The police officer asked me questions that seemed to echo through my head, just like they had those years ago after my encounter with Sam Barnes. I would nod occasionally, responding to everything and nothing at all. I remember only two things with clarity.

First, I remember seeing Kenny, Lily, and DJ running toward us, smiles shining on their faces. And when I saw them, I took a second to appreciate that they were alive; *we* were alive. The Krew began to chatter about the surreal evening, but I only caught jigsaw elements of discussion, pieces I would have to fit together when I had the energy. We knew one thing for sure: No one would believe the truth, because the truth was unbelievable. Simply, there had been an *incident* at Kamp Kromwell. Two counselors had gone insane and wreaked havoc on the campus and everyone there. Just two nutjobs. That was all. Nothing supernatural, nothing mystical, no occult.

I also remember Mossy. *Lois Greene.* I recall her standing amidst the flashing lights with that soot-covered face, looking like a hobo harlot. I had wandered to the square and sat on one of the benches, waiting for my parents to arrive to take me home. I was mentally rehearsing the story I would relay to my parents when Mossy's voice caused me to jerk with a start.

"I know you," she said. I looked up at her and smiled. She took a seat beside me and patted my leg. "You okay?"

"I suppose," I said. "As okay as everyone else."

The two of us sat there a moment, quiet, watching the light of dawn change the sky into pale violet.

"You need to do it," she said.

"What?"

Mossy's eyebrow arched. "I know you. I saw you in those cards. You got things around that watch over you. Good things. Now, I don't claim to know what happened to you, son. But I know something happened, all the same. Somebody tried to steal something from you, and if you stay quiet, they'll damn well take it." She pointed that wagging finger at me. "You have a chance to tell your story. If you do, I can guarantee folks'll listen. But . . . you gotta speak to be heard." Mossy rose to her feet, straightened her dusty clothes, and pawed at her wild hair. Then she gave me a wink and strolled toward Drummond, who was locked in conversation with the fire marshal. "Hey, Earl," she called to him. "How about you give me a little kiss?"

On October 17, 1995, I walked into the Knox County Courthouse in downtown Knoxville. That afternoon, I stared Sam Barnes in the face and told the courtroom what he did to me. A unicorn in a room full of mules. I did spy another horn in the crowd. Asia Demarco sat in the fourth row with his brother, Paul, on his right and Kenny on his left. Lily and DJ sat directly behind them. And when I told my story that day, I didn't speak to the courtroom. I talked to them. My friends. The Krew.

Before Sam's attorney had a chance to highlight my ugliness in cross-examination, I confessed I had initiated contact with Sam. When asked why I did such a thing, I told the courtroom that I was gay and was curious about others like me. That was the truth. When this fact became record, my father left the courtroom without looking at me. He was followed by my older brothers, who, like my father, slithered out of the courtroom in shame. I didn't care. I wasn't ashamed.

Not anymore.

My mother remained in her seat, and beside her sat my sister, Anne, and my brother, Bruno. As I told my tale, I expected Mom to look away and glance down at her hands. I expected to see at least some thin veil of disgrace. But no. No, she sat there on that bench, listening to me confess all my secrets, my sins. And she smiled. Not the kind of forced smile that one uses to hide discomfort, but a smile of pride I had never seen before. I have never, ever forgotten it. All these years later, whenever I feel gray, I close my eyes and picture that smile, and that memory rekindles my color.

I recounted the details of what transpired in the restroom at Landers Water Park, and when I did, my eyes moved directly to Sam Barnes. Not a single aspect was omitted. Not a word was ignored. I sat there, staring into the eyes of my monster, realizing that he was not the only creature I had conquered that year. I had fought loneliness. I had battled self-doubt. And I—*we*—went to war with demons, literal monsters. And we lived. Surely, if I could conquer those things, I could live my truth and experience the freedom it offered. *You gotta speak to be heard.*

Following my testimony, my attorney, Ms. Finch, approached the stand and took me by both hands. She squeezed them and nodded to me with satisfaction. The judge then asked Sam's attorney—a slick puppet of a man whose name eluded me then and still eludes me—if he would like to cross-examine me. The man glanced at me and then back to the judge.

"No questions, your honor."

In retrospect, I'm not sure what he could have asked me in Sam's defense. Would he go so far as to say a fourteen-year-old kid had lured a grown man astray? Cross-examination would have only led to echoes of damning truths already apparent to everyone present.

An hour after my testimony, the defense and prosecution rested their cases, and the jury entered deliberation. My mother urged me to leave, to go home and wait to hear from Ms. Finch, but I elected to stay. Something in me wanted to see Sam's face—more notably, his eyes when justice arrived at his doorstep. It took the jury less than two hours to declare a verdict.

Sam Barnes was found guilty of all counts.

He was sentenced to life in prison. Ms. Finch later explained it meant eventually Sam could be eligible for parole. That didn't mean he would ever receive it. That mattered little then. It matters less now. Sam Barnes died in prison three weeks before his first parole hearing. I would like to say that I felt some sympathy for his passing, some obscure sadness at the loss of human life. But I didn't. I didn't feel anything at all. I wasn't delighted or distraught by his death. The only word that ran through my mind when I heard the news was, "Well . . ."

Seasons have come and gone since that day in the Knox County Courthouse. As for the Krew, as with most young relationships, the obligations of time eventually contaminated our friendships. Hours transformed into months and months into years. Decades add distance.

Lily Wilkins (née Foster) eventually moved from Tennessee to Maryland, where she lives with her husband, George, three children, and seven grandchildren. Though we are not quite as close as I would like, we follow each other on social media and regularly trade updates.

Through my connection with Lily, I learned her brother, DJ, turned out to be a respected licensed clinical social worker in Atlanta, Georgia, working with troubled children. He married a woman named Lucille and had five children of his own. I was saddened to hear he passed away from liver cancer last year.

Kenneth Louve fell in love in college and married at twenty-two. He graduated from the University of Kentucky with honors and became a big-wig corporate attorney. As you can imagine, his talent for bullshit made him an excellent lawyer. He and his wife, Cynthia, have two great children, twins. As with Lily, Kenny and I keep up with one another via social media. He lives just an hour away. We try to get together at least once during the holidays each year to have dinner. Every now and again, when he's telling one of his courtroom stories, I spy that familiar glint in his eye, that sense of adventure. It always makes me smile.

I see Paul Demarco every now and again. He's been married and divorced—twice—and has four children, three of whom are great, and a daughter who's hell on wheels. He owns a successful car dealership, Demarco Ford/GMC, with two locations to serve you. I purchased my last car from him just three years ago—and at an exceedingly fair price, I might add. He calls me at least once a month to see if I'm ready to trade up. *Not just yet, Paul. Not just yet.*

Asia Demarco eventually chose to go by his "Christian" name, Alberto, or *Al.* Today, "Asia" is merely a stage name, a persona used when Al is in character at the Bijou Club downtown, which he owns along with Charlie, his partner of eleven years. When Al is away from his alter ego and the spotlights are dark, I am often moved by what a humble and kind man he has turned out to be. But when the make-up is on, and the hair is high—honey—that old Asia—the same extroverted soul I met all those years ago at Kamp Kromwell—shines brightly as ever. And Asia is a *star*.

As for me, life has been good. As with us all, there have been difficulties, peaks and valleys. My mother passed away when I was twenty-one, but she saw me graduate from the University of Tennessee before her final days. I did so without *ever* being called to the dean's office. I've lived longer without my mother than with her at this stage. After she was gone, my sister Anne and I broke with the family. Mom was the only thread holding the tattered fabric of our family together. With her gone, the cloth unraveled. Like many in the LGBTQ+ community who are cast out by their families, I sought out others, a new family, a chosen family. Over time, members have come and gone, but there is liberty in knowing you may choose the energy in your life.

Since one can't do many things with a liberal arts degree, I entered the police academy at age twenty-four. My ordeal with Sam Barnes left me wanting to be more to the world around me. Being a police officer would help me catch the other Sam Barnes of the world. By twenty-nine, I had become a detective. I'm not sure why. After the events at Kromwell, I developed this talent for finding *hidden* things. Things that no one else could see. I don't know how to explain it. I've just learned to listen to the voices that speak to me. Sometimes they're whispers, other times a scream. But I always hear them. Annie says it's intuition. But I wonder. I don't know who they are, and I don't care. I just listen to what they have to say. And they've never steered me wrong. They even told me about Chuck.

Chuck Gilroy was a medical examiner in Knoxville, a stocky guy with a sweet grin who was a little too nice for my tastes. I had no intention of involving myself with another man who meddled in corpses. But it didn't take long to see that Chuck wasn't dangerous. The guy didn't have a single tattoo, had never touched a cigarette, and the harshest thing to pass through his system was Gatorade. Everything he ate was "plain with cheese." During the first month of our spontaneous relationship, I tried *thrice* to break things off. Maybe I felt he was too good for a damaged unicorn like me. Each time I prepared to go on my way, one of those voices would murmur like a cosmic coincidence, and I would rethink my decision. It was all so confusing. I decided only one person could tell me what to do with the man, and I was overdue for a visit to Jasper Mill.

As she did all those years before sitting at that table in the Kromwell dining hall, Mossy handed me a deck of Bicycle playing cards and told me to shuffle my query into them. Once I returned the cards to her, she dealt them like a Blackjack dealer at Caesars Palace. She would pause now and again, eyeing a card and its position on the table before continuing. With the spread on the table, Mossy rendered her decision.

"Well, if you wanna know what I see, you'd be a fool to send him off," she said flatly. "Looks like your momma sent him your way. She's been tryin' to tell you, but you don't listen to shit." She sipped her coal-black coffee and pawed at that mane of hair on her head. "You got to listen to those voices, Joe. Not everyone can hear him like we do. You don't want to ignore them lest they find ways to get your attention."

"I listen, Mossy," I attempted.

"*Yeah, yeah, so you say*," she replied, waving her hand indifferently. She raised a crooked eyebrow. "If you wanna know what I see, stick with him. 'course, it's your decision and all. If you want to *whore* around bar hopping for the rest of your life, get rid of him. But if it's loyalty you're looking for—*love* and whatnot—then I'd tie that boy down and just let him out to graze." She took another sip of coffee and nodded at me. "You know if I were you and all that shit."

Chuck and I have been together ever since.

ABOUT THE AUTHOR

A.J. Grea is an author and screenwriter living in East Tennessee with his husband of twenty years, three snarky cats, and a meddlesome squirrel who will not stay away from the windows. A lover of 80s horror, he began writing short stories at the age of nine.

One of his first stories, "The Monster Who Ate My Brother," resulted in a parent-teacher conference, during which his mother had to assure the concerned faculty that his siblings were fine.

When not spinning hair-raising yarns, A.J. spends time as most middle-aged comic book fans do--playing video games and collecting childhood toys that remind him of when his only responsibility was being home before streetlights began to glow.

www.ingramcontent.com/pod-product-compliance
Lightning Source LLC
Chambersburg PA
CBHW022001290726
48835CB00045B/179